THE
ANNIVERSARY

LAURA MARSHALL

SPHERE

SPHERE

First published in Great Britain in 2021 by Sphere
This paperback edition published by Sphere in 2022

1 3 5 7 9 10 8 6 4 2

A CIP catalogue record for this book is available from the British Library.

ISBN 978-0-7515-7505-7

Typeset in Caslon by M Rules
Printed and bound in Great Britain by Clays Ltd, Elcograf S.p.A.

Papers used by Sphere are from well-managed forests
and other responsible sources.

Sphere
An imprint of
Little, Brown Book Group
Carmelite House
50 Victoria Embankment
London
EC4Y 0DZ

An Hachette UK Company
www.hachette.co.uk

www.littlebrown.co.uk

For Charlie and Arthur

Chapter 1

15th June 1994 | Travis Green

Travis sits in the front room, running his hands back and forth over his semi-automatic rifle, cool and smooth beneath his calloused fingers. He is calm, his heartbeat slow and even. In a few hours' time, eleven people will be dead.

He can hear the gentle clink of crockery from the kitchen. Elaine is emptying the dishwasher, closing the cupboard doors softly so they don't bang. He had thought about killing her too, but he wants her to know what he has done. He wants her to understand why. That will be a worse punishment for her than death.

Death. He hasn't thought much about it, although he's known all along it would be inevitable. He's not frightened, because he knows it will be a nothingness, like before he was born. If anything, he's looking forward to it.

She made him fried eggs this morning without being asked, the edges brown and frilly, just how he likes them. He wonders if she senses that something is coming. She can be like that. Her grandmother was supposed to have had the gift – people used to come to her to have their fortunes read, right up to the end of her life. People can be fucking stupid. As if knowing what's going to happen can make any difference, make things any better. If he had known what was going to happen to him and Elaine, could he have changed things? If he could, then that makes a mockery of the whole thing. No, we're in control of our own destinies. Elaine has sealed her fate as surely as Travis has his own.

Paul has left for school, and Travis is glad he is out of the way. He wouldn't want him to see anything. He'll be OK. Maybe in time he'll come to understand. Travis senses in him a certain quality, a quiet watchfulness that reminds Travis of himself. Last week, he caught Paul looking at him intently, almost as if he knew what Travis was planning. Their eyes locked for a moment, until Travis pulled his away and busied himself elsewhere. If he hadn't been so preoccupied with his plans, he might have been frightened.

There are folk in this town who think Travis is a joke. He's seen them laughing behind their hands, talking about him when they think he's not looking, whispering this and that, swapping rumours about why he lost his caretaking job at the school. They certainly won't be laughing when this day is over. Some of them will never laugh again.

The radio is on in the kitchen and he can hear the faint strains of Elaine singing along as she stacks the breakfast things into the dishwasher. It's been a while since he heard her singing. His resolve hardens as he thinks about what might be lifting her spirits.

In a few hours' time, eleven people will be dead, and it will *be time to turn the gun on himself. And if everything goes to plan – and surely Travis has done enough to ensure that it will – nobody except Elaine will ever know why.*

He stands up and tightens his grip on the rifle. It's time.

Chapter 2

It's the most innocuous of questions, but it makes my insides shrivel, curdling them like sour milk: *Where did you grow up?* If the person asking is under the age of forty, it's not so bad. Sometimes there's a flutter in their eyes, a brief microsecond of recognition – they know there's something significant about my home town, but they can't recall what it is. That's OK. But if they're older – ten years or more older than me – they'll wince and in an instant it's there between us, as if another person has joined the conversation. Only it's not a person, it's a place: Hartstead.

Sometimes – and these are the times I prefer – they won't say anything; they'll simply move the conversation on to safer ground. What I hate is when they say, *Hartstead? Oh, God, I remember that day so well. I know exactly where I was when I heard the news.* If they're around forty years old, it's often the first news item they recall with any clarity. They would have been in their mid-teens, beginning to engage with the world, to understand that what was happening out there could affect them. *I was frightened to go out for ages afterwards*, a woman at a party once said to me. *Me and my friends were obsessed with it.*

This I can cope with. I nod and smile, and say I was very young, keeping my fingers tightly crossed behind my back, hoping they don't probe me any further about it. Where I struggle is when someone goes further and says, *What about that terrible story? Of the last one before he … you know. It happened right in front of his wife and daughter; she was only about four years old.* I do my best to arrange my features into a semblance of calm and say, *Yes, of course, but it was a long time ago and our town has moved on. It's no longer defined by a tragedy that took place twenty-five years ago.*

This, of course, is a lie. How could we not be defined by it, when it's all the general public remember about us? There's nothing else memorable about Hartstead. If it weren't for what happened here on the 15th June 1994, nobody would have heard of the place. It doesn't have a cathedral like nearby Salisbury, or the coast. It doesn't even have any boutiquey little shops selling handmade pepper pots and bottle-openers shaped like otters. There's a Tesco Metro, a small W.H. Smith's and all the other faceless shops you would expect to find on the high street of a run-of-the-mill small town in the south of England. The only thing it has that you won't find in other towns is the memorial plaque in St

Thomas's church: a sombre, discreet brass plate with the names of the eleven victims engraved on it. It doesn't list the other casualties, though – the witnesses, and those left behind. There was talk at the time of something bigger – a community hall, or a memorial park – but those plans were swiftly shelved. It turned out the residents of Hartstead didn't want a daily reminder of the worst day of their lives, and it seemed futile to attempt to build something positive out of a tragedy in which no light could ever be found.

That can be the end of it and the conversation moves on; but, other times, a shadow falls over their face and they say, *I'm sorry, you didn't ... lose anyone yourself, did you?* They slacken in relief when I say no. But I am lying again. I lost everything the day Travis Green took a semi-automatic rifle and made his way around our town, indiscriminately pulling the trigger. The man they all remember, the very last person to be killed, was my father. The wife that looked on in horror was my mother. The child, clinging to her, distraught and blood-spattered, was me.

SOUTHERN GAZETTE

Friday 17th June 1994

TOWN IN MOURNING AS ELEVEN SHOT DEAD

ELEVEN PEOPLE WERE KILLED on Wednesday when 38-year-old Travis Green took a semi-automatic rifle and rampaged around his home town of Hartstead, before turning the gun on himself. The community has been rocked by the tragedy, and police and Social Services are working around the clock to support the families of the victims and other residents who watched the terrible events unfold.

The gunman's first victims were husband and wife Peter and Jane Frogmore, both aged 82, shot in their garden. The couple lived next door to the gunman, and were said to have had a civil, neighbourly relationship with him. They were due to celebrate their diamond wedding anniversary later this year.

Another married couple, Richard and Sheila Delaney, aged 45 and 43, were next in the firing line, killed on the pavement outside their house as they left for a shopping trip, followed by 54-year-old Graham Mooney, a driving instructor, mown down as he waited for a client. The gunman continued his rampage, shooting dead David Wilkes, 42, an estate agent, and 19-year-old Manisha Mehta, killed outside her parents' hotel where she worked part-time.

Travis Green then moved on to the high street, the news of the massacre not yet having spread. He killed Suzanne Persimmon, a 28-year-old case worker at the Citizens Advice Bureau, and Melissa Bradshaw, also 28, solicitor at a small law firm. At the end of the high street, he turned onto the recreation ground and shot a pensioner walking her dog, Maureen Featherstone, 65.

The gunman's last victim was 39-year-old Gary Colman, shot dead in his home in front of his wife, Sylvia, and their 4-year-old daughter.

As the police closed in, the gunman placed the gun in his own mouth and ended his reign of terror.

Neighbours of Travis Green described him as a loner. One, who preferred not to be named, said he had worked as a care-taker at St Margaret's High School in Hartstead until recently. 'He was asked to leave,' the source said. 'No one knew why, but he hasn't worked since.' Another local resident, who also chose not to be identified, said that Green was a regular in the Lamb and Flag on Hartstead High Street. He often drank with Dennis Glover, a local farmer said to be his only friend. Mr Glover has so far been unavailable for comment.

Hartstead residents are left shell-shocked by the traumatic events, and have been laying flowers and tributes at the sites of each murder. Teenager Hilary Masters, a schoolfriend of Manisha Mehta, laid a wreath and a card outside the hotel. 'It's just so awful,' she said, choking back tears. 'I can't believe what's happened. I feel so terrible. Manisha was supposed to be going to Cambridge. She had her whole life ahead of her.'

Outside the house of the last victim, Gary Colman, flowers are piling up too. The Colmans' next-door neighbour, Doreen Flitwick, told our reporter that the little girl was 'screaming and crying, soaked in blood' when the police arrived.

Green is survived by his wife Elaine and son Paul, 13. Sources close to the family suggest Mrs Green is being cared for at a psychiatric hospital and Paul has been taken into temporary foster care. Neighbours said she had always been polite but kept herself to herself. Paul was described as being a quiet boy with few friends, who spends a lot of time up at the disused quarry on the Farnwood Estate, the grounds of a stately home close to the town. It has been closed to the public since 15-year-old Adam Groundswell died there four years ago after experimenting with drugs and falling into the pit.

Chapter 3

Today is one of Mum's bad days. I've noticed since I moved in a few months ago how frequent they are. When I was in London, still working, it was easier for her to hide it from me, I suppose. She's always been so keen for me to be independent, to get out there and live life, that keeping the extent of her growing confusion from me came naturally to her. I was so busy all the time that I couldn't see what was going on – correction, I *thought* I was busy. If it wasn't so awful, I'd laugh now to think about how hard I thought it was to be pregnant and working a full-time job, moaning all the time about how tired I was. Jesus. I didn't know the meaning of the word. I didn't know that once I had a baby I would live in a fog where everything is off-kilter, where my limbs are so heavy it seems impossible to lift them; where my eyes sting all the time, as if several tiny insects have taken up residence in them.

Bedtime used to be my favourite time of day, but I

dread it now. There is no pleasure in it when you know, without a shadow of a doubt, that you will be awoken two hours later, often less. It's not even Amy's crying that rouses me. I wake as soon as she stirs, a familiar dread settling upon me before I'm fully awake. It can be almost nothing – a squirm, a snuffle – but there's no chance, none at all, that she will settle herself back to sleep. I'm in for at least an hour of feeding, rocking, pacing up and down the landing, rubbing and patting, until it's all I can do not to hurl her down the stairs.

Can't your mum help? Aisha said, when she came to see me soon after I had Amy. I wanted to scream at her, *No, she can't bloody help, she can't even look after herself any more!* But it wasn't Aisha's fault that she didn't understand. When I moved back here shortly before Amy was born, I told everyone I was doing it so my mum could help with the baby. I think I'd even had some idea myself that she could, that we would be able to help each other out. It took less than a day for me to realise that I had seriously underestimated how much she had gone downhill, and that not only would I be looking after Amy alone, I'd also be caring for Mum.

I try so hard not to resent Mum for it, because of course – *of course* – it's not her fault. But when Amy's had a particularly bad night and my body is heavy with exhaustion, and Mum asks me the same question for the tenth time that morning, or is refusing to eat, adamant she's already had her breakfast, it's hard. It's hard not to get angry, and at times I do, because if I swallow it down, if I move beyond anger, there's utter despair, and I can't allow myself to go there because then I'll be no use to anyone. It surfaces, unbidden, in the dead of night, when the house is finally still and I'm alone. When it's quiet, with nothing to drown out the voices that whisper to me about what it must be like for Mum to be like this. Mum, who has always been so independent, so strong. How does she feel inside? Does she know what's happening to her? Is she frightened? I can't stop myself imagining what it would have been like if she hadn't got dementia. She loves Amy, she really does, but I don't think she always knows she's her granddaughter. And Amy will never know her, not the real her. I let myself succumb briefly to these thoughts, weeping silently into my pillow, but after a while I have to force myself to stop, to think about something, anything else, in order to get back to sleep. I don't have the luxury of lying awake all night, tossing and turning and emoting. I need to squeeze in every drop of sleep I can while Amy's down, because, if I don't, there's no way I will get through the next day, and the next, and the next, each one more draining and monotonous than the last.

I think wistfully of my two best friends from school, Stella and Bec. If only they still lived here, I know they would help. But they're scattered to the four winds – Stella loved-up with Pete in Edinburgh, and Bec teaching scuba-diving in Australia. Even before Amy they weren't the greatest of correspondents, caught up in their own lives, just as I was in mine, in London.

I try not to think about Before, because a hole opens up inside me, threatening to swallow me. I try to think of that Cassie as a separate person: the Cassie who had well-cut suits and wore heels, who spent her days in a building made of glass and steel, holding meetings and issuing instructions. That Cassie had friends, and evenings in the pub, and cinema trips, and a boyfriend, even if he was married to another woman. She had a mother she could chat to on the phone, who was interested in her daughter's life and who had stories of her own. She had a life that existed outside this bubble of feeds and naps and cooking and cleaning and shopping. Amy only sleeps for a maximum of thirty minutes at a time during the day, and when she's awake she's never happy. She doesn't lie burbling in her pram like the other babies I see out and about. She's always crying, or writhing as if she wants to get out. I bought a bouncy chair for her but the longest she's ever sat in it without screaming is seven and a half minutes. It doesn't bounce any more, because one day I threw it across the room, hard, and the mechanism jammed. Amy wasn't in it.

What about Guy? Aisha had said next. *Amy's his daughter too.* But she's not, not in any real sense. He cried, when I told him. I'd never seen him cry before. I thought it meant he'd realised it was time to leave his wife. I should have known that an unborn child could never compete with a living, breathing one. That whatever I could offer him could never compete with a ten-year relationship, a shared history, a life inextricably intertwined. What did

Aisha think I was going to do, call him up and ask him to take Amy overnight? Even when we were together I was only allowed to call him at prearranged times when his wife wasn't there. Aisha had had that conversation about Guy with me too many times to pursue it, so she'd ended up giving up and just wishing me good luck.

I should feel that I'm well rid of him, I know. I want to feel that. But I don't. I long for him. Not only to share the burden of caring for our baby, which would be amazing, but just him. Talking for hours about anything and everything. Burying my nose in his neck and inhaling the scent of him. Curling up together in bed, knowing that despite everything I was finally in the right place, precisely where I was supposed to be.

Today, the doorbell goes and I pick Amy up as usual, hoisting her against my stomach. It'll be Mum's carer. I had intended to cancel them, but actually it's the only time I can leave the house without feeling any guilt. As the door swings open, I note without much interest that it's a new one, a woman of about my age, her glossy brown hair smoothed into a high, tight ponytail. Her eyebrows are thick and dark, immaculately groomed, like two fat slugs.

'Cassie!' Her face creases into a smile under the mask of foundation.

'Yes?' I say, uncomprehending.

'It's me, Chloe! Chloe Riordan . . . from school?'

'Oh, my God! I'm so sorry I didn't recognise you. You look so different.'

'Better, I hope,' she says.

At school she'd been mousy and spotty, her clothes always slightly too small or too large, and not quite hitting the mark fashion-wise. Unsure of how to answer without offending either her past or present selves, I fall back on a compliment. 'You look great.'

'Thanks – so do you! It's so good to see you!' She really does seem happy to see me, which gives me a guilty feeling. We were close throughout the five years we were at school together, although once she left at the end of Year 11 to study social care at college, and I stayed on to do A-levels, we drifted apart. Or, more honestly, I allowed us to drift, taking longer and longer to return her texts, coming up with excuses not to meet up – too much homework, Mum wouldn't let me go out … In reality I was busy with Stella and Bec, having got to know them better since she'd left, and finding I had more in common with them than with Chloe, who I'd unfairly begun to think of as dull and provincial.

'I thought you might be here – I heard you'd moved back to look after your mum, bless her. She's no age for it, is she? What is she, early sixties?'

'Sixty-three.'

Mum had had so many plans when she'd taken early retirement a few years ago from her admin job at the local council. When I was young, we had an ancient caravan that we'd hitch up to our equally ancient Ford Fiesta. We'd spend the summer holidays driving around the UK coast, pulling up at caravan parks and beaches, and, one memorable night, in a lay-by on the A21 near Hastings.

The caravan is long gone, but I know she'd been looking at second-hand camper vans, planning to spend this next stage of her life footloose and fancy-free, letting the wind take her. That was all stolen from her when, just a few months after retiring, she got the devastating diagnosis of early-onset Alzheimer's.

I used to wonder as a teenager whether she'd ever meet anyone else. A stepfather for me – big shoes in the hall, a razor in the bathroom, a deep voice asking what time his dinner would be ready. From time to time I'd ask her if she'd like to meet someone, and she always said she was happy as we were – the two of us against the world. I guess my dad must have been a hard act to follow. So it never happened, and now it never will.

'And who's this?' Chloe chucks Amy under her chin, eliciting a rare smile. 'Isn't she gorgeous?'

I suppose she is, but I never spend any time doing what the mothers in books do: staring adoringly at her, drinking her in.

'What's her name?'

'Amy.'

'How old?'

'Fifteen weeks.' Fifteen weeks of constant motion. Fifteen weeks of every single thing I do being for someone else. Fifteen weeks where every decision has been taken away from me, where everything I do is viewed through the filmy lens of motherhood.

'Oh, bless. My Phoebe's six months; we should get them together,' she says.

What for, so they can lie next to each other, unknowing, occasionally flinging out a hand wet with saliva and bopping the other in the face?

'I go to a baby group at St Thomas's church hall, it's on a Tuesday afternoon – why don't you come tomorrow?'

'Yes, maybe.' *Not in a million years.*

'What about her dad? Is he staying here too?'

'No,' I say shortly.

Mum was never a huge fan of my relationship with Guy, although she supported me, as she did in everything. If she could have met him it would have been different, I'm sure. She couldn't have helped loving him. He's charming, but not in a fake, smarmy way. It sounds crazy given that he was having an affair with me, but he's a genuinely good person. He just found himself in an impossible situation.

'Come through.'

She follows me into the front room.

'Hello, Sylvia!' she says to Mum. 'I'm Chloe! You won't have seen me before; I've been off on maternity leave.'

Mum looks at her without speaking, eyes glazed.

'She's not so good today,' I say to Chloe.

'Oh, bless,' she says again. 'I'm a bit out of practice, to be honest. It's my first day back after maternity leave. I hate being away from Phoebe – you know what it's like.'

I fix a smile to my face, but I'm consumed by a fierce jealousy of Chloe, who is going to get whole days on her own, away from the ceaseless demands of her baby. She

17

may spend it wiping geriatric bottoms, but it's a trade I'd gladly make.

'I'd give anything to stay home with her,' she continues blithely, 'but we can't afford it. I'm missing out on so much. Thank goodness I'm only part-time, though. I couldn't leave her every day like some do.'

I can never rekindle my friendship with Chloe, that much is already clear. I bet she has never sat on the floor sobbing while her baby screams and screams in her cot, the battery-powered mobile turning above her, plinking out its interminable tune. Twinkle twinkle, little star. I bet she's never pulled too roughly on her wriggling baby's arm when dressing her.

'What about you?' she goes on. 'Will you be going back to work?'

I think longingly of my quiet office, and of my assistant, Shanice, who would bring me coffee at regular intervals, huge coffees that I could drink in their entirety while they were still piping hot.

'No, I'm taking a bit of a break.'

'Oh, lucky you.'

Lucky me. Except I'd give anything to be able to go back. I'd be there tomorrow if I could. Amy would be better off at nursery – they'd know what to do, how to play with her. But I can't, not while Guy's there – and he loves that job. Used to say it would see him through to retirement. There's no way I could cope with seeing him every day and then going home to our child whom he refuses to acknowledge.

I'm going to have to do something, though. I was never able to save any money living in London, and the carers' fees are ripping through Mum's savings. Once they're gone, I suppose the house will have to be sold to pay for her care – and I can see the day coming, sooner than I thought, that she won't be able to live here, carers or no carers. Then I'll be homeless, with no job and a child, and a mother who doesn't know who I am.

'Right, shall we get you washed and dressed?' says Chloe loudly to Mum, who ignores her and continues to stare out of the window. Chloe takes her elbow, and Mum allows her to help her out of the chair.

'Did you hear?' she says to me. 'There's a journalist doing a big piece on Hartstead for the *Sunday Times*, to coincide with the twenty-fifth anniversary.'

'What? Who?' Jesus Christ, can they not give it a rest? I suppose I should have expected it, given the anniversary. Hopefully this journalist won't know I've moved back.

'Her name's Alison Patchett. She's local, and only a couple of years older than us, but I don't think she went to St Margaret's. Do you remember her?'

'No, doesn't ring a bell.' I'm sure I'll be meeting her soon, though. She may not be writing for a tabloid but they're basically all the same. It won't be long before this Alison is poking around here with her notebook and pen.

'No?' Chloe looks disappointed. I bet she prides herself on knowing everything and everyone around here. 'Anyway, she's doing this article on Hartstead, twenty-five years on. Not only on Hartstead, actually. It's about

19

how towns recover from … traumatic events.' She looks at me slyly from under her lashes. She always was keen to ask me about that day.

'Why can't everyone leave it alone? It was so long ago.'

'Oh, I totally agree, but I suppose people are always interested, aren't they? Especially when it's a big anniversary, like this year. It's one of those things you don't forget.'

I don't reply. At four herself, Chloe was too young to remember it – most people of our age are. I'm the only one who doesn't have that luxury.

'I suppose she'll try and talk to Paul Green,' she is saying.

'Does he still live around here? I thought he'd moved to London.'

I used to see Travis Green's son, strimming hedges or repairing fences, on my forbidden teenage trips to the quarry up at the Farnwood Estate. Stella, Bec and I, plus whatever boys we were hanging around with at the time, used to meet there, vodka poured into cans of Fanta, thinking ourselves so sophisticated as we puffed inelegantly on illicit cigarettes. The boys would dare each other to go ever closer to the edge, Adam Groundswell's tragic fall being ancient history to us; we'd only been babies when it had happened.

'Yeah, he did a few years ago, with some woman, I think. Dunno what happened, but he came back with his tail between his legs a year later.'

'Who was she?' I've never heard of him being involved

with anyone, although he must have been; he's in his late thirties.

Chloe and Mum have finally reached the door to the hall, and they pause.

'No idea. I doubt she was from round here, though; no one from Hartstead would touch him with a bargepole.'

'Why not? Because of what happened? It wasn't his fault.'

'No, but he's a bit weird, isn't he? Drinks too much, so they say. Shaun – that's my other half – says he sees him pissed in the pub all the time, but not, like, *fun* pissed. On his own, sinking pint after pint.'

'That's sad.' Poor man. His life must have been over-shadowed by what happened even more than mine has.

'And it's not just that,' Chloe says hurriedly. 'There were rumours that he knew what his dad was planning – even that he was involved somehow.'

'What? That's ridiculous. He was thirteen years old.'

'I don't know, that's what people said. He idolised his dad, apparently.'

Mum jerks her head up. 'She understood,' she says.

'What's that, love?' says Chloe.

'She understood,' repeats Mum.

'Who?' I say.

'She suffered like I did. She was the only one who understood.'

'Yes, that's right,' Chloe says to Mum. 'Best to agree with them, whatever they say,' she adds to me as if Mum isn't right there. 'They get ever so upset otherwise.'

'She can hear, you know. She's still a person,' I say coldly, as if I haven't been guilty of seeing her only as her dementia.

'Yes, I know,' says Chloe, flushing. 'Sorry.' She leads Mum from the room, and fusses over her in the bathroom, cajoling her as if she were a child.

In the hall, I tuck Amy into the pram and pull on my trainers. Maybe she'll sleep for a bit and I can walk in peace for half an hour. I'd love to stop for a coffee the way other mums do, but the pram has to be constantly in motion or she wakes up.

'Just popping out with Amy for a bit,' I call, manoeuvring the pram over the bottom of the door frame and down the steps. As I walk along the pavement, Amy starts to shift and grunt, always a prelude to a screaming session. My fingers curl around the navy handle, straining with the effort it takes not to give the pram one hard shove down the hill and simply let go.

Chapter 4

15th June 1994 | Paul Green

Paul watches his father clean his gun at the kitchen table. The muscles in his forearms twitch as he rubs the barrel up and down with an old piece of cloth. He hopes Travis is going to let him stay off school again and take him shooting squirrels up at the quarry on the Farnwood Estate, like he did on Paul's thirteenth birthday. Paul gets a warm feeling in his stomach when he thinks about that day. His mum had made herself useful for once and made them sandwiches, great thick doorstops of white bread with salted butter and ham from the butchers, not the pale floppy kind, and a flask of tea syrupy with sugar, the way his father likes it. Paul doesn't really like tea, but he'd gulped it down happily, lukewarm and tinny from the flask, sitting close beside his father on a fallen tree. He's not felt so happy since.

Travis hates Hartstead just as much as Paul does. He talked about it that day – the small-town gossips, poking their nose into people's business. You couldn't fart without everyone knowing about it, Travis had said, and Paul had laughed so hard that tea spurted out of his nose. He's getting out of here as soon as he's old enough, he's promised himself. Not for him this small life of trotting between work and pub, returning reluctantly each night to wife and kids. There's something better out there for him, he's sure of it.

The quarry is strictly forbidden, has been since Adam Groundswell smoked a joint that turned out to be a lot stronger than normal weed and fell into the pit. People still go there, though. A gang of kids a couple of years above Paul gather there on a Friday night, cans of cider clinking in carrier bags, weed hidden in their innermost pockets. Travis goes there too, shooting squirrels for fun, and the odd pheasant for the pot. Old Stan Fowler, the groundskeeper at Farnwood, turns a blind eye. He's known Travis since he was a boy. Paul can't imagine his father as a boy. It seems to him Travis must always have been as he is now – grizzled, dirt under his fingernails, smelling of earth and rolling tobacco.

Paul goes to the quarry too, when he can. His father doesn't know that. He's built a den in the copse near the drop, where he can secrete himself and watch the comings and goings. He watches Travis, wishing he'd ask him to go along with him.

He doesn't blame his father for wanting to get out of the house, away from his mother. There have been times where Paul hasn't liked the way his father treats her, but he's found out something recently that's changed his view. Paul knows more than he lets on about his mother, and when he lets himself think about it, he knows she deserves everything she gets.

Chapter 5

I'm out walking with Amy in the pram in the hope of getting a bit of peace, having left Mum dozing in her chair, surrounded by the Post-it notes she leaves for herself in a futile attempt to hold on to what remains of her life. Once she was standing again after the initial body-blow of her diagnosis, she took a typically practical approach, implementing all kinds of systems to make sure she ate, attended appointments, took her medication. As well as multiple Post-its, she put everything into her iPad, alarms going off at all times to remind her about various things. And it worked, for a while. She's past that stage now, but the Post-its remain. They're abstract now, though, mysterious. I found one this morning by the side of her bed that said simply, 'Remember'. Her handwriting, once bold and slanted, now wavery and shaky, pierces my heart.

I wasn't intending to go to the baby group Chloe mentioned, but as I'm passing the hall I can see in through the fire door, which they've left open to let some air in.

I pause for a second, looking enviously at the mothers chatting while their babies sit nicely in front of them on the floor, playing with blocks or cloth books. Maybe Amy will be easier when she can sit up unaided and do stuff. Or maybe she's just bored. I know I am.

Stupidly, I've stood here too long without pushing the pram back and forth, and she lets out a piercing wail. 'Ssshhh,' I say uselessly, jiggling the pram, but I know there's no point. I check the time. I've been out longer than I realised, and actually, she's probably hungry. I can either half run home and suffer ten minutes of screaming, or go in and feed her in there. I've got a carton of ready-made formula and a bottle in the enormous sack I have to lug around with me everywhere I go. Amy takes a breath and this time it's more of a scream than a wail, and it sends me scuttling into the hall. I keep my head down, inhaling furniture polish and instant coffee with a hint of dirty nappy. I take a seat as far away as possible from the little groups that have formed, and rummage in the changing bag. God, there's so much crap in here.

I gradually become aware of a presence, and I look up, my hand still searching the depths of the bag, to see a middle-aged woman with sensible shoes and small round glasses smiling at me.

'Hello, I'm Pat. Welcome. I'm the family and youth work leader here at St Thomas's. Would you like me to hold the baby while you sort yourself out?'

To my surprise and shame, hot tears press at the backs of my eyes at her kindness.

'Thank you,' I manage. 'I'm just trying to find her bottle.'

Pat lifts Amy gently out of the pram and holds her against her shoulder, swaying from side to side and rubbing her back. She quiets instantly, snuffling into Pat's neck. I fight the urge to run, leaving her in Pat's capable hands.

At last my fingers meet the smooth, curved plastic of the bottle, and, next to it, the carton of formula. I place the bottle on the chair next to me and rip the top of the carton open with my teeth, gagging at the sweet viscosity of the milk. I pour it into the bottle and hold out my arms for Amy.

'Do you want to warm it up in the kitchen?' asks Pat.

'Oh, no, it's fine, she takes it cold.'

'Really?' Pat's forehead furrows in concern.

'Yes,' I say, beckoning for her to pass Amy over. 'I read it's best to get them used to it cold, then you never have to bother about warming it up.'

'Alright,' Pat says dubiously, passing Amy to me.

As soon as she's in my arms she starts to cry again, twisting her tiny body so violently I almost drop her. Pat goes to lunge forward as if to catch her, then checks herself. 'I'll leave you to feed her in peace. Do come and have a cup of tea when she's finished.'

I smile in agreement, silently vowing to get her back in the pram and out of the door as soon as the last drop of milk is gone. It takes a while for Amy to settle to the bottle, but after a minute or two where she takes a few mouthfuls then pulls away, spitting and coughing, she stills, and begins sucking away contentedly. I look up, and my attention is caught by a poster pinned to the board on the wall next to me, among the notices for prayer groups and jumble sales. It's advertising a service and candlelit vigil in the churchyard on Saturday 15th June, to commemorate those killed in the tragedy of that day in 1994. Jesus, I can't get away from it. I know the twenty-five-year anniversary is approaching, but I hadn't thought it would be marked in any way. I don't recall there ever being anything like this before, although I suppose there were probably extra prayers in the church every year. There'd been a bit of a fuss ten years on, but Mum and I hadn't taken part in anything public; in fact I'd come home from university and we'd stayed in for several days, until the journalists who turned up hoping for 'the personal angle' had gone back to London.

I'm making a conscious effort to relax my shoulders, trying to enjoy the few minutes of peace I get when Amy's feeding, when I see Chloe making her way towards me, a chubby, smiling baby on her hip. She's in her 'mum' uniform today, rather than her carer's one – skinny jeans, white trainers, longline top to avoid any accidental display of midriff.

'You came!' she says delightedly.

'I was passing and she needed a feed, so . . .'

Her face falls. 'Well, it's nice to see you anyway. This is Phoebe.'

'She's lovely,' I say obediently, although she looks much like any other baby, only a bit fatter.

28

'Come and meet the others,' she says.

'I can't move at the moment. If I stop mid-bottle, she goes mad.'

'Oh, does she? It's easier with breastfeeding, I suppose: you whip your top up and off you go!' She probably doesn't mean to judge me, but I feel judged nonetheless. Another way in which I'm not a proper mother. 'I'll get them over here – girls! Come and meet Cassie!'

I start to protest but it's too late. Two women are making their way across the room towards us, both in different variations of the mum uniform. One of them is even more polished than Chloe, her honey-highlighted hair smooth, make-up flawless. I'd say she's a few years younger than me and Chloe; the other is older, I'd guess mid-thirties, although it's hard to tell. She looks a bit more like how I feel. She has dark circles under her eyes and I'm not convinced she's brushed her hair today.

I suspect they've recognised me already. I try to keep my life as private as I can. There are ghouls out there who feed on these kinds of stories, and I don't want them to be able to find out what I look like now. It's practically impossible, though. I don't have Facebook or Twitter or Instagram, but until recently I worked in marketing, and photos of me at work events, with my name attached, have slipped through the net. My friends live out their lives online and they assume I'm happy to do the same, gaily posting photos of me on their unsecured social media accounts. I've given up trying to control it.

'This is Della, and little Harry.' Della, the immaculate

blonde, picks up Harry's podgy hand in her manicured scarlet fingernails and waves it at me. I smile weakly.

'And this is Karen, and Theo.'

'Nice to meet you,' says the tired-looking woman.

'This is Cassie Colman,' says Chloe. 'We were at school together, at St Margaret's.' She doesn't raise her eyebrows, or load her voice with significance, but I've been playing this game too long not to hear it: she has told them about me already. *Guess who I ran into – Cassie Colman! Yes, the one who ... yes ... back then.* It won't be long before they work it into the conversation, wanting to pick over what I know, what I saw. Not much, as it happens. What does anyone remember from when they were four? I know I was found beside my mother as she cradled my dead father in her arms, the body of Travis Green beside her, gun in hand. But do I actually remember it? I think it's unlikely. Any memories I had have been overlaid with the little I've been told, and the reports I looked at online as a teenager. I devoured them in secret, finger hovering, poised to close the page if my mother should come in. Despite our closeness in every other way, Mum was always reluctant to talk about the details of what happened that June day, and eventually I stopped asking.

'Would you like a cup of tea?' asks Karen. 'I could bring you one over.'

'Oh, no, thanks, it's OK. I won't get the chance to drink it.'

'Can't you put her down on one of the mats for a bit,

when she's had her bottle?' says Della. 'She can have a little kick about.'

'She doesn't really ... do that,' I said. 'She's ... ' I tail off. What I want to say is *she's a total bloody misery guts*, but I sense that won't go down well here.

'A bit grumpy?' Karen fills in helpfully, and I give her a grateful smile.

'Yes.'

'It can be hard when they're like that,' she says, and I realise that, while the other two have sat down next to me, she hasn't stopped jigging from foot to foot. That's the only reason Theo's not screaming the place down. 'My husband can't stand it. He seems to think all other babies are like these ones.' She waves a hand at the happy babies playing on the floor. 'He says I must be doing something wrong.'

'They just don't get it, do they?' Della chips in. 'They don't spend all day with them like we do. Tom expects to roll in from work, throw Harry up in the air a few times and then have him quiet and in bed. If I ask him to do the bedtime routine for once, he says, *I've been at work all day*. What does he think *I've* been doing, painting my nails?'

To be fair, from the state of her, that would be a reasonable conclusion. I pull my sleeves down over my own ragged nails.

'What about your partner?' Della goes on. 'Does he help?' It's a seemingly innocent question, but I can't help suspecting she's been primed to ask it by Chloe, in the hope of extracting more info about Amy's missing father.

'We're not together,' I say, hoping to shut it down. I wish with all my heart I could join in with this casual moaning about useless husbands – although, from what Guy says, he was a pretty hands-on father with his son. I could have been the smug one who said, *Oh, Guy's great with Amy. He had her all last night and let me sleep. He takes her out every morning in the buggy before he goes to work to give me a break.*

'Oh, what a shame,' Della says, all *faux* sympathy.

'God, that must be hard,' Karen says with feeling. 'I mean, Simon's pretty crap but at least he's there, and he does help out a bit. There's no way on earth I could do this alone. You're a hero!'

She's the first person I've met who's given any indication that motherhood isn't a bed of roses, and I'm about to speak, to reach out and let her in, in the hope that she understands a tiny bit of how I feel, when Pat calls out.

'OK, everybody, it's music time!'

All the mothers (and they are all mothers, not a stay-at-home dad in sight) drift towards the centre of the room and sit down in a loose circle. Pat puts a cardboard box down in the centre and to my horror I see it's filled with tambourines, glockenspiels and other happy-clappy instruments.

'Oh, I won't stay for this.' Amy drains the last of her bottle and I lift her onto my shoulder, patting her back as other mothers do, although she never seems to bring up any wind. 'Amy's not really a ... fan of music.'

'Don't be silly, she's a baby!' laughs Della. 'How can she be a fan of anything?'

'I know, it's just … she'll probably cry, and it'll spoil it for the others.'

'There's always a minimum of three crying,' says Karen. 'Theo's usually one of them. Don't worry about it.'

'No, really, I'd better go. I'll see you another time.' I hastily tuck Amy into the pram and leave the way I came in without looking back.

As I hurry down the street, I wonder if moving back to Hartstead was the biggest mistake I've ever made. I'm completely alone. Stella and Bec are long gone. The only person I know from my previous life here is Chloe, and I can't see her and me becoming friends now. Mum's only going to sink further into dementia and away from me. What's more, to some I'll never be anyone other than 'tragic Cassie Colman'. It's been a quarter of a century since the events of 15th June 1994, but, however desperate those involved are to forget it, they can't. How can you forget the worst thing that ever happened to you?

Chapter 6

The high street has changed a lot since I last lived here eleven years ago. The mini-mart is a Tesco Metro, and what used to be a cosy little tea room is now an identikit chain coffee shop, its outside seats almost exclusively filled with well-heeled mums, buggies crammed around the tiny tables. I've no urge to join them, but I do experience a pang as I pass the Lamb and Flag pub. It looks the same as it did when I was a teenager, although I've heard it's changed hands. Despite us being blatantly underage, the old manager used to serve me, Stella and Bec up to a point, keeping a paternal eye on us and refusing us once he felt we'd had enough.

There's a beer garden at the side, and a few lucky souls are enjoying a cheeky daytime drink in the sunshine. There's nothing special about it – weathered wooden picnic tables on a patch of scrubby grass – but I'm pierced by a longing like physical pain for my old life. It's such a simple thing, to sit in a pub garden with a friend and feel the warmth of the sun on your face, the cool liquid slipping down your throat, the thrill of confidences shared.

I loiter by the gate to the garden, pushing the pram to and fro. I can't go in by myself, can I? It wouldn't be the same. So why am I still here?

'Can I get the gate for you?' The young woman at the nearest table stands, suspended in the space between the bench and the table. She's about my age, a bit younger perhaps, dressed in all black – chic, rather than Goth – with angular glasses that give her a sharp, enquiring look. There's a half-drunk glass of wine on the table in front of her, and a book – a new novel I've heard about but can't imagine ever getting the opportunity to read.

'Oh, no, thanks. I'm not coming in. The baby …' I indicate Amy, fast asleep, butter wouldn't melt.

'I'm sure they won't mind. It's not busy, and it's a fairly family-friendly place.'

She heaves herself out, flipping one leg and then the other over the bench and pulling the gate open for me. Maybe she recognises my desperation. I don't know why else she'd be so keen to help me.

I push the pram through and stand awkwardly by the table as she sits back down. 'I can't … she won't … ' That kindness, the tiny act of holding the gate open for me has undone me and a tear rolls down my cheek. I wipe it away furiously. 'Sorry.'

'That's OK.' She's remarkably sanguine. 'What is it?'

'I had been thinking I'd like a drink, but if I stop the

pram she'll wake up and start crying and I'll have to leave. It's just easier not to.'

'Not to what?'

'Not to do anything.' There's a dull finality to my words that makes the tears prick again. It's true: I don't do anything. Everything is so hard now, and so not worth it. It's easier to stay home, or just go for short walks.

'Would you . . . ' She hesitates, glancing at her wine and book, and I suspect she's already regretting her rash act of kindness. 'It's fine if you don't, but would you like me to jiggle the pram for you while you go and get a drink? Or I could go to the bar for you, if you'd rather?'

'Oh, God, would you?' For fifteen long weeks, the only other people to have held Amy or pushed her pram are professionals, apart from Aisha, on the one day when she came down from London to visit. She cooed over her and professed to want to hold her, but as soon as Amy began to cry she couldn't wait to hand her back: *I think she wants her mummy.* She pushed the pram for a bit when we went out for a walk, trying it on for size, to see how it would feel to be a mother. She doesn't have the faintest idea. I haven't heard from her since. I get the odd message from my other London friends, and from Stella and Bec, but I reply only briefly, having nothing to contribute any more. They don't want to hear about sleepless nights and nappies, and about my having the same conversations over and over again with my mother, who is not really my mother any more. That's all my world consists of now.

'Don't stop moving it,' I say, pushing the pram at her. 'Can I get you another one?'

'Oh, no, I'd better not, I'll be asleep by dinnertime.'

'You sure?' I say. I used to be the queen of making my friends have 'just one more' in my old life.

'Oh . . . go on, then. White wine – a small one.'

I smile to myself as I duck through the low doorway into the cool of the bar. Still got it.

'Won't be a minute,' the barman says to me from the floor. He's kneeling by the fridge, stacking mixers into it from a cardboard box. His T-shirt is riding up and I can see part of a tattoo on his lower back – Chinese symbols, I think, or Roman numerals; I can't tell from this angle. I'm rubbish at Roman numerals; I can never remember which is the C and which the M.

'No hurry,' I say, hoisting myself onto one of the torn red leather bar stools, savouring this small moment of freedom, relishing the smell of stale beer and the stickiness of the bar beneath my elbows.

'Right, what can I get you?' He rolls up his shirt-sleeves, revealing tanned forearms.

'Two small white wines, please.'

'Any particular one? We've got pinot grigio, sauvignon blanc . . .'

'You choose,' I say, and with a jolt of panic, or shame, I realise I'm flirting. What's the matter with me? He wouldn't be interested in me: he's gorgeous, and almost certainly several years younger than me. I pay and take the glasses with a minimum of further interaction.

Back in the garden, I blink in the sunlight, my eyes taking a second to adjust. My stomach drops away. There's no sign of the pram, Amy or the stranger I left her with. The glasses are slippery in my hands. I put them down on an empty table next to me, looking helplessly around. There's a young couple absorbed in each other on the adjacent table and I step on wobbly legs towards them.

'Have you seen a woman with a baby?' I blurt.

They look up blankly. The man shakes his head, but the woman's face creases in confusion. 'That was you, wasn't it, with the baby?'

'Yes, it's my baby, but she's with someone else now . . . a woman dressed in black, glasses.'

'Sorry, no,' she says, losing interest.

There's no one else in the garden. Oh God. My heart races and I struggle to draw breath, immobilised. I simply don't know what to do, where to go. I pull my phone out of my pocket, then realise I don't know who to call. I don't have anyone to call. The thought of dialling 999 occurs to me, and the scene unfolds in my mind as if it's actually happening: a sympathetic police woman becoming gradually more judgemental as I relate how I left my baby with a complete stranger. How I was glad to do it, purely to have a moment alone at the bar; how I flirted with the handsome young barman while a wicked woman stole my daughter.

Then my heart rate slows and I wipe the sweat from my upper lip, because she's there, the woman, emerging from behind the pub, smiling at me, pushing the pram along the path that borders the garden.

'I went for a turn around the garden,' she says. 'She was stirring and I knew how much you wanted her to stay asleep. I was terrified she'd wake up on my watch!'

'Oh, thanks.' I take a gulp of my wine, hoping she won't notice how much I am shaking.

'You didn't think I'd done a runner, did you?' She laughs.

'Ha! You're welcome to her,' I say, biting down hard on a grain of truth.

'Do you want to join me?' She nods towards her table where, as I would have seen if I'd looked a moment ago, her wine glass and book still sit, along with her jacket.

'Are you sure I won't be disturbing you? You've got your book.'

'No, it's fine. It's a bit hard going, actually. For some unknown reason the author decided not to use any speech marks. God knows why it won all those prizes. To be honest, I've no idea what's going on.'

'OK, if you're sure.'

We sit down opposite each other. She's still pushing the pram back and forth.

'Do you want me to take over the pushing?' I say, half-heartedly.

She looks at me closely, narrowing her eyes, which are brown with flecks of green. It's ridiculous, because we've just met, but it feels as if, unlike anyone else in my life, she *sees* me – how tired I am, how close to the edge. I hadn't realised how much I was craving that recognition.

'No, I'll do it,' she says. 'You drink your wine. You look as if you need it.'

I take another slug. 'God, I can't remember the last time I did this. It feels like a million years ago.'

'Big life change?' She looks at the pram.

'Yeah, you could say that. You don't . . . ?'

'Have kids? No. Not sure I'm the maternal type. I'd have to find a bloke first, anyway.'

'I'm not convinced I'm the maternal type either, to be honest.' My voice catches with the terrifying thrill of voicing this thought out loud.

'Maybe there isn't a type,' she says, unfazed. 'I mean, what do we mean when we say that? An earth mother who breastfeeds for five years and doesn't let her children watch any TV? There are all sorts of mothers. Who's to say one type is better than another? I mean, I'm no expert, but I would have thought if you make it to the end of the day and you're both still alive and healthy, that counts as a win. Especially when she's so tiny.'

'I feel like I'm failing her all the time.' Now I've let one uncomfortable truth spill out, more are following behind. 'I don't know what to do with her, and she's so . . . miserable.'

'Hey. I'm sure you're doing the best you can. What about her dad? Is he a help?'

'He's not on the scene.' I consider leaving it there, but

the wine has loosened my tongue, and I tell her what I was too ashamed to say to Chloe and the others. 'He's married. He has a child already with his wife.'

'Oh. That must be tough.'

'Yes, it is.' Understatement of the year. I try not to, but in my weaker moments I stalk his Instagram account, torturing myself with pictures of him and his wife and son at the zoo, and at restaurants, and tumbled together cosily on the sofa for a family movie night.

I take a gulp of my drink, unaccountably embarrassed at the personal turn the conversation has taken.

'Sorry, I haven't introduced myself. I'm Natalie,' she says, sensing my discomfort.

'Cassie.' No need to mention my surname. She'll find out soon enough, knowing this town. 'Do you live in Hartstead?'

'No, Tunston. I work freelance from home as a graphic designer. Sometimes I go a bit stir-crazy, so I jump on my bike and come over here for a drink.'

'Motorbike?' I have a vision of her in leathers, blasting around the country lanes, freedom personified.

'God, no, bicycle,' she laughs. 'Clears the head.'

The young couple have left and the barman comes out to clear their table. 'Can I get you anything else, ladies?'

'No, thanks,' I say. If I have any more, I'll definitely regret it when Amy wakes me in the night. He moves behind me, picking up discarded crisp packets and beer bottle labels from the grass.

'How about you?' Natalie says. 'Are you local?'

'Yes, I ... I grew up here. Then I went away to university and after that I was working in London. I moved back a few months ago, what with the baby and ... everything.' I've already said more than I meant to about Guy. I don't want to get into the situation with Mum.

Possibly it's my imagination, but I sense the calculations behind her eyes, the ones I see every time a new acquaintance hears where I'm from. *How old is she? So what age would that make her in 1994?* Although Natalie's surely not old enough to remember, unless she's taking an eternal youth potion.

There's a pause, and then I do something I never do. I volunteer the information.

'If you're wondering, yes, I am *that* Cassie. Cassie Colman, tragic tot, daughter of the last victim.' *Tragic tot* ... that's what the newspapers called me.

'Oh.' She looks down, clasping her glass. I seem to have knocked all the words out of her.

'You know what I'm talking about?'

'Yes, of course. Everyone round here knows the story. I'm so sorry.'

'Thanks.' In some ways what happened to me on 15th June 1994 is simply a fact of life to me now, but it's still nice to receive sympathy as opposed to morbid curiosity.

Natalie draws a breath, as if she's about to say something important, but there's a whine from the pram. Great. My time is up.

I stand up abruptly, almost knocking the tray of glasses

and other detritus from the passing barman's grasp. 'Oh, God, sorry.'

'No harm done. You off?'

'Yes, she's about to wake up and believe me, you do not want to hear her in full flow.'

'See you again,' he says, twinkling at me.

'You've got a fan,' says Natalie when he's gone.

'What? Oh, no, he was just being ... you know, barmen, that's what they do, isn't it?' I tuck Amy's blanket in needlessly.

'He wasn't so chummy with me,' she says, grinning. 'He likes you.'

'Yeah, right. I'm such a hot prospect, what with the bags under my eyes and baby sick down me. Anyway, I need to go.' Amy's cries are ratcheting up, and it won't be long before she's at her peak.

'It was nice to meet you,' Natalie says. I know she's going to pick up her book when I've gone and enjoy the last of her drink, and it should make me hatefully jealous, but, weirdly, it doesn't. She's the first person I've spoken to since I moved back to Hartstead that I could actually imagine being friends with.

'Shall I ... ?' I stop, unsure of the etiquette. I feel as if I'm asking her out on a date. 'Would you like to meet up again some time? If you need to get out one day.'

She looks pleased. 'Yes, sure, that'd be nice.'

Wow, that was easy. A throb of pleasure and pride pulses through me, at having reached out and put down a tiny new root. We exchange numbers and she says she'll let me know next time she's over this way. I set off down the street, a little fizz of happiness in my stomach for the first time in months.

There's something lingering below it, though, less fizz and more gripe. It takes me a moment to work out what's causing it, but I get there in the end. I may have opened up to Natalie about certain things, but I haven't shown her the worst of me. In that moment, when I thought she had taken my daughter, I felt a soul-crushing fear, I really did. And when she rounded the corner with Amy I was drenched in relief. But there was a tiny hint of something else below the relief. A minuscule fragment of me was thinking, however subconsciously, that, if Natalie had stolen Amy, I might get a full night's sleep. Yes, there was a microscopic, monstrous speck of disappointment.

Chapter 7

It's one of Mum's better days today. On these days, if I don't go out, she sometimes remembers who I am all day. And then, all I want to do is sit beside her and talk like I used to. I want to tell her about Amy, about how hard I'm finding motherhood. I long to ask her if she ever felt the way I do, or if it came as naturally to her as it seemed to; if our bond was there from the start, or if it took time to grow; if what I'm feeling is normal when your life has been up-ended by the arrival of a child, or if there's something wrong with me.

But I don't talk to her about any of these things. Her dementia has placed a wall around her and I simply can't relate to her in the way I used to, although I desperately want to. I want to see her as the same person – the mother who said it was alright for me to swear as long as it was in context, who bought wine for me and my friends and let us drink it at home where she knew we were safe, who let me know every day that I could be whoever I was, without fear. I know she's still in there somewhere, but I can't find her. I couldn't find her when I discovered I was accidentally pregnant and longed to discuss it with her – my fears about Guy, about bringing up a child alone; my uncertainty about whether I should keep the baby. I tried, but it quickly became obvious that she couldn't hold the thread of the conversation, and that it wasn't fair to make her keep trying. Instead, stupidly, I chose to talk to Guy.

It didn't take long for me to understand that his initial tears weren't joy for the baby I was carrying, or sadness at knowing it was time to leave his wife. He was crying for himself, because he realised how badly he had messed things up for all of us involved in the situation. He was also crying for me, because he assumed without asking that I would choose to terminate the pregnancy. And the truth was, I had been considering a termination. I'd already booked myself for a consultation, cancelled the appointment and then rebooked it. But the indecent haste with which he wanted to rush me to the clinic raised my hackles, and I found myself telling him I wanted to keep it, phoning the clinic in front of him to cancel the appointment for a second time.

You could say I had the baby to spite him. More fool me.

So, instead of pouring out everything that's in my heart, I chat lightly to Mum about what's on the telly. I'm sorry I have to go out, but by mid-afternoon I'm nearly out of nappies so I need to walk down to Tesco's. By the time I get back, she may have gone again. She's always happy to see Amy, though, even if she doesn't always know she's her granddaughter.

'I'm popping to the shops,' I say to her now. 'Chloe will be here soon.' That's another reason to go out. I haven't seen her since the baby group earlier in the week. I don't want to be pressured into going again next Tuesday.

'Who?' says Mum.

'Chloe. Your . . . ' I don't want to say *carer* to her. Who wants to think they need help with the basic tasks of living? 'The woman who comes for a . . . chat. She was at school with me.'

'Oh, *her*. Old . . . ' she points at her own eyebrows ' . . . beetle brows.'

'I should think she pays good money for a beautician to do them like that. They're all the rage now.'

'We used to have them very thin,' Mum says. 'Like this.' She draws an imaginary arch with her finger. 'Made you look like you had a poker up your . . . you know.'

'Mum!' I sound as if I'm telling her off, but actually I love the way her old self spikes up from time to time, rising above the surface like a dolphin and then plunging back down. 'I've got to go now, but don't say anything to Chloe about her eyebrows, will you?'

'I know I'm losing it but I've still got my manners.'

I'm not sure which are worse: the days when she knows something is wrong with her, when she understands her decline into unknowingness, or the days when she is mindlessly oblivious.

In Tesco's, all the baskets with wheels and a pull-up

handle have gone, so I hang an ordinary one over my arm, pushing the pram with some difficulty with the other. I stand in front of the nappies, debating whether to try a different brand. They're more expensive, but promise to improve your baby's sleep. Might it be worth a try?

'It's Cassie Colman, isn't it?'

A woman with impossibly smooth skin and auburn hair piled in a messy bun is standing to my left, slightly too close. I bet it took hours to arrange it that artlessly. She's wearing a casual but elegant black jumpsuit and a denim jacket. I step back and smooth my hair, feeling instantly frumpy in my leggings and tunic that covers a multitude of sins. I don't want to confirm my identity before I know who she is, although I have a pretty good idea already.

'Sorry to barge in,' she says, holding out her hand to shake. 'I'm Alison Patchett.'

Who else? I don't take her hand and she lowers it uncertainly. 'Who's this?' she says, reaching into the pram, thinking she's on safer ground here.

'Don't touch her,' I snap, jerking the pram away. 'She'll wake up.'

'Sorry.' She withdraws her hand. 'It's years ago, but those days are still fresh in my mind. I once flew into an absolute rage with the postman because he knocked too loudly and woke Katie up. Now I can hardly drag her out of bed for school, can I, Katie?'

I hadn't realised the red-haired teenager loitering a few metres away was with Alison. The girl barely acknowledges that Alison has spoken, merely raising one expertly groomed, heavy eyebrow *à la* Chloe, and tugging her school uniform skirt down. I can't help thinking that if she hadn't rolled it over so many times at the waist that it barely covered her bum, she wouldn't have needed to pull it down.

'How old is she?' I can't help but ask, even though I'm reluctant to prolong our conversation. I would do anything to have to wake my child, rather than the other way round.

'She's thirteen now, God help me.'

Blimey, I'd thought her older than that. I suppose they learn how to do make-up from YouTube. I was still daubing at my eyelids with a bright blue eye pencil at that age.

'I had her very young, but I guess it got it out of the way,' Alison goes on. Chloe said Alison was a couple of years older than us, but she doesn't look it. I would have put her at least a couple of years younger, but I suppose lack of sleep has aged me considerably.

'But it gets better loads before that. This is the worst bit, honestly. Katie was a horror at first, but by six months she was sleeping right through.'

'Really?' These stories are like a drug to me: I can't get enough of them.

'Yes. It will pass, I promise.'

I stamp down an absurd urge to fall on her neck sobbing. She's just trying to butter me up so she can interview me for her article.

'I know what you're doing,' I say, trying to re-establish my initial enmity.

49

'Yes, I'm shopping for groceries.'

'Oh, very funny. You recognised me from your research. I know about this anniversary article you're writing.'

'Yes, I'm writing an article, but it's not simply about Hartstead. It's a wider piece about how towns move on from traumatic events, what sort of a mark they leave. It's for the *Sunday Times*, not some tabloid rag.'

'I don't care who it's for. Do you know how many times I've been approached over the years by journalists? And how many times do you think I've spoken to them? None.'

'Alright, I get it.' She holds her palms up in mock-surrender. 'I wasn't angling for that, I promise. Obviously if you wanted to talk to me that would be great, but I understand if it would bring back too many traumatic memories.'

'Oh, for God's sake, I thought you said you weren't writing this for a tabloid. I don't have any *traumatic memories*. I don't have any memories at all from that day.'

She takes a step closer. 'Nothing at all?'

'Well – little flashes. But I don't know if they're real memories or just what I've read, or been told, or—' I snap my mouth shut. There's a gleam in her eye that tells me she's thinking this is *gold*. 'Don't contact me about this again,' I say, grabbing a pack of my usual brand of nappies from the shelf and flinging them into my basket.

'I'm interested, that's all, because I've come across a few ... discrepancies in the reports from that day. About what happened to you, particularly.'

Discrepancies? My stomach tightens. I long to ask more, and she knows it, but instead I steer the pram around her and make my way towards the tills.

'If you change your mind, Chloe Riordan's got my number,' Alison says to my retreating back.

'Chloe?' I turn. 'What's she got to do with it?'

'Nothing,' says Alison evenly. 'I'm talking to lots of people, about what impact the tragedy has had on the town, how the effects are still felt twenty-five years on. I'm not only interested in those directly involved.'

'Really? Or are you interested in people who know me? And my mum? If you come anywhere near her . . . '

'I've no intention of bothering her. Cassie, I'm not the enemy. It's not going to be a sensationalist piece, picking at old wounds, trying to make them bleed. It'll be sensitive.'

'Whatever.'

This time she lets me go. I pay for the nappies and head home, needing to be inside where nobody can stare at me. Whatever Alison thinks she has found out, the only one who really knows what happened to me that day is my mother, and her memories have gone where no one can find them.

Chapter 8

15th June 1994 | Peter and Jane Frogmore

They've had it for the last twenty years or so, ever since they became commonly used in schools. 'Peter and Jane? Like the books? Oh, how funny!' When they met in 1932 the books didn't exist, but now it seems like fate that he should have found his Jane, his other half. Peter knew the moment he first saw her, working behind the counter in Shepherd's, that she was the woman he was going to marry. It was a good decision, one that saw him through the war, and found her still waiting for him in Hartstead, with their children, when he came home forever changed.

She has her faults, of course, like everyone. She's a terrible cook, which, although it has given them a laugh over the years, has been quite difficult; she can be nosy, prone to gossip, which he has never liked and always discourages in her; and there was that man who had been hanging around when Peter came home from France in 1945. He had never got to the bottom of that. There have been times in the past sixty years when she's felt further away than others, their relationship ebbing and flowing like the tide. It's more a steady stream now, though, and here they are, pushing eighty and still together, still happy. Still making each other laugh every day.

They're managing in their own home, which is lucky considering where many of their friends are. Peter still does the garden, and, although Jane's arthritis won't allow her to help him, she sits in her deckchair and chats to him while he weeds and plants and waters. He has to take a break every twenty minutes or so, so today they're both sitting in their chairs with a cup of tea, admiring his handiwork. He does more in the front garden than the back these days. No one can see in the back apart from Travis and Elaine next door, and they don't care. Peter has seen their son, Paul, staring out of his bedroom window, but Peter doubts the boy was criticising their gardening, or lack of. He's a funny one, that Paul.

'That needs pruning,' says Jane, pointing a gnarled finger at the lavender that separates the garden from the pavement.

'Alright, add it to the list,' he says genially. She's been compiling and adding to this mental list for years, since before the war. However much he does, it never gets any shorter.

A shadow falls across Peter's face and he looks up. 'Oh, hello,' he says, seeing only the man and not the rifle in his hand, his brain unable to translate the reality of the situation into something he can understand.

The last emotion Peter experiences is not fear, but a sort of baffled confusion. It's Jane who feels the fear rising in her like the unstoppable urge to vomit. Her voice isn't strong enough, as it would have been years ago, to fully scream. What comes out of her mouth is little more than a whimper, and the man with the gun soon silences that. A wisp of smoke rises, dissipating almost instantly into the clear, warm air. Travis Green doesn't look back. He lets the gate click shut behind him and strides away down the street, leaving Peter and Jane slumped in their deckchairs. In this quiet street, in this sleepy town, it will be a while before anyone notices they are dead.

Chapter 9

'You talking to Alison Patchett, then, for her article?'

'What?' I look up from the box file I am rifling through.

'Della said she saw you, in Tesco's,' says Chloe as she helps Mum into her chair.

I'd forgotten what it was like, living in a small town. God help you if you had any actual secrets. 'No, she basically accosted me. I told her I won't help with the article.'

'Oh, OK. Are you looking for anything in particular in there?'

'Mum's birth certificate. I've made an appointment to go and see Oakdene House, and they said they'll need it.'

'Oh, no.' She looks down at Mum's wiry grey hair.

'Not ... any time soon.' I try to communicate that we shouldn't discuss it in front of Mum. I have talked to her about it but I'm not sure how much she understood, or if she's been able to hold it in her mind since. 'But I'd rather go and look round now and take my time making the right decision when it's not an emergency.'

'Oh, I know. I understand. It's a shame, though, isn't it?'

'Is it?' I say coldly, focusing hard on the papers in the file – bank statements from years ago, insurance policies long-since expired. *A shame* hardly covers what I feel at the prospect of having to put my mother into a home, of admitting that I can't care for the woman who has spent all of my life caring for me.

'Right, I'll see you tomorrow, then. Bye, Sylvia.'

Mum doesn't look up. She seems to have gone rapidly downhill recently. It may have been a mistake mentioning Oakdene to her.

When Chloe has gone, I go into Mum's bedroom. I've looked in every single file in the spare bedroom that serves as an office. I've found details relating to the car she no longer has, the house, insurance, finances and more, but no birth certificate. Maybe there are more files in here. I step quietly, half holding my breath, as if expecting to be told off. I don't know why, I was never forbidden from coming in here as a child, but I always felt it was off limits, very much 'hers' as opposed to being just another room in our house. I haven't cleaned in here much since I've been back, and the surfaces are covered with a fine film of dust.

I open the drawers, one by one, finding clothes she hasn't worn in years. A beautiful silk dress with a pattern of flowers and butterflies gives me a sharp stab of recognition. I reach out a finger and stroke it, cool and soft to the touch. A memory sparks – Mum in this dress, glass in hand, twirling around and laughing, the full skirt

56

billowing around her. In the wardrobe, I run my hands lightly over a rich brown fake fur coat. She would go out wearing this on winter evenings, a hammered silver necklace glinting at her throat. Where was she going? I didn't care enough to ask at the time, too excited about inviting my friends over in her absence, and I'll never know now. I wonder how many other childhood memories lie buried, waiting to surface.

There are shoe boxes in the bottom, but they either contain shoes or are empty apart from the crackle of tissue paper. There's nothing belonging to my father. Does she have a few of his special things tucked away elsewhere, or did she throw everything away in one fell swoop, unable to bear any reminders of him in the house? Along with the details of the shooting, it's the one other subject on which she remained tight-lipped: my father. Every now and then she'd feed me a titbit of information, but it was never enough to satisfy me.

It's not a big room and her bed is pushed up against the wall to create more floor space. She's never needed a bed with access on both sides, not since my dad died. Was she ever lonely? She must have been, living with only me and her grief to keep her company all those years. I guess what they had was so special, she felt she couldn't or didn't want to replace it.

I peer under the bed, but it's too dark to see all the way across. I switch on my phone torch and kneel down again. There's something there, on the far side, pushed right up against the wall. I lie down on my stomach and slide beneath the bed, trying not to breathe in the dust. I pull it towards me and wriggle back out. It's a faded purple cardboard envelope file, the fold-over flap torn and ragged. I sit cross-legged on the floor and lift the flap, revealing the original brighter purple beneath. I pull out the contents, a thick wodge of newspaper cuttings, letters and other papers. So this is where all the personal stuff is. There's a bundle of letters on the top, an anachronism in this digital age. I haven't written a letter since the thank-you notes Mum forced me to write as a child. I can't recall ever having received a handwritten letter. By the time I went to university, even Mum had moved on to email.

I open the top one. It's dated 1985, the year after my parents met and two years before they married. *Dearest Sylvia*, it starts. Must be from Dad, although I flip it over and check, half expecting – hoping, in a weird way – to discover a shocking secret. But no, it's signed *All my love, Gary*. I study my father's handwriting, spiky and defined, as if it will allow me to know him. Phrases jump out at me: *never felt like this before, you're all I need, it's us against the world*. I was right, they really did love each other. Like most people, I don't have any clear memories from before the age of five or six, by which time Mum hadn't appeared to be grieving. She was simply my brilliant mum. I grew to realise that her life had been affected in the same way mine had, by being viewed as the tragic widow of Travis Green's final victim; but, because I had no personal memories of my father, I sometimes forget that she did. That she lost the love of her life on 15th

June 1994. There must have been times when her cheerful demeanour was a front for her grief and pain, but she never let me see it.

I had honestly believed Guy was the love of my life. Maybe I was stupid and naïve, maybe it was the oldest story in the world – a married man who wanted to have his cake and eat it too – but I did. I'd had boyfriends before, and thought I was in love with several of them, but it had never felt the way it did with Guy. I'd never felt truly seen before, as if he could cut through all the outward confidence, the veneer, into the true heart of me. I knew it wasn't an ideal situation, but I also understood that it wasn't easy for him to walk away from his son. I never pressured him to leave, but deep down I'd always thought he would. I know I should be angry with him now. I know Mum would be if she could understand what has happened. But I'm not. I just miss him.

I put the letters on the floor beside me, looking round guiltily in case Mum is watching me through the open door. Underneath the letters is a collection of newspaper reports. I leaf through them. They all relate to the shooting. Most of them I've seen before, although never in this house. There's a picture of the senior police officer in charge of the investigation, DI Barraclough, in one of them. I recognise the name from my frantic teenage googling and peer closely at the grainy black and white picture of a middle-aged man with hooded eyes and a lustrous moustache. The next one has a photo of Travis Green and his wife, Elaine, sitting on a beach. It must have been taken in the 1980s, but it looks much older, a relic from a bygone age of kiss-me-quick hats and strolls down the promenade. Travis raises a bottle of beer to the camera and Elaine smiles widely, holding tight to the arms of her deckchair. I search her face. Did she have any idea what sort of man she was married to?

At the bottom of the pile is a packet of photographs, another thing that doesn't feature in modern life. In a few years' time, if I show this to Amy, she won't know what it is. I open it up. The first one makes my heart contract. It's a picture I've never seen, of my dad in the garden, the one that's still there outside the back door, holding what must be me as a tiny baby. He's looking down at me with such tenderness, such pride, one strong arm cradling my body, his other hand resting protectively on my chest. There are a couple of albums of family photos in the lounge, but Mum has always said that was all we had. I'm hit by a wave of impotent anger that she never spoke to me about him, never allowed me to feel the love he so clearly had for me. That she didn't allow me to know him, through her. He is a closed book, and now there's no one left who remembers him, no one who can open the book, even a crack. I also ache with a fierce sadness for Amy, who will never have a daddy who looks at her like this.

I leaf through the rest of the photos. They're a motley collection, from different times. There's a wedding photo of my parents that I've seen before. A couple of me as a baby and young toddler. Scenery I don't recognise, the grandparents I never knew. Then I get to the last one.

I drop it as if it's burning my fingers and sit very still, my eyes glued to it. My mum, on a windswept, grassy area that looks like it could be a clifftop, a wide expanse of blue sky above her. She is smiling, her face open, strands of hair whipped by the breeze. She's arm in arm with an attractive woman of about the same age who sparkles at the camera. If I hadn't just seen her picture in that newspaper report I wouldn't have recognised her, but it's definitely her – although she looks different here, happier.

Mum never mentioned knowing any of the other victims of the tragedy. None of the newspaper reports said there was any link between any of those killed; in fact they specifically state that the attacks were random, and that none of the victims had any connection to each other.

But the woman in the photo, arm in arm with my mother, is Travis Green's wife. It's Elaine Green.

Chapter 10

I still haven't asked Mum about the photograph. Every time I go to do it, I lose my nerve. This morning I'd decided I'd make myself sit down with her and go through all the photos in the folder, in the hope of sparking a memory, but Amy is more crotchety than usual and I don't get the chance. The four walls are closing in on me, so I take her to the park. There are mothers there, proper ones with toddlers, throwing bread to the ducks. One of them smiles at me as I pass with the pram, thinking that I'm like her, another normal mum, enjoying her time with her child. I wish I could feel like that about Amy.

I've only been out for half an hour, but the minute I walk back through the front door I know something's wrong. The telly is blaring from the front room and there's an acrid smell, like burnt rubber. I run to the kitchen, leaving Amy squirming in her pram in the hallway. There's a pan on the hob, black smoke issuing from it. I grab a tea towel, snatch the pan off the heat and chuck it into the washing-up bowl, which still has the water in it from the breakfast things. It hisses and spits at me, charcoal fragments floating to the top like scum.

I switch off the hob and sink down at the table, head in my hands, bone-weary from head to toe. I'm exhausted from lack of sleep, yes, but I'm also tired of everything being my responsibility. Of not having anyone else to bounce my decisions off, let alone make any of them. A wave of misery at Guy's absence crashes over me, although whenever I try to imagine him being here, involved in Amy's life and care or helping with the decisions about Mum, I find I can't. I've always told myself he wouldn't leave his wife because he didn't want to hurt or lose his son. But in the small hours of the night, when I stand at the window, Amy squirming and squalling against my shoulder, when the voices in my head that I try to ignore are at their strongest, I know that's not the reason. Guy just doesn't love me, or not enough to up-end his entire life.

So, once again, everything is down to me. I've known the day would come when Mum can no longer live at home, but I didn't expect it to arrive so soon. There's a small, selfish part of me that wonders where I will live if the house has to be sold, but the most pressing issue is going to see Oakdene House, and somehow (although I have no idea how) deciding whether it's the most appropriate place for her. In the hall, Amy's working herself up for a full-blown wailing session. I stand up and move towards her. The photo will have to wait for another day.

Later, I find myself standing in reception at Oakdene House, Amy strapped to my chest in a baby-carrier that I've decided might be easier than bringing the pram. Chloe will only be with Mum for the next hour, so I can't be long. The GP recommended Oakdene because they will take those at Mum's stage of dementia. Naïvely, I had thought a care home was a care home, but no: I've entered a whole new world of acronyms denoting different levels of care.

A middle-aged woman in an ill-fitting skirt suit bustles out.

'Cassie? I'm Anthea Newland. Welcome to Oakdene House.' She holds out her hand and I give it a limp shake. 'Right, if you'd like to come through this way,' says Anthea, 'I'll show you our communal areas first. This is the day lounge.'

It's a bright room, afternoon sun streaming through the windows onto comfortable chairs and freshly painted mint-green walls. It's uncomfortably warm, but it certainly doesn't have the lurid swirly patterned carpets and faded velour sofas of my imagination. There are a few women sitting around the television, ancient, hunched and silent. None of them look our way.

'This is nice,' I say, as a response seems to be required.

'Let's go and see one of the rooms,' says Anthea.

I follow her obediently down the corridor.

'This is our dementia floor, so, pending assessment, this is where Mum would be.' She's got an annoying habit of saying 'Mum' instead of 'your mum'. It's like the health visitor who refers to me as 'Mum', even when speaking directly to me. After she weighed Amy the other day, she said, *And how's Mum?* I thought she meant my mum at first, and began to talk about her dementia, until she broke in and explained she'd meant me. *Me? Oh, I'm fine*, I said, plastering on a smile and self-consciously stroking Amy's head.

'We've got an empty room along here I can show you.'

We pass an open door and I peek in.

'No!' shouts a tall, strong-looking woman, lashing out at the young girl trying to help her out of bed.

The girl steps back calmly out of range. 'Alright, Vera,' she says. 'Let's try that again, shall we?'

'Our patients can have challenging behaviours,' says Anthea. 'All our staff are highly trained to deal with it, and we work very hard to ensure these behaviours don't impact the other residents. Now, here's the room.'

It's pleasant but plain. It could almost be a mid-price hotel room if it weren't for the telltale handrails and commode, and an indefinably institutional air that gives it away.

'This is nice, isn't it?' I say again, feebly.

'We are very strong on person-centred care here,' says Anthea. 'We ask families to put together memory boxes with key items in them, and to bring photos to put up on the walls and so on. We understand that our residents are still the same person they always were – that they have interests, likes and dislikes. We see the person, not the dementia.'

I put my lips on Amy's soft little head, my eyes hot with unshed tears. God, I wish I could still truly see Mum as a person. I know she's in there, but I can't reach her, and sometimes I think I've stopped trying.

'That's good,' I say. 'But she wouldn't be on this floor, would she?' I think of the grey heads in the day room, the woman I saw in the bed who must have been eighty plus.

'Oh,' says Anthea, looking puzzled. 'I thought you said on the phone . . . and your GP's report . . . Alzheimer's . . .'

'Yes, but it's early-onset. She's only sixty-three. She'd be with the other younger dementia patients, surely?'

'I'm afraid we don't have any in residence at the moment. Obviously it's more common in older patients.'

'But the GP told me about this place! Why didn't she recommend somewhere more suitable for someone of her age?'

'I'm afraid there's no such thing, not round here anyway.' Anthea has the sympathetic, discomfited look of someone breaking bad news. 'There are a few places that specialise in early-onset around the country, but nothing in this area.'

'So she'd be with all these old people?'

'Yes. I can't say for sure what level of care she would need. There would need to be a full assessment, but if our findings are in line with what you and Mum's GP have told me, then yes, she would be placed here.'

I thank her, but make my excuses as soon as I can. I can't let Mum go there. They're all about twenty years older than her. She's still young. She was planning to set off round the country in a camper van. This is not the right place for her.

Chloe's about to leave as I get back. She fills me in on what Mum's had to eat and how she's been.

'You'll never guess who knocked on the door while you were out.'

'Who?'

'Alison Patchett!'

'Jesus, you're joking. You didn't let her in, did you?' I can't believe the brass neck of her, turning up here.

'Only for a minute. I thought ...'

'Mum's not well enough to be interviewed by a journalist! What on earth were you thinking?'

'No, she wasn't here to see Sylvia. She wanted to talk to you.'

'She was sniffing around, trying to dig something up about Travis Green. Why the hell did you let her in?'

'I'm sorry, Cassie, I didn't realise. You won't tell my boss, will you?' There's fear on Chloe's face, and I realise I know nothing about her circumstances. Is she the breadwinner in her family? Care work is notoriously poorly paid.

'No. But please don't let her in again. Did she talk to Mum?'

'They were chatting while I made a cup of tea. I couldn't hear what about.'

Dear God. I hope Alison realises that whatever Mum said is likely to be untrue. Or some of it will be; she does have the odd moment of lucidity, but it's not always easy to tell the difference. I can't help wondering, though, whether she said anything about Elaine. This could be my chance.

When Chloe's gone, I go into Mum's bedroom, retrieve the folder from where I stowed it back under her bed, and take out the photo of her and Elaine. In the lounge, Mum's watching television. She was never much of a one for watching the telly before. She was a reader, but she hasn't picked up a book in the few months I've been living here. I suppose she can't follow the thread. I sit down next to her on the sofa and take her hand self-consciously. We always hugged and kissed before, but since I began to lose her I've felt weird about it, as if I'm touching a stranger. Will I be with Amy like Mum was with me, always hugging her or stroking her hair, cuddled up together as our default position? I can't imagine it. One of the reasons I don't touch Amy as much as I could is that I am afraid of waking her if she's asleep, or setting her off crying if she's awake.

'Was Chloe here today?' I ask, for something to say.

'Yes, I think so,' says Mum vaguely.

'And Alison? A woman with red hair?'

'Yes.' She sounds less sure. At times I think she agrees with me as a way of trying to hide the extent of her confusion, as she did in the early days, before she was diagnosed.

'I couldn't help it,' she says, looking away from me, out of the window.

'What? Talking to Alison? I know. It's not your fault. She should never have come here.'

'I couldn't see another way out. I'm sorry.' She looks straight at me, her watery hazel eyes unaccustomedly sharp.

'What do you mean? Mum?' She seems closer than normal, within touching distance of making sense. But then her face clouds over, and she's gone again.

I can't silence the questions that crowd my mind. My mother knew Elaine Green. Was friendly with her, by the looks of the photo. But according to all the reports, none of the victims were connected. What does it mean? Does it even mean anything? But if it doesn't, why did she never mention it? Why didn't she tell the police at the time? Mind you, she rarely talked about the tragedy at all, so why would she break her silence to tell me about her friendship, if that's what it was, with Elaine?

Mum stares numbly at the telly. I know I ought to be trying to engage her more than I do, rather than being grateful when she's quiet and not bothering me. It's a bit like how I feel about Amy. Great. Another thing to feel guilty about. I'll add it to the ever-expanding list.

'Mum,' I say, hesitantly – she can get quite cross at being interrupted.

'Hmm?' Her eyes don't stray from the screen.

I sit down next to her on the sofa and screw up my courage.

'I found this photo the other day. Who's this with you?'

She looks down, impassive. 'I don't know.' She sounds vaguely annoyed, as if I'm being unreasonable.

'This is you, isn't it?' I point at her.

'Yes, of course it's me.' She's closer to anger now, but I won't give up.

'But you don't know who this is?' I tap Elaine's smiling face.

'How on earth should I know?' She snatches the photo from me and throws it to the floor.

I give up. This is getting me nowhere and upsetting Mum. 'OK. Sorry.' I stand and pick the photo up. 'I'll make a cup of tea.'

She turns back to the television, ostensibly relaxed, but, when I look down, her hands are clenched tight in her lap, her knuckles white like bone.

Chapter 11

gamerboy: hows it going

katiekat2006: alright

gamerboy: u ok to talk, is your mum there

katiekat2006: yeh but shes working. She works all the time. It's alright tho cos she doesn't take any notice of what Im doing!!!

gamerboy: parents r so stupid

katiekat2006: ikr

gamerboy: what does she do then

katiekat2006: shes a reporter

gamerboy: she doesn't check your messages does she

katiekat2006: no she's big on TRUST. Lots of conversations about she must be able to trust me

gamerboy: have you told her about me

katiekat2006: no. Theres nothing to tell is there

gamerboy: not yet maybe 😉

katiekat2006: !!!

gamerboy: mad that you live in the town where that Travis Green thing happened. My mum remembers it from when she was young

katiekat2006: yeah same, actually that's what shes writing about

gamerboy: maybe she'll find out something crazy about it that no one knows

katiekat2006: nah it's not that kind of thing. Just a boring story about different places where bad stuff has happened

gamerboy: tell me if she does find out something cool though

katiekat2006: yeh ok

gamerboy: gotta go, what you doing later

katiekat2006: nothing its so boring here. Chat later?

gamerboy: yeh def

gamerboy: xxx

katiekat2006: xxx?

gamerboy: yeh!!!

Chapter 12

It's mildly uncomfortable sitting at the pub garden table with Amy squashed against my front, but it's worth it for the peace. I lift my face to the sun and give a little sigh of pleasure. Against all the odds, she appears to like the baby-carrier. She'll sleep for much longer in there than she will in the cot or the pram.

I had felt a little thrill of excitement when I saw Natalie's name come up on my phone earlier. I can't remember the last time I felt pleased about anything, so when she said she was going to be in Hartstead this afternoon and suggested meeting for a drink, I nearly bit her hand off. I was ten minutes early to the pub, which made me a bit sad for myself, realising how starved of adult company I am. The twinkly barman is here again, and he recognised me from last week. James, his name is, I've now discovered. Even though I know without a shadow of a doubt that he's not genuinely interested in me, it's still nice to be lightly flirted with, to be reminded that that part of my life is not as over as I had thought.

'Hi!' Natalie sinks down opposite me. She's only wearing black jeans and a T-shirt, but she somehow manages to look immaculately put together. I put a self-conscious hand to my limp, unwashed hair. 'No pram-pushing duties for me today?' she asks.

'No, I've got this brilliant thing. She actually stays asleep in it. It means I have to do absolutely everything with her attached to me, but it's a small price to pay. How are you? Did you get cabin fever again?'

'No, I've given myself the day off. I had to visit a friend who lives out in the countryside over the other side of Hartstead, so I was coming back this way and thought you might want to get out.'

'Oh.' Is my neediness so obvious?

'Oh, God, sorry, that came out wrong. I don't see you as a charity case – I thought it'd be nice to see you, that's what I meant to say.'

'I am a charity case,' I say ruefully. 'You're absolutely right.'

'Can I bring you a drink out?' James appears beside us.

'Oh, yes, please. White wine. How much do I . . . ?' She rummages in her bag.

'It's alright, you can come in and pay at the bar before you leave. I trust you,' he says. 'Not so sure about this one.' He points at me.

'No, she's a total reprobate,' says Natalie. 'I think I've

fallen in with a bad crowd. Look at her, baby strapped to her front, swigging away at a glass of wine.'

'I'll only have one.' I put my glass down abruptly, smile fading. Does everyone think I'm as bad a mother as I do?

'Oh, Cassie, I was only joking. God, I keep putting my foot in it today. As far as I'm concerned you could get hammered. I don't care.'

'I think getting hammered might be beyond the pale,' I say, relaxing. 'Mildly pissed, maybe. Oh, God.' Alison Patchett is approaching on the other side of the street. Hopefully she'll take one of the side roads, but if she doesn't, she's going to walk right past us.

'What?' Natalie follows my gaze.

'Just this woman I don't want to see. I might go and hide inside for a minute ... Oh. It's too late. She's seen me. Damn.'

'Who is she?'

'I'll tell you in a sec. Hi, Alison.'

'Hi.' Alison eyes me warily across the gate, clearly thinking about last time we met. I've got something else on my mind, though.

'Please don't come to my house again. You upset my mother.' This is stretching it a bit. I don't know for sure that she upset her, and, even if she did, Mum certainly doesn't remember anything about it.

'I'm sorry, Cassie. I didn't realise ... about your mum, I mean. I would never have questioned her if I'd realised she was ...'

'Completely gaga?' It comes out harsher than I intended.

'Confused,' she says. 'I know what it's like. My grandmother had dementia. She lived with us for a while before she had to go into a care home. It's so hard.'

'Yes, well . . . ' I am wrong-footed by her sympathy.

'Can I buy you a drink? I really want to talk to you – I know, I know, you don't want to be interviewed for the article, and that's absolutely fine, but there's some stuff I'd love to discuss with you, off the record.'

Has she found out something about me that I don't know? Or could it be that she knows something about my mother and Elaine Green? I think of her talk of 'discrepancies' when I bumped into her in Tesco's. There was a time, when I was about fourteen, at the time of the ten-year anniversary when it was briefly in the news again, that I became obsessed with the events of 15th June 1994. As a child I'd accepted that it wasn't talked about, but as I got older I began searching for anything to do with the tragedy. I read news reports, feature articles, Wikipedia entries, discussions on forums years after the event. I was hungry for any little titbit. Googling my name brought up even more articles and blogs. The authors of these would go on to contact me in years to come, but I'd always refused to speak to them. Alison Patchett needn't think I'm going to change my mind. And there's no way I'm telling her about the photo I found.

But the small, empty chamber inside me, the one that

sent me to search the internet and scroll through the microfiche in the library to find the original news reports, still wants to be filled. I need to find out what she knows.

'I'm having a drink with a friend, but if you don't mind . . .' I look at Natalie.

She raises her eyebrows, mutely asking: *Do you want me to say yes or no?*

I give an almost imperceptible nod.

'That's fine. I'm Natalie, by the way,' she says to Alison. 'Can I get you a drink?'

'Allow me.' James is behind me, holding Natalie's wine. He places it on the table. 'What can I get you?' he asks Alison as she comes through the gate and takes the seat opposite me.

'Oh . . . er . . .'

'You can come in and pay at the end.'

'Great, thanks. Diet Coke, please.'

He gives a mock bow and goes inside.

'This is Alison,' I say to Natalie. 'She's writing an article for the *Sunday Times* about the twenty-fifth anniversary of the Hartstead shooting.' As always, the words lie thick on my tongue. Calling it *the shooting* seems harsh, almost disrespectful to those who died, but what's the alternative? 'The Hartstead tragedy' is overdramatic, laying it on thick like a tabloid newspaper. 'The events' cloaks it in too much mystery, as though it's a dark secret that must not be named.

'It won't only be about Hartstead,' Alison corrects me. 'It's about how towns recover from tragic events such as a mass shooting – what the impact is on those left behind, and those who come after them.'

Natalie sits up straighter. 'Oh, I'd heard someone was doing that. Sounds ... interesting,' she says, although I sense something else behind her words. I shoot her a sharp glare. 'If handled sensitively,' she adds quickly.

'Absolutely,' says Alison, detecting an ally. 'And it will be, I promise. Cassie, I had no intention of interviewing your mum. I just wanted to see you.'

'But you did talk to her?'

'We had a quick chat.'

'Did she say anything?'

'What do you mean?' Her eyes sweep to Natalie.

'It's OK, Natalie knows ... who I am,' I say. 'Mum was a little strange – stranger than normal – when I got back. Did she say anything about ... all that?' About Elaine Green, and the day she sat smiling with her on a clifftop.

'No,' says Alison. 'She wasn't making a lot of sense, I'm afraid. I was only there a few minutes.'

'What did you want to talk to me about, anyway?'

'A few things.'

I bet.

'Did you ever hear anything about what happened to Travis's wife, Elaine?' she says.

Oh.

'Not really.' I try to speak naturally, to not give away what I know – or don't know. 'Just that she moved away from the area.'

'Yes, that's all I can find, too. I've searched online, but

I can't find anything more recent than the reports from the time.'

'That's not so surprising, though,' says Natalie. 'After an experience like that, you'd want to hide away, wouldn't you?'

'Yes, of course. It's more frustrating than surprising. I'd love to talk to her.'

'I highly doubt she'd let you anywhere near her,' I say, thinking, *if she has any sense*. Unlike me, apparently.

It seems Alison doesn't know about Elaine and my mother, anyway. Surely she would have mentioned it by now.

'Quite likely. I've asked around a bit, but no one knows anything. I'm going to keep digging, though, in the hope that I'll find something. I tracked down the original Senior Investigating Officer, a DI Barraclough, but he wasn't giving anything away about her.'

Barraclough. The name gives me a jolt: the newspaper reports under Mum's bed; the photograph of Elaine and my mother . . . I force myself to concentrate on what Alison's saying.

'He's retired now, but he agreed to talk to me – although not about Elaine. Most of what he told me is a matter of public record, but there were a couple of things that were new to me, and that I can't find anything about online or in the original reports.'

'Like what?' asks Natalie, before I have a chance to.

'Firstly, he said there was a rumour going around at the time – never proven – that Travis Green had a collaborator who planned the attack with him, was possibly going to do it with him, but never took part for some reason.'

'People have always said that.' I'm disappointed. This is not new news. 'It's one of those mad conspiracy theories, though, isn't it?'

'Maybe. Barraclough said they did look into it at the time. He was at pains to stress they never found any evidence to suggest anyone else was involved, but he did say one of the rumours was that the accomplice was Travis's friend Dennis Glover.'

I recognise the name from the news reports I'd read. 'Oh, yes, Tom Glover's dad.' Tom had been three or four years above me at school. 'He was a bit of a weirdo, wasn't he? Managed Gladstones' farm?'

'Yes, that's him. Dennis died years ago, but Tom still lives in Hartstead. He had a kid when he was only about nineteen. Ryan, I think his name is.'

'Imagine having a child that young. What a nightmare,' says Natalie.

'It's alright, actually,' says Alison in a clipped tone. 'I had my Katie when I was very young. Lots of advantages.'

'Oh, God, sorry.' A blush spreads across Natalie's face. 'I'm terrible for putting my foot in it.'

'It's fine. Your face, though!' They laugh together, and I have a stupid pang of jealousy that they're having a shared moment. *I brought you together*, I want to say. *You wouldn't even know each other if it weren't for me.* Pathetic. Neither of them is my friend. It's only the second time

I've met Natalie, and I need to be very wary of Alison. I mustn't let my guard down around her.

'Anyway,' Alison goes on, 'I asked around and Ryan lives with his dad. His mum's an alcoholic and he's not allowed to live with her. Tom's married again, with a baby – about the same age as your little one, I think. I tried to talk to him, but he wouldn't let me in.'

'You can't blame him,' I say. 'He won't want all that stuff dragged up again.'

'Exactly,' Natalie says.

'Barraclough told me something else, though,' Alison says. 'Oh, thanks!' James sets her drink in front of her.

'You're welcome.' He moves away, loading empty glasses from a nearby table onto his tray.

'What?' says Natalie.

'They did look into the Dennis Glover thing, and, as I said, they never found any evidence that he was involved, or anyone else for that matter. But there was another rumour going around at the time, which was that the accomplice was one of the victims. That one of them had helped him plan the whole thing, but it had gone wrong and Travis had turned against them.'

'That's crazy.' I mentally scan through the victims. 'Where on earth did that come from?'

'I don't know. Barraclough didn't know either. It's probably total rubbish. It was just . . . something I hadn't heard before. Something to think about, to question.'

'How would you go about finding out, though?' Natalie asks.

'Talking to people who were around at the time, the ones who were involved.'

'Does it matter?' Natalie looks from Alison to me and back again. 'I mean, I'm not trying to create an argument, I'm genuinely asking. Is it worth causing real distress by dragging up painful memories?'

'You're right,' I say. 'It's bad enough that this town is only known for this one awful thing.'

'I know,' says Alison. 'I understand that, I really do. I'm from here, remember.'

'What school did you go to? You weren't at St Margaret's, were you?' I'd know her, surely, if she had been.

'No, I was at Callenden. My parents travelled a lot, so they wanted me to board.'

That explains her self-confidence. It's what parents pay £30,000 a year in school fees for. My best friend Janine Murphy left St Margaret's to go there when her grandfather died and left her parents a load of money. I never saw her again.

'What was that like?' Natalie asks. 'I go past there occasionally; they still make the girls wear boaters and those awful dresses.'

'It was alright,' Alison says. 'It was … school. Katie's there now, as a day pupil.'

'You say you understand, but did you lose anyone, in the shooting?' I say, unwilling to let it go.

'No, I didn't.'

'It's not the same for you, then. You *can't* understand.'

'OK, fair enough.'

'Do you remember your dad at all?' Natalie asks me. 'You were, what, four?'

'Yes, four.' I'm uncomfortably aware of Alison, unwilling to divulge anything intimate in front of her.

She can read me like a book. 'I won't put anything in the article that you tell me in a personal conversation, I swear. We're talking as . . . friends, at the moment.'

Are we friends? For a moment I feel wary again – journalists have these tricks, don't they, to lull you into divulging more than you meant to? But she does seem genuine, and I realise I want to talk about it more than I thought.

'I remember someone, I think. Swinging me round, lifting me up high in the air. I don't think it was Mum. It's snatches, tiny fragments of memories, but I don't know if they're real or not. A pink plastic teapot. I think he used to play with me with it, but I don't know if that's a real memory, or if Mum told me about it . . .'

'My dad wasn't around when I was growing up,' says Natalie. 'It makes you close, doesn't it? When it's just you and your mum.'

'Yes.' *Close* almost isn't a strong enough word, not for me and Mum. That's what makes it so hard to be grieving for her while she's still alive, the mother I'm losing, day by day, piece by piece. I don't, would never, wish her dead, but, if she were, I could feel uncomplicatedly sad, instead of conflicted, trapped and guilty.

'So, are you local, Natalie?' asks Alison. Such an innocuous question anywhere but Hartstead. Here, it's loaded, and contains within it many other questions.

'I live in Tunston, so yes, local-ish.'

Not really. It's not the same for those who live in nearby towns and villages. They don't get the sympathetic head-tilt, the sharp intake of breath, the macabre curiosity.

'Did you grow up there?' God, Alison never takes a minute off. I suppose that's what made her so successful so young. That and the private education, and the contacts in the industry it no doubt conferred. Plus I keep forgetting she's not as young as she looks.

'Yes,' Natalie says. 'A Tunston High survivor.'

'What was that like?' she says, intrigued, and I want to laugh. Alison wouldn't have lasted a minute at Tunston High. The kids had to be searched for weapons on the way in even back then, and I saw a headline in the local paper recently about kids there getting involved in drug-trafficking.

'As you said, it was school.' She grins. 'Bit different from Callenden, though. Do you still live around here?' She turns the question back on Alison.

'Yes, not far,' Alison says.

'Is it just you and your daughter, or . . . ' Natalie leaves a delicate pause.

'Yes. Her dad and I broke up a long time ago.'

'Does he live nearby?' I ask, thinking longingly of the alternate weekends off that a divorced mum would get.

'He was from round here originally,' she says. 'In fact . . . oh, it doesn't matter. I haven't seen him for years now.'

'What?' says Natalie.

'Oh, it's no big deal,' Alison says, picking at a thread of

loose skin around her fingernail. 'He knew Paul Green, when they were kids, that's all. Before the shooting. I think they were at primary school together. But honestly, it's neither here nor there. We're not in touch. Katie doesn't see him.' She speaks with an air of finality, cutting off the possibility of any further questions. I don't mind, because something she said earlier is still pricking at me, the craving for information that drove me to the news reports as a teenager still gnawing inside me. If only Mum had talked about it more, or at all, maybe I wouldn't be like this.

'You said there were a couple of things that DI Barraclough told you ... ?'

'Yes. So there was the thing about the accomplice, and then there was something else.'

'Yes?'

She hesitates, and the penny drops. 'Is it about me?'

Amy stirs and shifts in her pouch. I haven't got long before she'll wake and want feeding.

'Yes.'

'Go on.' Everything is very still and quiet apart from the gentle clink of glasses, as if all three of us are holding our breath.

'It's not anything major; it's ... you know how all the news reports said you were found next to your mother, covered in blood?'

'Yes.'

'You don't remember that, do you? It's OK, I'm not asking as a journalist. This is all off the record.'

'No, I don't remember anything about that day. At least, I don't think I do.' Just flashes again: sirens and blue lights; a forbidding grey sky; sitting in a car with a woman in uniform, the seat scratchy against my legs. The pink plastic teapot. I frown. A flash of something else comes into my mind, but as soon as I try to focus on it, it slips beyond my grasp.

'Well, DI Barraclough told me that you weren't found in the house at all.'

'What?'

'All the papers reported it that way – either because it sounded more dramatic, or they simply didn't know – and no one bothered to correct them, because what did it matter?'

'Where was I, then?' Blood races around my body, beating out a tattoo that gets faster and faster.

'You were outside in the garden, by yourself.'

'What? Where was Mum?'

'She was in the house with your dad, as they said. But you were wandering about outside. And another thing: you didn't have any blood on you.'

'What do you mean?'

'All the papers described you as blood-soaked or blood-spattered, didn't they? Well, that was embellishment on their part again. Barraclough said you didn't have so much as a drop on you.'

'So, what does he think?' says Natalie, frowning. 'That Cassie wasn't in the house at all when it happened?'

'Dunno. He wouldn't speculate, just said they were

the facts. He was one of the first on the scene, so he would know.'

Natalie and Alison continue discussing it, but I drift away mentally, my mind whirling. Mum has never spoken to me about that day, but I've always assumed the reports to be true; assumed I witnessed my father's murder, and Travis Green's suicide too. If I didn't – if she somehow managed to get me out of the house – why wouldn't she have told me, instead of letting me believe something so awful? And if she's effectively lied to me, not only about that but also about knowing Elaine Green, can I trust anything she ever told me? What else has she lied about?

Chapter 13

15th June 1994 | Richard and Sheila Delaney

Will this be the last time? The last time Richard watches Sheila stowing her canvas bags in the boot of the car. He knows she's right to use them on their regular Wednesday morning shopping trip – God forbid they should go shopping another day, or another time – just as she's right to dutifully take the glass to the bottle bank every week. But part of him burns to help himself to as many plastic bags as he likes at the supermarket checkout, loading up his trolley with a hundred of them, each with one solitary item inside.

'Ready, love?' he says. Funny how easily the endearment trips from his tongue. He hasn't felt anything close to love for her for years. Had forgotten what love felt like at all until recently, when it exploded into his life like a firework. It wasn't so much familiarity breeding contempt, what had happened to him and Sheila, but familiarity breeding indifference. He is sure she is equally miserable, if that's the right word for the creeping weariness, the heaviness that has dogged him for the past few years, like a lead weight in his heart, leaving him

unable to feel happiness, even when something ostensibly wonderful happens. Until now. Now something truly wonderful has happened, and for those few hours a week, any he can steal, the weight is lifted and he experiences joy again, fizzing like a burst of sherbet on his tongue.

'Oh, hang on, I've forgotten the list,' she says, and scuttles back into the house.

Richard leans against the car and breathes in the warm morning air. It's going to be a hot, shimmering day. He thinks about what the woods will be like later, dry and hard underfoot, ferns unfurling between dog roses and honeysuckle. An illicit hand slipped into his; warm lips, soft skin. It will be the last time they need to hide away in the woods, though he thinks they'll always go back there, to where it all began. He knows they'll be together forever, that they'll never slide into silence, the way he and Sheila have. He won't make the same mistake twice.

Lost in thought, he barely notices the man striding down the pavement towards him, and certainly doesn't register what he's holding. As Travis stops in front of him, Richard, like Peter before him, doesn't realise what he is going to do until his world explodes in a shower of pain. Lying on the pavement, he is aware of Travis Green's feet in their black boots. He wills them to move on. Despite the new life he was planning without her, there is still a husk left – a shattered ruin of the love he once had for Sheila. He doesn't want this for her. But the boots stay put, and Sheila's heels are clipping down the path, and then there's the click of the gate. A scream. Another shot.

The boots move on.

Chapter 14

Alison's revelation about the discrepancies between the news reports and what DI Barraclough told her have roused my curiosity, long dormant but never completely dead. I keep going back to the folder under Mum's bed and gazing at the photo of her and Elaine, as if by looking I can understand their relationship. The need to know what happened is like an unbearable itch that my fingernails keep creeping back to.

Alison gave me her number the other day in the pub, gagging for me to change my mind and talk to her on the record. On the one hand she's the obvious person to talk to about all this – she may have discovered something from her research for the article which would explain this photo; on the other, she's the last person I should talk to. If there is something that was never reported at the time, never discovered, it's going to make her article yet more newsworthy. Journalists will come pouring into Hartstead, raking through the muck. Isn't it better to let sleeping dogs lie?

Even as I have this thought, I know I can't. My fingers are texting asking to meet before I've fully decided what I'm going to tell her. She replies straight away, saying she's free now if I can make it. I wrestle with indecision. Chloe's already been, so meeting now will mean leaving Mum on her own. Frustration surges through me. Not only am I trapped once by having a baby on my own, there's a double layer of barbed wire around me that I have to fight my way through every time I want to do any little thing.

Sod it. Mum will be alright.

Alison's already there in the pub garden when I arrive, Amy strapped to me as ever. I've put her facing outwards in the hope that being able to see the world go by will distract her. Alison coos over her briefly, but she's plainly not a baby person.

'I got you a glass of wine – I hope that's OK.'

'Thanks.' I take a sip, careful not to spill any on Amy. That really would make me a bad mother.

'So …' Alison is bubbling with barely suppressed excitement. 'You said in your text there was something you wanted to talk to me about.'

'Yes, but it has to be off the record.'

'Oh, come on, Cassie, throw me a bone. Let me quote you in the article, saying something – even if it's nothing revelatory. You can have full copy approval.'

I swivel the glass ashtray round and round on the table, looking away from her pleading stare. James is on the far side of the garden, clearing tables. He gives me a wave and I smile distractedly.

'OK,' I say. 'But you have to tell me everything you find out.'

'Deal! So come on, what is it?'

I reach into my bag and bring out a white envelope. 'You know how it says in all the reports that the victims were random, and not known to each other?'

'Yes.'

'Have you heard anything to the contrary?'

'No. In fact, Barraclough confirmed it again when I met with him.'

'I found this in my mum's room.' I slide the photo out and pass it to her.

'That's Elaine Green, isn't it?' she says. She knows her stuff. 'Who's the other woman?'

'That's my mum.'

Alison's head snaps up. 'They knew each other?'

'Looks like it. But Mum never mentioned it – although she never talks about the shooting at all. Never has.'

'Have you asked her about this?'

'I did, but she ... well, she didn't even recognise Elaine.'

'Ah.' Alison drums her fingers on the table.

'Have you got anywhere with finding Elaine?' I say.

'No. I tried Barraclough again but he still wouldn't tell me anything. Fair enough. All I know is, she moved away right after it happened. I don't even know if she goes by the same name.'

'What do you think this means? You don't think ...' I swallow down nausea. 'You don't think Mum had anything to do with it, do you? Those rumours that he had a collaborator … ?'

'Hey, no.' Alison puts a hand on my arm. 'Don't be silly. You're jumping to wild conclusions. Just because they knew each other, that doesn't mean they were involved in it. There was never any hint that Elaine knew what he was planning. Barraclough wouldn't say much, but he did say she was absolutely destroyed by it, and that I should by no means go after her. I wonder, though …'

'What?'

'Can I get you anything else, ladies?' James appears at our table, as if out of nowhere. I jump, causing Amy to give a little squawk.

'No, thanks, we're fine,' says Alison.

'OK, give me a shout if you want anything,' he says, smiling at me and going back into the pub.

'What?' I repeat, handing Amy my keys. She flaps them up and down and tries to put them in her mouth. Might keep her quiet for a bit. 'What do you wonder?'

'What if it wasn't random?' says Alison. There's a strange light in her eyes and I can sense her hunger for the story, the prickling in her fingertips that tells her she's close to something big. 'If your mum knew Elaine, who's to say the other victims didn't know each other, or were known to Travis Green?'

'It wouldn't change anything, though, would it?' I have the sense of being on a galloping horse that I have no means of controlling. 'They'd still all be dead. Our town would still be infamous. Even more so.'

'Don't you want to know the truth, though? Don't you think the other families who lost their loved ones would want to know? Don't they deserve to know?'

'I'm not sure, Alison.'

'Well, I am. Come on, let's have a look.' She reaches down and pulls a blue folder out of her bag. 'I brought my notes with me, when you said you had something to tell me.'

'I don't think—'

'Right.' She ignores my futile protestations. 'The first to be killed were Peter and Jane Frogmore. The next-door neighbours.' She lays a photocopy of a newspaper article on the table. An elderly couple look up at us, blissfully incognisant of their eventual fate. 'They were known to him, for a start.'

'Yes, but they didn't know him in any real sense. Only to say hello over the fence.'

She looks up in surprise. 'How do you know?'

'I got bit . . . obsessed with it, I suppose, when I was a teenager. Looked up all the reports, read everything I could get my hands on.'

'That's understandable. Especially if your mum never talked about it.'

Amy throws my keys to the ground and bangs on the table. Alison picks them up and gives them back to her. She flings them down again, straining and twisting against the bonds of the baby-carrier.

'Oh, God, she's going to start crying in a minute.' My heart rate is rising. 'I'll have to go.'

'I'll come with you. She'll probably calm down if we walk – give her something new to look at.'

'I doubt it,' I say grimly, standing up and swaying from side to side in a motion that has become as natural to me as breathing since becoming a mother.

'Let's give it a try. Come on.'

'Are you off?' James is out in the garden again.

'Yes, she's about to kick off,' I say, still swaying. 'Don't want to put the other punters off their drinks.'

'OK, hope to see you again.' He opens the gate for us.

'He couldn't wait to get us out of there,' I say to Alison as we walk towards the high street. She was right: Amy has quietened down now and is looking around with what passes for interest in a four-month-old baby.

'That's not true,' she says, looking at me strangely. 'I know it's difficult for you, when you have to take a baby everywhere. Believe me, I've lived it. I was a single mum – and I was a teenager. You can imagine the looks I got. But other people generally don't mind babies, unless they're screaming their heads off. You don't need to get so stressed about it.'

'That's easy for you to say. James practically pushed us out of there.'

'No, he didn't. He was being nice and holding the gate open for us. If anything, I think he likes you.'

'Don't be ridiculous! Look at me.'

'You look fine, Cassie. You look great. Life's not over because you've got a child.'

'It feels like it,' I say shortly. 'I should get home.'

'Hang on – have a look at these before you go. Let's sit here for a sec.'

We balance ourselves on the seats in the bus stop. I bounce Amy up and down.

'So, there was Peter and Jane. Then the next ones were Richard and Sheila Delaney.' She shows me another photo, again photocopied from a newspaper article. 'Do you recognise them?'

'No. Only from the reports. How could I? I was only four when they died.'

'I know. I just thought looking at them might spark something,' she says. She takes me through the other victims – names and photos that are as familiar to me as if I did know them personally.

'This is Graham Mooney, the driving instructor killed while waiting for his next client.'

'His wife was a history teacher at my secondary school,' I say. 'They said she was off for a year after it happened.'

'Oh, yes. Anne Mooney. I didn't realise she'd taught you, though. Would she talk to you, d'you think? If she's still alive.'

'What do you mean, talk to me?'

'Oh, nothing, just a thought.' She hands me the next photo. 'David Wilkes, the estate agent. Then this is Manisha Mehta. She lived in a flat above the hotel, a bit further down the road.'

I search their faces for clues. It's pointless.

'Travis Green moved on to the high street,' Alison goes on. 'The next victims were Suzanne Persimmon who worked at the Citizens Advice Bureau and Melissa Bradshaw, a lawyer. Then it was the dog-walker, Maureen Featherstone.'

I know all this. I've read everything there is to read. It was then that he made his way up the hill towards my parents' house.

'The police had been called,' says Alison, 'so he knew he was running out of time. The streets were largely empty, as friends called each other, told their neighbours what was happening, hid in their houses.'

Did nobody tell my parents? Dad was killed in the house. Did they let him in?

'And the last one was your dad.'

'Not quite the last,' I say, thinking of Mum watching the violent death of not only her beloved husband, the man who wrote those tender letters I found under her bed, but of the gunman himself, too. What she must have been through, seen. What *I* must have seen. Memories scrabble for ascendancy. My mother screaming at me. A noise louder than any I'd heard before.

'Are you OK?' says Alison, catching my arm as I sway forward.

'Yes, sorry . . . ' I put my arm around Amy, although she is safe in the carrier. 'Felt a bit dizzy.'

'Was it a memory?' Alison asks eagerly.

'No! I told you, I don't remember anything. And I need to get back to Mum.'

I stand up and walk away without saying goodbye. There was a ghoulish edge to the conversation that I've encountered too many times before. Alison may be aiming for professional detachment, but she's no more immune to prurient curiosity than anyone else. I don't feel comfortable telling her that more and more new memories are edging their way into my consciousness: the sound of the helicopter as it hovered menacingly in the iron-grey sky; the pink and white check of my gingham dress; a warm wetness in my knickers, nobody having thought to ask if I needed the toilet until they saw the damp patch on the back seat of the police car. And something else too. Something that doesn't make any sense at all.

Chapter 15

15th June 1994 | Graham Mooney

Graham is feeling grateful. Hopeful, too, that this new client will be the beginning of a turnaround for him. The recently opened driving school in Tunston has hurt his business, but it's nice to know past clients are recommending him – that he still has that all-important word of mouth.

He mentally sorts through what still needs to be paid: mortgage and council tax have already gone out this month, so that's OK. There's the credit card bill, but that's going to have to be the minimum payment again. At least Anne doesn't know about that. Yet. His mind strays to the tax bill looming at the end of July, but he forces it away. That's six weeks' time. Anything could happen by then.

He checks his watch and sighs. The client is late. Not a good start. He'll have to finish the lesson at the allotted time regardless of when it began, because for once he's got another lesson straight after, but clients don't like it if they don't get the full hour, even when it's their own fault. He'd go and knock on the door but the bloke didn't tell him his address, just to meet him here, on the corner of Wordsworth Street and Chaucer Close. Maybe he hasn't seen the car. Graham gets out and looks up and down the road, stretching his arms behind him and wincing at the clicks and cracks. All these years hunched in the passenger seat, feet poised over the dual controls, have played havoc with his joints. There's no sign.

He's tired to the bone, mentally as well as in his aching muscles. They tell him things, his clients, as they reverse round corners and into parking spaces. It has to do with the curious mix of intimate proximity, and the anonymity of never looking directly at each other, focusing only on the road and potential hazards. Sometimes he senses that they're saying things they've never told another living soul, as if he were a priest in the confessional, or a counsellor. It's information he doesn't always know what to do with, but they don't seem to expect answers, or even any response. They're happy with the occasional murmured 'turn left here' or 'pull over as soon as it's safe to do so'. It leaves him exhausted, though, as if in giving him this information, in lightening their own load, they have weighed him down.

He's looking the other way, so he doesn't see the man striding down the street towards him, a man with no intention of taking a driving lesson. A man in heavy black boots. A man with a gun.

Graham's just thinking how he would love to retire, if he's honest, but there's no hope of that, not with the state of his finances. He has one last thought before the bullet smashes into the back of his skull: knowing my luck, I'll be working till I drop dead.

Chapter 16

I hear Mum stirring around nine-thirty – hours later than she would have woken in the old days – so I take her up a cup of tea. She had her dinner in bed last night – she's been eating less and less recently, and I've noticed that if she has it up here, she sometimes manages more. I realise as I come in that I forgot to collect the tray, which sits on her bedside table. She's had less than a quarter of the tiny portion of roast dinner I gave her. She looks up blankly as I come in. I assume it's one of her foggy days, so I decide to leave her to it. She's often groggy first thing, but it usually clears once she's had her tea. I place the cup on her bedside table, but, as I do, she shrinks from me, cowering on the far side of her bed, duvet pulled around her protectively.

'What the fuck are you doing here?' she snarls.

I spring back as if she's slapped me. She's not averse to a bit of swearing but I've never heard her use the f-word.

'It's me, Mum. Cassie.'

'Get away from me. Get out!' She's shouting now, a bead of spittle on her chin. She lunges towards last night's abandoned plate and grabs the steak knife I gave her to make it easier to cut the meat, brandishing it in my direction.

I walk out, aiming for steadiness, and stand on the landing, waiting for my heartbeat to slow. I lean against the wall, feeling every bump and whorl of the flocked wallpaper through the thin fabric of my T-shirt. I breathe, in through the nose and *whoosh* out through the mouth. This is what you do, isn't it? To calm yourself down? But what if there is no calming you? What if your own mother has shrunk from you as if you were a violent stranger? I cover my mouth with my hand as if that will hold back the waves of despair. And then I hear a reedy, wavering cry like a hurt bird.

'Cassie? Is that you?'

I rush in, waves of warmth flooding through my veins. She's back. The knife has been replaced neatly on the tray.

'Mum.' I kneel down by the bed, unsure if my legs can hold me any longer.

She reaches out, and I steel myself not to flinch, but she simply strokes my hand with a paper-dry finger.

'Where's the baby?' she says. 'It's Brenda's boy, isn't it?'

Who the hell is Brenda?

'The baby's downstairs. But it's not . . .' I tail off, conscious of all the advice I've read about how distressing it can be for those with dementia if you insist they are wrong all the time. 'Yes, it's Brenda's boy,' I agree.

'Thought so,' she says, continuing to stroke.

I bite back tears. 'Drink your tea,' I say. 'I'll come back in a bit to give you a hand getting ready.'

I stand at the kitchen sink, surveying the garden. The lawn needs mowing and the flowerbeds, once Mum's pride and joy, are such a mess I can't tell which are flowers and which weeds, although I've never understood the difference. I add sorting out the garden to my endless mental to-do list. The moment where Mum didn't recognise me sits in my gullet like vomit. I knew it had to happen one day, but it was worse than I'd ever imagined. If she doesn't know who I am, I can't help her. This is a journey she is taking alone.

And then in my back pocket, my phone rings. It's Alison. I hesitate. There's an addictive pull to the information she's been feeding me, but I'm conscious that it's not necessarily good for me. Unhealthy. I can't resist, though.

She starts speaking before I've said hello.

'Guess what?'

'What?'

'I found your history teacher, Mrs Mooney. She lives on Wilson Road.'

A memory pops. Huge, clear-rimmed Deirdre Barlow-style glasses and a long, straight nose.

'So she's still alive?'

'Yes, she was only in her early fifties in 1994, although

she would have been near retirement by the time you were at secondary school. She'll be late seventies, I suppose, but she's *compos mentis*.'

'How did you find her?'

'Facebook. I messaged her and she's agreed to speak to me for the article.'

'Does she know what you're writing about?'

'Yes, and she was fine, although ...'

'What?' Why do I get the feeling I'm not going to like this?

'I did tell her I was working on it with you.' The words come out in a rush, as if the quicker she says them, the more likely I'll be OK with it. 'I said you'd be coming with me to see her.'

'Oh.' I suppose I should be angry, but I'm swept up in this. I thought I'd put it to bed long ago, that I'd come to terms with my past, but I realise now I'm nowhere near. These feelings were sleeping, waiting for a prince, or a gobby journalist, to wake them with a kiss. I realise with a jolt that I want to go and see Mrs Mooney as much as Alison does. More, probably. 'What time?'

'Oh, right.' Alison had obviously been expecting me to put up more of a fight. 'Four o'clock.'

'I'm meeting Natalie for a drink.' I don't want to cancel; it's the only thing I have that bears any resemblance to a social life.

'Can't you make it later? Say five? We won't be more than an hour at Mrs Mooney's.'

'OK, I'll ask her.'

'Great. I'll pick you up from yours at quarter to.'

'No, it's OK, I'll meet you there.' It'll only take me ten minutes to walk to Wilson Road.

I text Natalie asking if we can meet later, briefly explaining why, thinking as I do how laborious it is having all these conversations via text instead of calling. It's so rare for anyone to phone that I always assume something's wrong if they do. A minute after I text her, though, Natalie does call me.

'Hi, I started to text but then I thought it'd be quicker and easier to call,' she says. I smile to myself. 'That's fine, I can meet you at five, but . . . I hope you don't think I'm poking my nose in, but . . . are you sure you want to do this?'

'Go and see Mrs Mooney?'

'Yes, that, and all the rest of it. Helping Alison with this investigation of hers. I can see why you would – you've obviously got unanswered questions; I totally get that. But I think you need to be careful about whether Alison is really on your side.'

'Yeah, I've thought about that too. And thank you, for caring about it,' I say. 'But she's going to write this article whether I help her or not. This way I'll have some influence over how she does it.' This is true, but it's not the whole truth, which is that I'm sucked in, helpless in the face of the possibility of finding out something, anything about the day I thought was a closed book.

'OK, if you're absolutely sure,' she says. 'In which case I thought . . . ' She trails off. I pick absent-mindedly at a chip in the *faux*-granite worktop. 'I understand if you're not comfortable with it, but . . . I could have Amy for you, if you like? While you go and see this woman?'

My finger halts, the sharp edge of the broken piece pressing into my skin. I don't speak.

'Sorry, it was a silly idea,' she says quickly into the silence. 'I'll see you at five.'

'No,' I say, slightly strangled. I clear my throat and try again. 'No, that would be . . . amazing.' An hour. A whole hour without having to think about whether she's going to cry, whether to put her in the pram or the sling, whether she needs a bottle, or a nappy change, or a sleep. 'Are you sure, though? She's not . . . easy.' I think of Natalie, drinking her wine in the sun, free of care. Does she know what she's letting herself in for?

'It'll be fine, Cassie, honestly. It's only an hour. What's the worst that could happen? Even if she cries the entire time, I'll cope.'

Oh, God, I think. What if she does? Maybe I should take her with me after all.

'Look, if there are any problems, I'll call you, OK? Let me know where you're going to be and I'll stay close, so if I need you, you won't be far away.'

I don't realise how tightly I've been tensing my shoulders until I make a conscious effort to drop them. 'OK. Thank you. Could you maybe come to mine, and we could walk over together? It's only ten minutes but it'll give me a chance to explain about feeding her and stuff, in case you need to?'

106

'Of course. Whatever you like.'

'Thanks.' I can't say much more because I'm so close to tears, and I don't want her to know what a terrible mother I am, how much it means to me to get an hour off.

When I hang up, I can't stop thinking about what Natalie said. Am I making a huge mistake getting involved with Alison? Am I letting my overriding need to know what happened that day overtake my sense of what's right, or good for me? And humming below that is the knowledge that Mum's getting worse; I can't stop reliving that terrible moment where she shrank from me in fear.

It's five minutes before I notice that I've picked off a big patch of the veneer from the worktop. What was a small chip five minutes ago is now a bare patch of exposed MDF, rough beneath my fingers.

Chapter 17

gamerboy:	hey baby, hows it going
katiekat2006:	K. You?
gamerboy:	missing you
katiekat2006:	soz, not been on. Mum took my phone and ipad cos I got in trouble at school
gamerboy:	where do you go
katiekat2006:	Callenden
gamerboy:	posh school
katiekat2006:	its crap
gamerboy:	what did you do
katiekat2006:	called out my teacher. Shes a right cow
gamerboy:	cool. I hate teachers

katiekat2006: me too.

gamerboy: thats so bad she took your phone. Bet she wd go mad if you took her ipad!!

katiekat2006: yeh right, Id have no chance, shes never off it. Working all the time.

gamerboy: she find out anything yet?

katiekat2006: don't know

gamerboy: don't you want to know?

katiekat2006: I guess

gamerboy: you could look at her emails or what shes writing, see if shes found anything out.

katiekat2006: why do you care???

gamerboy: I don't. Doesnt matter. Gotta go.

katiekat2006: no wait

gamerboy: what

katiekat2006: I can have a look if you want

gamerboy: up to you

katiekat2006: she's going out later, if she doesn't take her ipad I can look then

gamerboy: 🖤

katiekat2006: what does that mean!!!

gamerboy: 😉 talk later?

katiekat2006: K 😘

Chapter 18

I chew my lip as we watch Natalie push the pram away from us, weighed down with the changing bag into which I've stuffed everything she could conceivably need during the next hour, along with a written list of instructions covering every eventuality.

'She'll be fine.' Alison squeezes my arm. 'It's good to have some time away. You need it. You'll have to get used to it as well, for when you go back to work.'

I don't reply, preferring to keep my head buried firmly in the sand, away from the incessant worries about money and work and Mum, and what I'm going to do when my maternity pay runs out.

'Shall we?' says Alison.

There's no doorbell at Mrs Mooney's, which is one of a row of terraced houses that open straight on to the street, so she gives a smart knock. There's a high-pitched yapping from behind the door, and a shape gathers on the other side of the frosted glass. As she opens the door, Mrs

Mooney bends down to hold the collar of the small, fluffy white dog that's attempting to jump up at our knees.

'Calm down, Walter.'

She's smaller than I remember, her body hunched in on itself, her skin lined and her hands curled with arthritis. Her eyes, though, behind what surely can't be the same massive glasses, are bright and alert. She must be a good fifteen years older than Mum, but I can tell instantly that she has all her faculties. She's still here.

'Hi, I'm Alison Patchett.'

The dog has calmed down a bit, so Mrs Mooney lets it go and takes Alison's outstretched hand. 'Nice to meet you.'

'And this is Cassie Colman.'

'Cassie.' Her eyes, the colour of melted chocolate, look very large behind the thick lenses, and her fingers feel lumpy and misshapen as they grasp mine. 'Lovely to see you, dear.' Her tone is fractionally different from how it was when she addressed Alison. I don't know if it's deliberate – wanting to let me know she knows who I am, so I don't have to explain – or whether, like most people old enough to have been there on that June day, she simply can't help it.

She takes us into a small, immaculate front room. There are little wooden cases all over the walls filled with dozens of thimbles – a lifetime's work. I wonder if she actually wanted all of them, or if she'd just thought of getting a few and then every birthday and Christmas, every time a friend took a holiday and brought her back a little present, the collection expanded independently of her wishes. *Not another bloody thimble.*

Alison and I sit in silence on the edge of a pristine beige sofa while Mrs Mooney boils the kettle in the kitchen. When she's handed us our tea in bone china, flower-patterned cups, she takes a seat in the armchair by the window, the dog settling itself at her feet.

'So. You wanted to talk about … what happened to Graham.'

I am struck by the thought that I've never spoken to anyone else affected by what Travis Green did that day. Selfishly, I haven't given proper consideration to what the families of the other victims went through. Yes, I lost my dad, but I was so young I hardly remember him. The main impact it had on me relates to how it affected Mum, and my relationship with her. Mrs Mooney lost her husband, her soulmate, the man she thought she would spend the rest of her life with. She's had to live without him for almost the entire length of my life.

'Yes,' says Alison, after a pause in which I realise she had been expecting me to speak. 'As I said, I'm writing an article about how towns recover from tragic events. Cassie's working with me on it.' I look at her, but she remains fixed on Mrs Mooney, offering no sign that she is in any way embarrassed by this semi-lie. 'Do you mind if I record our conversation?'

'Sure. I'm happy to talk about it.'

Alison taps at her phone and puts it on the coffee table. 'I know, for many, it's too hard,' Mrs Mooney goes on. 'They hate it when journalists drag it up, when all they're trying to do is move on. But you can't move on, not really. Not those of us who lost a loved one. And, if you don't talk about it, it festers away, goes inward. I've always talked about it, otherwise it's almost as if it never happened. As if Graham never lived.'

Another way in which she's different from Mum, I think.

'So, could we talk a bit about how you think Hartstead has been affected by the tragedy – as a community?' says Alison.

'Well, these things leave a mark, of course they do.'

I think of the times I would catch Mum with a faraway look, would have to pull her into the present with my chatter about school, or friends.

'You have to accept that for those over a certain age Hartstead will always be synonymous with the tragedy. But in some ways I think it made us more of a community. I think we understood that the way back was to support each other, to come together. Groups sprang up that are still going today – not the counselling ones, although those were helpful for many, I know, but other things: baby and toddler groups, the gardening club, the fish-and-chip supper nights at the town hall. Those were all things that began then, and they're still going strong. I've never lived anywhere else to compare it to, but I think there's more of a sense of community here than in many other places.'

I think of Pat in her owl glasses at the baby group welcoming me, and consider the likelihood of me ever going back.

'So something positive came out of the darkness?' says Alison. 'That's interesting – I've never read or seen anything about that in the press coverage.'

'You wouldn't have, because they're not interested,' says Mrs Mooney tartly. 'That's not the story they're after, is it? They want the tragedy, the despair, the anger, the weeping families. And we've got all those, that goes without saying, but we have something else too. We have people who raised thousands of pounds to support the families of the victims; we have support groups; and Hartstead has a rich history, as well. The tragedy isn't the only thing that's ever happened here.'

'Of course,' says Alison, scribbling in her notebook. 'Would you be happy to talk a bit about Graham, Mrs Mooney?'

'Yes, right.' She has been speaking passionately about Hartstead, but now her face smooths itself out, and I get the sense that she's slipping on a mask. It's something I've been used to seeing with my mother, although she wore hers all the time. I suppose she's taken it off now. I wonder if that's in any way a comfort for her.

'So, he was waiting for a client that day – someone was coming for a lesson?'

'That's right. It was a new one; I know because he was pleased about it. The business wasn't doing all that well, so getting a new client was good news. He had some ... to be honest he was in a bit of debt that he hadn't told me about. I only found out ... after.'

'That must have been hard,' says Alison.

115

'Yes,' says Mrs Mooney shortly, not falling for Alison's sympathy act, if it is an act.

'Did Graham know Travis Green?' says Alison.

'No, not at all. What makes you ask that?'

'Oh, nothing. Just wondering. What about Paul Green?'

'That poor boy? No, we didn't know him, although I've always felt desperately sorry for him.'

'We heard there was a rumour that he knew what his dad was planning?'

'Oh, for goodness' sake, I've never heard anything so ridiculous. The boy was thirteen years old. I thought you said your article was about how the town has coped, not a sensationalist tabloid piece. The shootings were random; the police looked into that at the time. You can drive yourself mad thinking about why. Graham was in the wrong place at the wrong time, that's all.'

'I promise it's going to be a serious, respectful piece,' says Alison, leaning forward, elbows on her knees. 'However, there are a few things that have come to light that don't quite add up. I doubt any of it will make it into the article – it's more for Cassie's sake that we're looking into those.'

Mrs Mooney looks at me over the edge of her teacup. 'You surely can't remember anything from that day, can you?' she asks me.

'Not really . . . bits and pieces.'

'Do you still have any of Graham's stuff?' says Alison. 'I mean, records from the business, that sort of thing?'

'I've still got his work diaries,' says Mrs Mooney. 'I should have got rid of them, but . . . I don't know, something about seeing his handwriting, I couldn't ... ' She wavers, then tightens, closing herself in.

'Could we see them?' Alison asks eagerly.

Mrs Mooney looks from one to the other of us. 'I suppose so ... they're only appointments and things, not personal journals.'

'That's fine, anything that will give us any information – for Cassie, I mean,' she adds.

'They're in the study. Come up.'

We follow her into the hall and upstairs to a box room. The desk is bare apart from a laptop, and the room is empty of any other furniture apart from an office chair and a set of cheap MDF bookshelves loaded with folders and box files, all neatly labelled with things like INSURANCE and WILLS. The top shelf has several faded blue A4 diaries, and she takes one from the right-hand side.

'This was the last one,' she says, smoothing the cover as she holds it out to me. I open it and leaf forward to 15th June. There are several appointments written in capitals, the black biro pressed hard into the paper. The first one is for ten o'clock.

Alison puts her finger to it. 'Nigel Waterford. That's the one ... '

' ... he was waiting for, yes,' says Mrs Mooney.

'You said he was a new client?' Alison asks.

'That's right. Graham was so pleased. There was a driving school opened up in Tunston and they were offering all these deals for new customers. He couldn't compete.'

Alison skims back through the pages. It doesn't look

117

good – some days Graham hadn't had any appointments at all, and others only a few.

My stomach turns over and my hand shoots out to the page. Alison looks at me. 'What is it?'

'There.' I nod towards the page, the word sticking in my throat.

'What?' Mrs Mooney comes closer on Alison's other side, craning to see.

'On the Thursday,' I say. It's a couple of months before the shooting. 'Sylvia Colman. That's my mother.'

'Oh,' says Alison. 'Did you know Graham was her driving instructor?'

'She didn't have a driving instructor.' My voice comes from somewhere else, somewhere far away. 'She learned to drive when I was eight, so we could get the caravan. I remember her saying she'd never had a lesson before in her life'

As I say it, I feel a flicker of doubt, and am disconcerted. How can there be this thing about my mother that I don't know? Maybe it's not that important in the scheme of things – but why wouldn't she have told me? Why would she have lied back then and said she'd never had a lesson?

'Did you know Cassie's mum was a client of Graham's?' Alison asks Mrs Mooney, excitement bubbling.

'No,' she says. 'But I didn't know who any of them were. I mean, he used to talk about them a bit, but he didn't mention their names, or if he did I didn't take it in. Anyway, even if he had said her name, it wouldn't have meant anything to me, not before . . .'

Before my mother and I became unwitting bystanders to the tragedy that fascinated the nation.

'And then, after, I was in no state to be thinking about his clients, or anything else for that matter.'

Alison turns the pages back through the weeks. 'Looks like she had a regular appointment. Every Thursday at eleven o'clock, and – oh!' Alison stares at the diary as if she's seen a ghost.

'What?' I say distractedly, still trying to get to grips with this new knowledge about my mother.

'The same person had the lesson after your mum every week. Well, up until the end of February.'

'There's nothing strange about that,' says Mrs Mooney. 'People like to have their lesson at the same time each week.'

'No, but … the name … look.'

'Elaine White,' I read. 'So what?'

'You said you found a picture of Elaine Green and your mum, so we know they knew each other. It's not that much of a stretch, is it?'

'What, you think Elaine White is Elaine Green? But why wouldn't she use her real name?'

'Because she was taking the lessons in secret for some reason? Maybe Travis didn't like it. They stopped after February anyway. Did Graham ever mention an Elaine?' she asks Mrs Mooney.

'No, I don't think so,' she says.

'So if she *was* having her lessons in secret—'

'We don't know that,' I say hastily.

119

'No, you don't,' says Mrs Mooney, taking the diary from Alison and snapping it shut. 'This is all pure speculation. I think I've said all I want to say to you. You say you're not muck-raking, but I don't know what else you'd call it. You can't change what happened, and every time the media reports on it like this you're picking at the scars, hurting us all over again. I thought this was going to be a positive piece about moving on.'

I start a fumbling apology, but she bustles us out of the room.

'Did the police ever see these diaries?' Alison asks, refusing to give up as Mrs Mooney herds us down the hall towards the front door.

'No, why would they? Graham was an innocent victim.'

'Of course he was,' I say firmly. 'Thank you so much for your time.'

As we walk down the street, Alison speculates, coming up with ever wilder theories, but I'm not listening. All the time we were there, there was a part of me that was silently worrying about Amy, a little tug of anxiety that has now transformed into an energy force, pushing me along, faster and faster, until Alison reaches out. 'Hey, slow down. I can't run in these shoes.'

'Sorry, it's … Amy. Natalie's had her for ages; she's probably kicking off.'

'She'll be fine. It's only been an hour. Where are you meeting her?'

'At the pub.'

'We're nearly there. Honestly, don't worry. I know what

it's like, but you needed a break. You've got so much on your plate.'

'I'm alright,' I say automatically, and I am. I am coping, and I will keep on coping, because I don't have any choice. I don't even know what me not coping would look like. I try to picture what would happen if one morning I didn't get out of bed, if I just pulled the duvet over my head and closed my eyes, for one little morning. I see Amy screaming and hungry in her cot in a dirty nappy, Mum angry and confused at this strange baby in her house, putting a pan of beans on the stove to heat and forgetting it, walking out of the house in her nightclothes, the beans a blackened, smoking mess. Nope, I can't switch off for a single minute, let alone a whole morning.

I increase my pace as we approach the pub, almost tripping over my feet in an eagerness to see Amy that I don't fully understand. I tumble through the gate and across to the table in the garden where Natalie sits, an empty glass in front of her.

'Hi, Natalie! Was everything OK?' I peer into the pram. Amy looks exactly as she did when I left her, her head slightly to the left, rosebud lips pursed.

'Yes, lovely. She didn't wake up.'

I sink down onto the seat next to her, my legs wobbly. 'Thank you so much. I really appreciate it.'

'I didn't do anything.'

'You did. Let me get you a drink.'

'Go on, then. I'll have a white wine. I didn't dare have an alcoholic drink while I was responsible for her.'

There's no one behind the bar, so I slide onto a stool to wait, assuming whoever's working today is down in the cellar. I take a look around, and that's when I see James's familiar curly dirty-blond hair. He's got his back to me, and hasn't noticed there's anyone at the bar. He appears to be deep in conversation with a dark-haired man at the corner table, a man who is vaguely familiar to me. The man drains his pint untidily, beer spilling from the side of his mouth and down his chin. James looks to be asking him a question, leaning forward intently. The man slams his glass on the table and gets unsteadily to his feet, wiping his chin with the back of his hand. He leans down and says a few words into James's ear. I can't hear what he says from here, but it doesn't look altogether friendly. He stumbles past me and out of the door towards the street. James sits at the table for a few seconds, rigid, then stands and heads towards the bar. When he sees me, he puts on a smile but it doesn't quite reach his eyes.

'Hi, Cassie. What can I get you?'

'Three white wines, please. Is ... everything OK?'

Foolishly, I'm struck by a twinge of disappointment. I was hoping that what Alison and Natalie said might be true, that he likes me, but now he seems distant, going through the motions.

'Oh ... yeah. He'd had a bit too much to drink, that's all. I was subtly suggesting he call it a day.'

That wasn't what it looked like. He has to open a new bottle, and I cast around for something to fill the silence. 'Is he a regular?'

'Yes. A bit too regular for his own good. Actually ...'

'What?'

He stops wrestling with the corkscrew for a moment and puts the still unopened bottle down on the bar. Why do I feel as though he's going to tell me something I'm not going to like?

'That's Travis Green's son, Paul.'

'Oh.'

That's why he was familiar. It's been a long time since I've seen him. I'd catch a glimpse of him on those teenage trips to the quarry, or in town, passers-by casting surreptitious glances at him when they thought he wasn't looking. I used to feel a weird sense of kinship with him, both of us notorious thanks to the Hartstead tragedy, through no fault of our own. Both children who became a subject of fascination by the tabloids. Both left behind by our fathers.

'Yeah. He's alright, but a bit of a drinker. Can't blame him, I suppose.'

'I heard he moved to London with a girlfriend, is that right? A few years ago? Then came back?' I'm asking because I can't not, because I can't resist a chance to further my knowledge about Paul Green – but also, I have to admit, because I want to forge a connection with James, to give us a common interest.

'Yeah, that's what I've heard.'

'Was she from round here?'

'No, she was this posh, arty woman he met up at Farnwood when they had a sculpture exhibition in the grounds. She ...' He pauses a minute to pull the cork out. 'I probably shouldn't say this . . . ' He lowers his voice further. 'It was only ever a rumour.'

'What?' I lean in closer, shifting Amy's weight forward.

'No one knows what happened to her. She upped and left him and then . . . disappeared into thin air. Next thing you know, he's back from London, and back working up at Farnwood.'

'What's supposed to have happened to the girlfriend? Surely people don't think Paul . . . did anything to her?'

'I don't know. As I said, it was only a rumour.' James puts three glasses on a tray and fills them with elaborate care.

'What happened to him, after the shooting? Did he carry on living with his mum?' A memory surfaces from the newspaper reports.

'No,' says James. 'He told me about it once, when he'd had even more than usual to drink. That's what people do to barmen, we're like priests.'

'Not entirely,' I say, grinning. 'I don't think priests tell tales about what they've heard in the confessional.'

'Ooh, you'd be surprised. Terrible gossips, all of them. Anyway . . . ' He grows serious and leans over the bar towards me, close enough that I can see the tiny flecks of stubble on his chin. I have to stop myself reaching out and touching his face. 'He told me he was taken into foster care locally, after the tragedy. It was supposed to be temporary – his mum was in a terrible state and wasn't able to look after him – but it stretched out longer and longer, and she kept saying she still wasn't ready to have him back. He ended up living in care till he was sixteen, and then he moved out and got a job on the Farnwood Estate. He's been there ever since, apart from that year in London.'

'He's a gardener up there, right?'

'He's the groundskeeper. He started out as a sort of apprentice, I think, when he was sixteen, then he was a gardener. When he came back from London, old Stan Fowler was retiring, and he'd always had a soft spot for Paul. Paul got Stan's job. Been there ever since.'

I wonder how that felt, returning to Hartstead having finally got away from the notoriety that must have dogged him here. I don't wonder, actually. I know. He felt the way I do now.

I can't stand here much longer without it seeming ridiculous, so I pick the tray up. 'I'd better get these out to the others.'

'Sure, OK. Hope to see you soon.'

I sit quietly in the garden as Alison tells Natalie what happened at Mrs Mooney's. I don't tell them about my conversation with James. Alison tries to draw me in a couple of times, but eventually gives up. There's a warmth in my stomach when I think about James – the way he smiled at me, how close he was, the scent of sandalwood and citrus that I caught when he leaned over the bar – but I can't help thinking about what he didn't say. What was he really talking to Paul about? It didn't look as though he was telling him he'd had enough to drink. But why would James lie to me? And, more than that, why does he know so much about Paul Green?

Chapter 19

I toss and turn all night, running over and over what James told me about Paul. In the morning, as I blearily make up Amy's breakfast bottle, I come to a decision. I need to talk to someone about this if I'm ever going to sleep again. I text Alison and ask if she can meet later. She replies immediately, suggesting the pub.

When Chloe arrives for Mum, I'm so preoccupied by my thoughts about James and Paul that I barely register that she's not her usual ebullient self – quiet and watchful where she's normally chatty and open. I'm in the hall strapping Amy into the baby-carrier when she comes out of the lounge with the air of a person who has a piece to say.

'You should be careful,' she says without preamble.

'About what?'

'People have noticed that you're hanging around with Alison Patchett, helping her with her story. They don't like it.'

'What people?'

'People who were there, who went through it.'

'*I* was there.' I stand up straighter. 'If anyone has the right to know what happened, surely it's me.'

'But you don't remember it, do you? You were only a kid. For those who were there as adults, these articles and things, they bring back bad memories. They don't help anyone. The opposite, in fact.'

I clip the final strap of the carrier in with unnecessary force. 'I don't think it's any of your business, Chloe, to be honest. Alison is going to write the piece, with or without my help. If I want to be involved, that's up to me.'

'I know,' she says. 'I'm just saying it's not going to win you any popularity awards around here.'

'I hardly think I was in line for one of those in any case,' I say, hefting Amy up and adjusting the straps before sweeping out of the door without saying goodbye to Chloe or Mum. Where does she get off, thinking it's OK to speak to me like that? I know for a fact she talked to Alison when she was first sniffing around – Alison told me so in Tesco's that first day. Why has she changed her mind about it now? I know as well as anyone what these articles can do. I watched the lines around my mother's mouth deepen every time something similar happened and they showed footage of Hartstead on the news. I watched her switch the channel without saying a word. I saw the change in her at every anniversary, every time there was a casual mention on the radio of 'the Hartstead massacre'.

This is different, though. Alison has awakened a need in me for the truth, a need that, if I'm honest, has been bubbling away most of my life.

When I get to the pub, there's no sign of Alison in the garden, so I step into the dark interior.

'Hello again.' James is behind the bar, shirt-sleeves rolled up, a tea towel slung over one shoulder. He really is gorgeous. I give myself a mental shake. His large, elegant hands and deep brown eyes are neither here nor there.

'Hi. I'll have a Coke, please.'

'Coming up.'

I take a quick look around to make sure Alison's not sitting inside for some reason, and see the familiar figure of Paul Green, sitting in the same spot as yesterday, a pint of beer and an open newspaper on the table in front of him.

James puts my Coke on the bar. 'He's in here most lunchtimes, and then again in the evening,' he says. Amy, still in the carrier on my front, reaches for my glass, and he moves it out of the way. 'Hey, that's not for you.'

She picks up a beer mat and waves it around, thrusting it into her mouth. I remove it absent-mindedly. James busies himself putting my money into the till.

'Alison mentioned that you're on your own with Amy. That the father's not on the scene, I mean,' he says without looking at me.

'Oh, great, what was it – pity poor single Cassie day?' The bubbles from my Coke fizz painfully on my tongue, and I force thoughts of Guy away.

'No, not at all.' He sounds both surprised and hurt. 'It must be difficult for you. I was raised by a single parent myself, so I do have a tiny idea of how hard it is.'

'Yeah, it's hard,' I say shortly. Being raised by a single parent and being one are not the same thing at all.

'I'm sorry, Cassie. I didn't mean to ...' He hands me my change. 'Forget it.'

We seem to have had an almost-argument, one which I don't quite understand. I don't want to fall out with James; he's one of the only people I know in Hartstead. I think of our last conversation, how keen he was to talk about Paul. Perhaps talking about it again will get us back on a better footing, and it will also give me a chance to ask about Elaine.

'I don't suppose ... oh, sorry.' Amy's got hold of the beer mat again and has gummed one corner of it to a mush.

'Doesn't matter.' He smiles and I feel lighter. 'What do you not suppose?'

'Do you know anything about Paul Green's mother?'

'Like what?' He takes a cloth from the sink and runs it over the surface of the bar, scooping up stray peanuts and scraps of beer bottle labels and emptying them into the bin.

'I think ...' I stop, suddenly unsure whether I should share this information with him.

'What?' He stops wiping for a second, and turns his attention on me. I melt a little, and the words are out before I can give them proper consideration.

'I think my mum and Elaine knew each other – were friends. I can't ask her about it because she's got dementia.'

'I wouldn't know anything about that. But he might.' He jerks his head in Paul's direction. 'Why don't you ask him?'

'Oh, I don't know.' Paul has finished with the paper and is now studying his phone, frowning, his long legs stretched out in front of him. 'He looks busy.'

'Don't be silly. Go on. I'll hold Amy for you – I promise I won't drop her.'

'What if someone needs a drink?'

'It's not exactly Piccadilly Circus in here today, and you're only going to be over there – I'll give you a shout.'

I shouldn't, I know. I should tell James not to be so ridiculous and that we should leave the poor man to enjoy his pint in peace. But the inescapable desire to know more urges me on, whispers in my ear, tempting me with what Paul Green knows, what he might tell me. I lift Amy out of the carrier and pass her across the bar. Her face lights up as James takes her, dimples pockmarking her fat cheeks.

'She likes you,' I say in wonderment.

'No need to sound so surprised.'

'No, it's just . . . I've never seen her like anyone before.'

'She likes *you*,' says James, blowing a raspberry that elicits a chuckle I've never heard.

'Not really,' I say without thinking. 'She needs me. Not the same thing.'

James frowns, suggesting a ghost of a worry, gone before I can be sure it was there at all.

'Sorry, I'm just tired,' I say, the catch-all excuse of the new mother. 'Wish me luck, then.'

Paul looks up enquiringly as I stop at his table, ready to say I can have a chair, or the salt and pepper pots, or whatever it is I'm after.

'Hi. You don't know me, but—'

'Let me guess. You're a journalist, writing a terribly sensitive piece, and you'd love to give me the opportunity to tell my side of the story. No, thanks.' He returns to his phone, swiping briskly at the screen.

'I'm not a journalist. I'm Cassie Colman.'

'Oh.' He stops swiping. 'Sorry, I didn't realise.' He's immediately warmer. It may be the first time my identity has worked in my favour.

'Can I sit down for a minute?'

'OK.' He's still guarded but it's progress. I take the seat opposite him.

'For various reasons I won't go into,' I say, knowing if I mention Alison and the article he'll close up again, 'I've been trying to find out a bit more about what happened that day. To me, particularly.'

'I don't think there's any dispute, is there?' he says. 'My dad rampaged around Hartstead shooting anyone who got in his way, including your father.' His delivery is dry and unemotional, his body language indicating no trace of discomfort.

'I know the police thought so – that he was shooting

at random, I mean. But there are a few things I've found out that have put doubts in my mind.'

'Such as?' Is he clutching his pint a little more tightly, or is it my imagination?

'I found a photo of your mum and mine together. I don't know when it was taken, but I had no idea they knew each other. Mum never mentioned it.'

'Why don't you ask her?'

'I have, but she's got early-onset Alzheimer's. She couldn't tell me anything – I don't think she even recognised Elaine.'

'I'm sorry to hear that,' he says, but again it's flat, emotionless. I don't think he's particularly sorry to hear it; he just knows that's what you're supposed to say when you're told something bad, or sad. 'I've got no idea if they knew each other. I was thirteen when it happened. I was more interested in going out on my bike with my mates than who my mum was hanging out with.'

'There's something else. Did she ... was she learning to drive back then, d'you know?'

'No, not as far as I know.'

'Oh, are you not ... ?'

'In touch with her? No, I haven't seen her for years.'

'So you don't think she was taking driving lessons from Graham Mooney?'

He looks at me sharply. 'The one who was killed?'

'Yes. I've recently found out that my mum was, and there was a woman calling herself Elaine White who had the lesson after her every week, and I wondered if that was how they met?'

He shrugs, aiming for nonchalance, but he seems rattled. 'Can't help, sorry.'

The door swings open and a group of women come in, chatting and laughing. I throw a quick look at the bar and James holds Amy up apologetically.

'I need to go,' I say. 'The barman's holding my baby.'

'Words you never thought you'd say,' says Paul wryly, and I realise there is a person in there, behind the barriers he's had to erect.

'Can I leave you my number, in case you think of anything?' I take the opportunity while he's apparently human.

'If you like,' he says. I scribble it on a beer mat and he pops it in his shirt pocket, while I hasten to retrieve Amy, who's starting to whinge and wriggle. James doesn't look quite as enamoured of her as he did a few minutes ago.

'I'll wait for Alison outside,' I say, forcing her legs through the holes in the carrier.

'Yes, probably best,' he says. 'Did he know anything about your mum?'

'No, he said not.'

'Did he tell you anything else?'

'No, he said he hasn't seen Elaine in years. Listen, James—'

'Sorry, I need to serve these ladies,' he says, smiling at the group of women. One of them nudges her friend below the counter.

'OK, well, maybe we can ...' The words die on my tongue. He's already moved across to serve them. I slink out without saying any more. I'm not even sure what I wanted to say to him. Was I going to ... ask him out? Why on earth would he be interested in me?

Alison is sitting at what I've begun to think of as 'our' table, her face raised to the sun. She turns at the sound of Amy's squeaking.

'Hey, you two.'

'I don't know how long I'll be able to stay; she's already a bit restless.'

'Shall I hold her for a bit?'

'Oh, God, yes please.'

I untangle her from the carrier and pass her to Alison. Amy quiets instantly, almost nestling into her.

'Shall I get you a drink?' I feel I have to ask, as she's holding my baby, but I don't want to go back in there and see James flirting with those women.

'In a minute. Tell me about James and Paul first.'

I fill her in on what James told me, and tell her about the encounter between him and Paul that I witnessed yesterday, as well as my conversation with Paul just now.

'So, what's going on there?'

'I don't know. Paul said he didn't know anything about Elaine having driving lessons, but I'm not sure if he was telling the truth. Listen, Alison ...'

'Yes?'

'You said the other day that your ex was friends with Paul when he was a kid – did they stay in touch as they got older? I mean, was he still friends with him at the time of the shooting? He might be able to tell us—'

'No.' She stops bouncing Amy, who yelps in protest and grabs for a fistful of Alison's hair. 'I told you, we don't speak. And I'm pretty sure they were only friends as kids, not later. So anyway, what about this Nigel Waterford, who was meant to have the lesson at ten?'

'Maybe he was late.' I allow her to change the subject, although she's definitely being cagey about Katie's dad. 'Lucky for him.'

'Maybe. Hey, what's wrong with you?' she says to Amy, who is snuffling and squirming.

'She's getting tired. I should get her home, I might be able to get her to nap in her cot.'

'OK.' Alison passes her over swiftly, although I don't know if it's because she doesn't want to talk about her ex, or because she's fed up with holding Amy.

'Oh, God, sorry, you didn't even get to have a drink.'

'It's fine, Cassie. I'm happy to be able to give you a bit of a break. Shall we meet in the café tomorrow afternoon? Make a change from this place.'

That evening, once I've got Amy down to sleep, I sit and watch telly with Mum, agreeing with everything she says no matter how absurd, my mind full of James and Paul and Elaine. I want so much to ask Mum about Elaine again, but I know there's no point. I fall into bed around ten, more exhausted than I ever thought possible. The night goes by in the usual haze of wake-ups, feeds and pacing the floor. In what passes for the morning in my new life, otherwise known as the middle of the bloody night, I lift Amy out of the cot next to my bed and take her downstairs. In the hall, I notice a letter on the doormat. Surely the postman hasn't been yet? It's only five-thirty.

I plonk Amy in her broken baby bouncer in the kitchen, hand her a mini rolling pin she's taken a recent fancy to and go back into the hall. The envelope, a cheap brown one obviously from a multipack, is addressed to me, no postal address or stamp. Whoever delivered it has done so by hand. I run my thumb under the flap and pull out a sheet of A4 paper. I unfold it, and my bemusement slowly morphs to unease. There are four words written in neat capitals in black biro: LEAVE THE PAST ALONE. Then I notice there's another, smaller piece of paper in the envelope. I take it out and unease deepens into something worse. I force myself to take a breath, but it catches in my throat, fear permeating through me. Amy is grizzling now in the kitchen but I ignore her, my eyes inexorably drawn to the headline cut from a newspaper, the words smudged but horribly legible: *Baby dies in mysterious circumstances*.

Chapter 20

'You got one too?' Alison looks puzzled, and something else I can't quite identify.

'Yes – you mean you got a letter?'

She reaches into her bag and pulls out an envelope the same colour and size as the one my letter arrived in. She pulls out a piece of A4 paper and a scrap of newspaper. The writing is almost identical, LEAVE THE PAST ALONE. Her newspaper headline is different from mine: *Teenage girl missing*, it says.

'Have you told the police?'

'No,' she says. 'But now I know you've got one too, I think we should.'

'What difference does it make that I've got one too?'

'Oh, well ... ' She traces a pattern with her spoon in the froth on her cappuccino. 'It's more evidence, isn't it?'

'Can they do anything, do you think?'

'I don't know, but we should at least log it. In case ... '

'In case what? Something happens to Amy or Katie?

Jesus, Alison. Do you think this is real?' I put my hands round my cup, shivering despite the warm weight of Amy, asleep on my chest in the carrier.

'No, I don't think there's any real threat. It's someone trying to scare us off. I've had worse in my time.'

'What do you mean?'

'Oh, you know journalists, we ask too many questions. People don't like it!' The brightness of her tone doesn't match her expression but I can't worry about that now. 'The question is,' she says with a hint of relish, 'who sent them?'

'This is not a puzzle, Alison. It's not an episode of *Columbo*.'

'I know, that's why I said we should go to the police,' she says, injured.

'It's just, you seem to be enjoying this a little bit too much.'

'I'm not, Cassie. Yes, I have that instinct for a story, I can't deny that. But that's not what this is about. This is personal for me too.'

'What do you mean?' Does Alison have a vested interest she hasn't told me about?

'I'm from Hartstead, I know what it's like to be from a town that's notorious for all the wrong reasons. I wouldn't exploit you, or this town. But something's not right. There was something else going on back then – don't you want to understand? For your mum's sake, and your dad's? For you, too?'

Outside the café window, Hartstead looks like any

other small town in the sunshine, flowers spilling from hanging baskets outside the shops. And, for most people, it is. Those too young to remember, or those who have moved here since 1994, for whom it is not the backdrop to the worst day of their lives.

Of course I want to know, and Alison knows it.

'I've been thinking,' she says. 'We should go and see Tom Glover. This rumour that his dad was involved – I've heard it from a few different people now, although no one can say where it started.'

'When you say *we* should go and see him . . . '

'He's more likely to talk to you, Cassie. This rumour's been floating around for years, so he must have been approached by journalists in the past, yet he's never spoken out. He won't be about to start now. You, though . . . '

Tragic Cassie Colman. Who could turn her away? It sickens me that I'm willing to use it to my advantage, this traumatic thing that happened to me, but I know I will.

'You could go tonight, once he's home from work. I'll take Amy for you,' Alison offers, holding a palm up to stem the protest which is about to spill from my lips. 'Cassie, I've managed to get Katie to the age of thirteen all by myself with no major mishaps. I think I can manage a baby for an hour.'

'What about Mum? I've already been out too long.'

'If you think she'd be OK with it, I could stay with her. That way you could put Amy to bed before you go, and I can be there in case she wakes, or there's a problem with your mum.'

139

'Really?'

'Sure. If you think your mum'll be happy.'

Back at the house, Alison and I sit and have a cup of tea with Mum, chatting away almost normally. It reminds me of the nights where as a teenager I'd get in from a party, with Stella and Bec if they were sleeping over, and Mum would have waited up for us. She'd make tea and toast and the four of us would sit around the tiny kitchen table, Mum keen for the gossip, Stella and Bec telling her more than I would have done about the events of the night. When I go up to settle Amy to sleep I can hear Mum laughing like a drain at something Alison has said. For a moment I can almost forget that I've lost a part of her. Once she's drifted off in my arms, I gently set her down and switch on the mobile over her cot, creeping out of the room to the strains of 'Twinkle Twinkle, Little Star'.

When I come down, Alison joins me in the kitchen, where I'm heating up some casserole for Mum's dinner, vainly hoping she'll eat more than her usual few meagre mouthfuls. 'Everything OK?'

'Yes, Amy's asleep. I've left the mobile playing for now, but maybe go up in twenty minutes or so and turn it off. She should be in a deep sleep by then. Are you sure you're happy to stay here? There's fruit salad in the fridge for after.'

'Yes, Cassie. Don't worry.'

We get Mum seated at the table and picking at her food. After a few more minutes of me flapping and Alison reassuring me, I walk away down the street, strangely weightless without Amy strapped to me. I keep returning to the moment earlier when I told Alison about the note. She'd appeared surprised that I'd got one as well as her, which is strange in itself. If someone was trying to warn her off, it makes sense that they'd be trying to do the same to me. There was something else, though, and as I make my way into the small, new-build estate where Alison (through her witch-like journalistic powers) discovered Tom lives, I realise what it is. She didn't only seem surprised. She seemed relieved.

Chapter 21

I stand on Tom Glover's doorstep, heart fluttering in my throat. This estate used to be an area of wasteland behind the mini-mart. We were forbidden to play here as children, so naturally we came every chance we got. It's quiet, the residents all settling down for the evening, although I can smell a barbecue and hear the faint sound of children playing in the distance. I find myself hoping Tom is out.

The door opens and a familiar blonde stands there, although it takes me a few seconds to place her. It's Della, from the baby group. The one who told Chloe she'd seen me in Tesco's with Alison. Shit. She must be the new wife Alison told me about.

She looks at me in confusion for a few seconds, and then recognition dawns.

'Hello,' she says. 'It's Cassie, isn't it?'

'Yes, hi, Della. How are you?'

'I'm alright,' she says, mystified. Am I about to try and sell her tea towels, or a gadget for cleaning the windows?

'I'm sorry to barge in – it's probably a bad time,' I say, thinking of Harry. 'I always find this the worst time of day with Amy.' It's a deliberate attempt to curry favour, forge a bond, which backfires on me.

'Oh, no, Harry's always fast asleep by seven. Routine is so important.'

'Yes, absolutely.' I try unsuccessfully to unclench my teeth. 'I wanted to know ... is your husband in?'

'Tom? Yes, he's here. Do you know each other?' Doubt skims across her face. What has her husband been up to?

'No,' I say. Confusion replaces worry. 'We were at school together, but we didn't know each other.'

'Della?' A slight, heavily freckled man emerges from the room at the back of the hallway. He comes and stands next to her. 'Can I help you?' There's a slight belligerence there. He too thinks I'm selling something, or spreading the Lord's word.

'This is Cassie Colman,' says Della quickly, and I can tell it's not the first time they've spoken about me between themselves.

'Oh. How can we help you?' He's still wary but the rudeness has gone. Alison wasn't wrong: my name opens doors.

'I wanted to talk to you. Can I come in? It won't take long.'

'Della said she saw you with Alison Patchett,' says Tom, his hand on the door, making no move to let me in. I was right, they have been talking about me.

'Yes, I know her. But this isn't about the article. It's

about me trying to find out a bit more about ... my history ... what happened to me. Please, can I come in, for a minute?'

'Alright.' He steps back and Della does the same. 'Keep it down, though, Della's only just got Harry off to sleep and I don't want him waking up again.'

Ha, looks as if he's not such a perfect baby after all.

I follow them through to the kitchen, and we cram ourselves around a small, square dining table overlooking the garden. Everything is spotless and there's a collage of photos of Harry painstakingly arranged in a frame on the wall: Harry smiling; Harry peeking out from under a blanket; Harry holding his toes. There's also a large square photo on canvas of Tom and Della on their wedding day, Della stunning in backless ivory silk, Tom dazed, unable to believe his luck. There are no photos, indeed no evidence at all, of the teenage son Alison mentioned.

'So?' says Tom, his hands, incongruously large for such a small man, splayed on the table in front of him. 'You'll need to make it quick, I'm going out in a minute.'

'Alison's told me a couple of things that don't fit with what I thought I knew about that day.'

'I'd take anything she says with a pinch of salt,' Tom says.

'One of them was ... it was something to do with me, but the other ... it was about a rumour that was circulating afterwards, that ...'

Tom's hands curl into fists. 'That my dad was involved?

For fuck's sake, how many more times?' He's obviously forgotten he asked me to keep it down. 'Just because my dad had the occasional pint with Travis Green, it doesn't mean he had anything to do with it. Right, if that's all you want, I'm out of here. You can leave now, and don't think about bothering us again.'

He pushes his chair back with too much force and it clatters to the floor. Della jumps up to right it, and as she does so there's an unmistakable wail from upstairs.

'Oh, great, he's awake. You can sort him; I'm going out.'

He flings the kitchen door open, almost hitting a teenage boy, who must surely have been listening on the other side.

'For God's sake, Ryan, what are you doing there?' says Tom.

Della squeezes past them both and hurries up the stairs. Tom doesn't wait for an answer from his son, and a few seconds later the front door slams behind him.

I stand, and find myself face to face with Ryan Glover. From what Alison told me I know he must be around fourteen, but he looks younger apart from the telltale teenage acne. He's wearing black skinny jeans and a T-shirt with the name of a band I've never heard of on the front.

He takes a step closer. I try hard not to wrinkle my nose against the sour smell of old sweat and unwashed clothes, overlaid by the musk of cheap deodorant.

'Are you really Cassie Colman?' he says in a low voice. I recognise his yearning. It's not the first time I've got that reaction to being who I am. I bet he reads a lot of true crime.

'Yes,' I say shortly. I want to leave, but he's in my way and I don't want to get too close to him.

'Wait! Do you know Paul Green?'

'Not really. I've met him once.'

'What was he like?' he says. 'I tried to talk to him once when I saw him in town, but he wouldn't speak to me.'

'He was fine,' I say. I'm not surprised Paul wouldn't talk to Ryan. His intense interest is disconcerting.

'Do you think he knew what his dad was planning?'

'No, I don't. Look, I need to go now.' I take a step towards the door but he doesn't make any move to get out of my way.

'People say he did. They say he helped his dad plan the whole thing.'

'I'm sure that's not true.'

'They say it about my grandad too.' It's little more than a whisper, and he flicks a glance towards the door, as if his father might reappear, shouting at him to shut up. 'He was friends with Travis Green, you know.'

'Yes, I heard that.' Reluctantly, I'm drawn in. 'Did you know your grandfather?'

'No.' He looks disappointed; he wants to impress me, and I'm reminded that he's just a boy. 'He died when I was little.' He moves nearer still. There are dark shadows beneath his eyes, and the pallor of his skin highlights the pus-filled pimples that scatter his forehead and nose.

I push past him into the hallway. 'I'll just tell Della I'm going.'

I call up the stairs but there's no reply. I feel weird about leaving without saying anything, so I make my way up the stairs. I can hear Harry crying and Della murmuring softly in the bedroom at the far end of the landing, so I gently push the door open. She's standing at the window with Harry in her arms, rocking from side to side.

'I'm going now, Della,' I whisper.

'Alright,' she says, tersely.

I tiptoe down the landing. One of the other bedroom doors is wide open. It's immediately evident this is Ryan's room. It has the same foetid smell he does, its appearance in stark contrast to the rest of the house. Clothes are strewn all over the floor, there's a filmy glass on the bed-side table containing an inch of orange juice and another half-inch of green mould, and dirty cups and plates litter every surface apart from a desk under the window, which is pristine and empty except for a battered cardboard box. I can't see what's in it apart from a square of faded green cloth that lies on top of the contents.

Something inside me clicks, like a switch being flicked. I step into his room, hardly breathing. I'm halfway to the desk when the floorboards creak behind me.

'What are you doing?'

I spin round. Ryan is framed in the doorway, looking taller than he did downstairs.

'Get out of my room.' He sounds more frightened than angry. 'Come away.'

Away from what? I sneak a look at the box, feeling an inexplicable pull to see it again. The green cloth has dark, rusty stains on it and is sitting on top of what looks like an old newspaper.

He comes towards me and plucks at my arm, his bony fingers surprisingly strong. 'Get out!' he repeats. 'This is my room. It's ... private.'

'Sorry.'

What the hell am I doing? I disentangle myself from his grasp and walk swiftly back to the landing. Ryan says nothing, but stands stock-still, staring at me. I hurry down the stairs and out into the street, my heart hammering in my chest.

The air has cooled while I've been in there, and goosebumps pimple on my arms as I hurry down the road. My mind keeps returning to what I saw in Ryan's room, like a dog that's found something unpleasant in the bushes. The small green square of material, the darker patches which produced such a visceral reaction, sending a chill through me that reached all the way to my insides. I have no idea what that piece of cloth is, but I'm sure I've seen it before.

Chapter 22

katiekat2006: I found something

gamerboy: ??

katiekat2006: on Mum's iPad. Looked when she was asleep the other night

gamerboy: what did you find

katiekat2006: shes trying to find relatives of people who were killed that day

gamerboy: yeh obviously. That it?

katiekat2006: she found one. Anne Mooney, wife of Graham Mooney, shes been to see her

gamerboy: anything else? I have to go soon, homework

katiekat2006: no wait

gamerboy: what

katiekat2006: she said they found out something at
Mrs Mooneys

gamerboy: like what

katiekat2006: she's written something about driving lessons,
and then Did Elaine and Sylvia know each other?

katiekat2006: you still there?

gamerboy: yeh. Anything else?

katiekat2006: it says Driving lesson, Nigel Waterford 10am

gamerboy: that it?

katiekat2006: shes written some stuff about Paul Green, saying
girlfriend? And then Paul Green – James? That's
all I can remember

gamerboy: Cool 🖤 🖤 Talk later

katiekat2006: 🖤 🖤 🖤

Chapter 23

'So Tom wouldn't say anything about his dad?' Alison takes a sip of her wine. 'God, that's good. Don't let me have any more, though; I can't drink in the afternoon.'

'No, he got pretty angry, said people were always asking about it, but there was no truth in it. Then he left.' I take a sip of my own drink, pushing the pram back and forth with my other hand, praying Amy stays asleep. I couldn't face the baby-carrier today; she was up half the night and my back is killing me. When I'd got back from the Glovers' last night, Alison had been anxious to know what had happened, but Amy had been screaming her head off and Mum was refusing to go to bed and I'd shooed her out, saying I'd tell her all about it tomorrow. 'There was something a bit weird, though.'

'What?' asks Natalie. We feel like a little gang, the three of us, WhatsApping and meeting up for sneaky afternoon drinks. I'm actually beginning to allow myself to be a bit happier about moving back to Hartstead, despite the weirdness of what's going on.

'Tom's teenage son, Ryan, was there. He sort of ... cornered me in the kitchen and started asking me stuff, like if I knew Paul Green. He's a bit ... odd.'

'Odd how?' says Alison.

'It's hard to explain. He's very interested in what happened that day. When I went upstairs to tell Della I was leaving, I saw his room and ... oh, I don't know. I'm being ridiculous.'

'What?' asks Natalie. 'Don't worry about looking silly. Tell us.'

'His room was a mess apart from his desk, which was empty except for a cardboard box. I couldn't properly see what was in it – mostly papers, I think, like old newspapers. On the top there was this square of faded green cloth with darker stains on it.'

'What was it?' says Alison.

'I don't know. But it made me feel uncomfortable. I felt as if I recognised it, somehow, but I don't know how or why.'

'What sort of cloth?'

'I don't know – material. Cotton, I suppose.'

They both look bemused. I suppose I can't blame them.

'And you said you know his wife?' Natalie asks.

'Sort of. I met her once at a baby group. She's a friend of my mum's carer, who I went to school with. Oh – shit, there she is now!'

Della, Chloe and Karen are walking along the street

with their buggies. They're going to pass right by us. It's Tuesday; they'll be on their way to baby group.

'Hi, Cassie!' calls Chloe when she spots me. 'Are you not coming back to the group? Were we that awful?'

'No, I'll come another time, it's just today I'm ...' I gesture to the table, the drinks, my friends.

'Ooh, lucky you,' she says. 'Those were the days, when I could sit around all afternoon drinking.' She doesn't sound envious, though. She sounds as though she pities me, overlaid with the merest hint of judgement. 'You remember Della? Oh, and Karen?' she adds as an afterthought. Karen smiles tightly. Theo's quiet for once, his legs kicking merrily away.

'Yes. Hi.'

'Could I have a word?' Della says stiffly. 'In private.'

'Um, OK. Can you keep an eye on Amy?' I ask Natalie, who takes the handle and rocks the pram back and forth.

I walk to the gate and out into the street. As Della and I move away from the pub garden, I see Chloe leaning over the pram, all over Amy. She'd better not bloody wake her up; I haven't finished my wine, and I might need it after this: Della's clearly going to have a go at me. Karen puts a hand on Chloe's arm and draws her away and a surge of gratitude sweeps through me.

'I wanted to apologise,' Della says, fiddling with the little pearl buttons on her cardigan.

'Oh.' I wasn't expecting that.

'Tom gets a bit funny about people asking about his

dad. He used to get teased about it at school. It's kind of a sore spot for him.'

'Yeah, I can see how it would be.'

'He doesn't usually react like that.' Red splotches creep onto her neck and chest and she doesn't meet my eye. 'But all this twenty-five-year anniversary stuff is bringing back bad memories for him.'

'I can understand that.'

She hesitates, plainly wanting to say more. I wait, not inclined to make it easier for her.

'Will you talk to Alison, then?' she says, finally.

'About what?'

'Not writing this article.'

'What? I can't do that. I mean, it's her job. What difference would it make anyway? It's still going to be the anniversary. Everyone's still going to be talking about it.'

'I know. But he's got this bee in his bonnet about the article, how it's dragging everything up again, making it worse.'

'I can't ask her not to write it, Della. For one thing, I'm sure she wouldn't listen to me. I could ask her not to mention the rumour about Dennis Glover, though? If that would help?'

'Yes, please. Oh, that would be great, thank you. And Cassie ... about Ryan last night. Did he ... say anything to you?'

'Not much,' I say cautiously.

'He's at that awkward age, and with me not being his mum, and the new baby and everything, I think he's struggling. Tom finds it very hard – which I totally understand,' she says quickly.

'Right, OK.' I'm beginning to feel slightly awkward myself about this conversation.

'Ryan's real mum's an alcoholic, you see. He had to come and live with us a year ago, but him and Tom don't really see eye to eye. It's not easy. For Tom ... for any of us.'

'I'm sure.'

'I do my best, but Harry takes up a lot of my time.'

'Of course.' Why is she telling me all this?

'OK, thanks, Cassie.'

'That's OK.' I don't know what she's thanking me for, but I'm keen to end this rather uncomfortable conversation.

We walk back to the pub garden. I can't see the pram at the table, but I don't panic this time. I've only been away a minute. Sure enough, when I get closer, I can see James pushing it around the garden.

'Sorry,' says Natalie. 'She was stirring and he offered to take her for a couple of turns around the garden.'

'It's fine,' I say. 'Thanks.'

'She's asleep,' says James, returning to the table. 'Mission accomplished!' He gives a little bow and heads back inside.

'Thanks,' I say after him, unexpectedly moved. For the first time, there are other people who know how difficult Amy can be, who are invested in keeping her asleep, in making my life easier.

'Are you sure you won't come to the group?' Chloe says, fussing with Phoebe's blankets.

'Yes. Another time,' I say.

Karen casts a longing look at the glasses on the picnic bench.

'Do you want to stay for a drink?' I say, ostensibly to all of them, but really to her. She looks as though she could use a drink, or at least a conversation that doesn't revolve around babies.

'Oh . . .' She looks at Chloe.

'No, thanks,' says Chloe firmly. 'Baby group starts in five minutes. Come on, girls.'

The three of them move off, Karen trailing reluctantly in their wake.

'Let me get you another one,' I say to Natalie, whose glass is almost empty.

'Oh, go on, then,' she says, draining the last drops. 'I'll have a G&T.'

I'm on my way back out with her drink when a figure looms out of the darkness in the corridor between the bar and the garden.

'Jesus!' I jerk to a halt, gin slopping onto my hand. It's Paul Green, carrying an empty pint glass.

'You again,' he says. 'I felt it, you know.'

'What?' I suddenly feel very isolated despite the chatter from the bar. He sways slightly and puts out a hand to steady himself against the wall. His eyes are bloodshot.

'Your disapproval the other day. It's always mothers who disapprove.' He's over-enunciating every word,

156

the way people do when they're trying to disguise how extremely drunk they are.

'Sorry, I don't know what you—'

'You think I'm terrible because I haven't seen my mother for years. But she didn't want me, couldn't cope with me, whatever the hell that means.'

I know what it means, even though teenagers are a different kettle of fish from needy babies. I feel a sneaking sympathy for Elaine. 'I wasn't disapproving.'

'You were. Flora was the same. *She is your mother, after all*. Well, look how that turned out.'

'Flora?'

'My ex-girlfriend. Don't pretend you haven't heard about her. How she mysteriously disappeared. There was no mystery about it. I moved to London to be with her, and then she pissed off like everyone else does. Couldn't stand to live with me for another minute. I drank too much, apparently. Although I wouldn't have needed to if she'd been a bit fucking nicer to me.'

'I'm sorry . . . '

'You've got no idea what my mother was like.' It's as if I haven't spoken, almost as if I'm not here. 'Everyone felt so sorry for her. Poor Elaine, living with that awful man. She was no angel.'

'What do you mean?' He wants to tell me something, I'm sure of it, but he'd never do it sober. This is my best chance.

He draws closer, his breath sour with beer fumes. I try not to inhale too deeply.

'She was fucking someone else.'

I draw back, my pulse racing.

'You weren't expecting that, were you?' he says with satisfaction. 'Saint Elaine Green, the wronged wife. She thought I didn't know, but I was thirteen, not stupid. Sneaking out to meet him, lying to us both. No wonder my dad went crazy.'

I can't get any further away from him; I'm already pressed tightly up against the wall. I can see the stains on his teeth, the pores in his skin, a gash where he's cut himself shaving.

'Are you alright, Cassie?'

Thank God. James stands at the end of the corridor, wiping a glass with a tea towel, his voice deliberately light.

'Yes, I'm . . . OK.' I am now that Paul has pulled away from me and staggered past James towards the bar.

'Everything OK?' James casts a wary eye at Paul's retreating back.

'Yes – he's had a bit too much to drink, I think.'

'He didn't hurt you, did he?

'No, he didn't touch me.'

'What was he saying?' James asks.

'He wasn't making much sense, to be honest.' I say airily, trying to disguise the lie I don't know why I'm telling. 'I'd better get this out to Natalie.'

In the garden, I plonk the drink down on the table and flop into my seat, my legs unable to hold me up any longer. 'Jesus.'

'What's wrong?' Natalie asks nervously.

'I just ran into Paul Green again.'

'Oh.' She grabs for her glass, taking a gulp. 'What happened?'

'He was blind drunk, for one thing.'

'I've heard that's not an uncommon state of affairs,' Alison says. 'What did he say to you? God, Cassie, are you OK? You're shaking.'

'I don't know. He told me something.'

'What?' Alison leans forward. Natalie's eyes are wide, fixed on mine. There's been a palpable shift in atmosphere around the table.

'He said that Elaine was having an affair. At the time of the shooting.'

'What?' Alison lights up like the Blackpool Illuminations. I've never seen her so animated. 'Who with?'

'He didn't say.'

'How did he know? What else did he say?' Alison asks, agog.

'He was really angry about it. It was horrible.'

'Don't you think he could have got it wrong?' Natalie says. 'I mean, he was only a young teenager, wasn't he? He could have seen something and misinterpreted it.'

'I guess so. But whether it was true or not, Travis obviously believed it too. Paul said, *No wonder my dad went crazy.*'

'So, what – he's saying this had something to do with why Travis went crazy? Oh, my God, this is huge. Did anyone else know, d'you think?' Alison taps her nails on the table.

I think of the photo of Mum and Elaine, arm in arm, hair whipped by the wind. Did Mum know? I could ask her but I'll never be able to trust her answer.

'But how has nothing ever come up about this before?' says Natalie. 'Surely someone would have said something before if it was true?'

'I suppose nobody knew,' says Alison. 'Except those who had a vested interest in it not becoming common knowledge.'

There's a moan from the pram. Amy is waking up. To be honest, I am itching with the need to be by myself to process this new information, or as by myself as I ever am with Amy, so I make my excuses and leave. Nonetheless I feel a pang as I shoot a quick look back at the two of them, glasses in hand, their heads bent together over the table.

By the time I get home, Amy has miraculously fallen asleep again, so I leave her in the pram in the hall. I look in on Mum, who is glued to the TV and barely acknowledges me. I fling myself down on my bed, meaning to think about what Paul said, but exhaustion, as ever, is not far away, and I drift off into an uneasy, dream-filled sleep.

I'm woken later by a piercing scream from Amy. It normally takes her a while to reach that pitch. I sit bolt upright, head spinning, and am off the bed and down the stairs before I'm fully awake. Mum is standing over the pram, her hands inside it. The hood is up and I can't see what she's doing in there.

'Be. Quiet,' she is muttering, her voice low and insistent, almost ferocious.

'Mum!'

She looks up, startled.

'Where's Gary?' she says in distress.

It's the first time she's asked for my dad. I've been dreading this day. To have to say those words to her, for her to have to bear his loss all over again – and now it's come to it, I can't do it to her.

'He'll be back later,' I say, banking on the fact that she won't remember this conversation, but she doesn't look reassured. 'It's OK,' I say softly, knowing I mustn't get cross with her about things like this, I must keep reminding myself that she can't help it. 'You go and watch the telly,' I say, hating how I have to speak to her like a child, or an imbecile. My proud, capable, free-spirited mum. 'I'll sort the baby out.'

She makes her way slowly into the lounge, looking so old and helpless, hopeless, that I have to steel myself not to weep.

'Come on, you,' I say, lifting Amy out, her face puce, actual tears rolling down her cheeks. 'What's the matter with . . . '

The words dry in my mouth and I hold Amy away from me in horror, checking her body all over for any injuries or blood. I can't see any, which feels like a miracle because where she was lying, right under her solid little body, which I now see with new eyes – all dimples and soft, sweet skin – is a penknife, the largest of its blades pulled out, shining silver against the baby rabbits that gambol across the pram sheet.

Chapter 24

15th June 1994 | David Wilkes

Normally they'd be in when he goes round to value a house, but this geezer asked David to meet him outside. Probably doesn't live there. Looks like an old girl's house – nets at the window, china figurines on the sill inside – maybe it's his mum's, carked it or gone into a home. Either way, it's good news for David. That probably sounds callous but that's the nature of it, and you have to get used to it. For every lovely young couple, dewy-eyed about finding their first house, there's a bitter divorcée being forced out of the home she's made and loved for years, the place she brought up her children. For every happy nuclear family moving into their perfect four-bedroom forever home, there's a grey-haired man-child who's lost his beloved mum and his childhood home in one fell swoop. Circle of life, innit?

David's not the only one waiting around today. There's a driving instructor fifty metres down the road standing by his car, looking at his watch. He wouldn't fancy that game, teaching stroppy teenagers to drive. Sod that for a game of soldiers. He gets enough of that at home with his two. Sometimes he envies the divorced blokes he gets coming in looking for crummy one-bed flats. Yes, they've lost their homes (the ones who didn't have the swanky lawyers to ensure the wife had to move out), but look what they've gained. Coming home every night to a place that looks exactly like it did when they left in the morning, pulling a beer out of the fridge, football on the telly, no one to nag at them if they drop their curry on the sofa. No hormone-crazed teenage boys slamming doors and moaning about homework and arguing over the TV remote. Sounds like bloody heaven.

Then there's other ones he envies. Showed a couple round a flat the other day, not young, about his age, he supposes. But the way they were with each other ... He doesn't think him and Michelle were ever like that, not even in the early days. They were nervous, especially when they were outside the flat – looking round, as if someone might be watching them. They calmed down once they were inside, though. They were so nice to each other, asking each other's opinions, laughing at each other's jokes. Probably not been together that long, although they were wearing wedding rings. Mid-life newlyweds, second-time-rounders. David gives 'em six months.

He's looking the other way, so the first he knows about it is the shot, ringing out into the clear summer air. He assumes it's a car backfiring. Even when he turns and sees the man with the gun, it doesn't register. It's not something you expect to see. But then there's a terrible scream, like the vixens he hears in the garden at night, but it's not a fox, it's a woman. David can't tell where it's coming from. The man is running now, running towards David, and his stupid brain won't catch up, won't tell his feet to move. He is rooted to the spot, his body on fire with fear, and the man is raising the gun now and this is it, he's going to die here outside this crummy old lady's house and the last thing he said to Michelle was to tell her to stop the bloody kids arguing or he'd start having his dinner in the pub.

Chapter 25

'So, can you be absolutely sure this penknife wasn't placed there by your mother?' The young policeman's eyes move briefly to a burbling Amy, arms and legs flailing in the baby-carrier on my chest, unaware of her central role in this unfolding drama.

'No, I've already said I can't be sure. I don't recognise it, I've never known her to have a penknife, but I don't know every single thing she owns.' I place a protective hand on Amy's head, and try to force an image from my mind: my mother brandishing a steak knife at me, some-one she took for a total stranger.

'And when you questioned her she didn't know either, despite the fact that you came across her standing over the baby, complaining that she was crying?'

He seems unable to grasp the extent of Mum's con-dition. Let's hope he never gets anyone with dementia wandering into the station. His lack of understanding is staggering.

'She has *dementia*. Alzheimer's. She doesn't know what she had for breakfast. Sometimes she doesn't even know who I am – her own daughter. She forgets words, and what the telly is, and whether she's eaten all day. It's impossible for any of us, her included, to know whether that's her knife and whether she put it there.'

'So it's possible she put it there and forgot?' He's unquestionably decided this is what happened, confident he can blame it on her and have this all wrapped up by teatime.

'Yes, but it doesn't seem likely, and, as I said, I don't recognise it.'

'Was there anyone else in the house?'

'No, it's just me and Mum, but ... '

'Yes?' He looks up with a glimmer of interest.

'I don't know how long it had been there.'

'You mean someone else could have put it there, before you got back to the house?'

'I suppose so.' I shiver, thinking of the people we were around this afternoon. Chloe, Della, Karen. James. Paul was in the pub, but I don't think he could have got near Amy, could he? Unless ... while I was talking to Della?

'To be honest, even if you think it was slipped into the pram while you were out, there's not a great deal we could do. No crime has been committed.'

'What about the notes? With the headlines?'

'They're not specific threats, though, are they? It could be a practical joke – one in very poor taste,' he adds hurriedly, seeing my expression. 'Plus there's absolutely no reason to suppose that whoever sent the notes also put the penknife in the pram.'

'Right, so what you're saying is, go home and wait until someone physically hurts my baby, and then you'll do something?'

He looks worried, obviously envisaging this scenario playing out, and the trouble he would be in. 'Do you have any reason to suppose someone wants to hurt your baby?' he asks.

I stare at a darker spot on the pale grey wall behind him. 'How old are you?' I say.

'I'm not sure why that's relevant,' he says, bristling.

'You're clearly not old enough to remember the Hartstead tragedy.'

'No, I'm not. I know *of* it, of course.'

'Well, I am. My father was one of the victims.'

Realisation dawns. 'Oh . . . you're . . . '

'Yes, I am.' I press on quickly. 'The woman who got the other note, Alison Patchett, is a journalist. She's writing an article about the shootings. I think there's someone out there who doesn't want us to look into it too deeply.'

He looks doubtful. 'Why do you think that would be?'

'I don't know. I think there was more to what happened that day than meets the eye. My mum . . . she knew Elaine, but she never told me.' And Elaine's son believes she was having an affair, but I don't tell the policeman that. Those smiles on my mum's and Elaine's faces in that photo hold me back, as if I'd be betraying my mum's friend by letting Paul Green's poison spread any further.

167

He leans forward, elbows on the table. 'I understand it was traumatic. But it was a long time ago. People have moved on. Hartstead has moved on. If you think there's a chance someone is targeting you and this journalist because you're digging up what happened all those years ago, why don't you just stop? Cut off contact with the journalist?'

'But don't you understand? This could be huge, if it's true – if Travis Green specifically targeted his victims, if it wasn't random?'

'I'm not sure how you've come to that conclusion, but even if that's true ...' he pauses, and I understand in that moment there is no part of him that thinks I'm right ' ... then no, I don't think it's huge. It won't change anything. Leave it be, let the journalist get on with it if she wants to.'

The journalist is one of my only friends, I want to tell him. *If I stop seeing her, I'm cutting my friend tally by fifty per cent.* I don't, though; it'll only make things worse.

'Look,' he says, sensing the waves of stress emanating from me, 'there's not a great deal I can do at the moment, but I'll log all this, and if anything else happens that gives you cause for concern, don't hesitate to call.'

'OK.' What else can I say? I stand, shifting Amy into a more comfortable position. He puts his hand inches from my elbow and steers me from the room.

Outside the police station, the sun slips behind the clouds and I shiver, wishing I'd brought a jacket. It's one of those early summer days where the weather can turn on a sixpence. The policeman's words are ringing in my head: *cut off contact with the journalist.* I take out my phone.

Alison and I are sitting in her car outside a neat bungalow on the outskirts of Hartstead, the first of our two stops today. When I called her yesterday to tell her about the penknife, and say that instead of being frightened off it had made me more keen to get to the bottom of whatever was going on, she had found it hard to hide the delight beneath her concern.

'You should definitely ask Barraclough if he ever heard anything about Elaine having an affair,' Alison says, turning off the engine.

'Do you think?' It still feels like a betrayal of this woman I've never met.

'Absolutely! I'd do it, but, as I said, I think it's better if you go in on your own,' she says. 'He was helpful to me, up to a point, but I felt as though he'd told me all he was going to when I was here last time. But when I mentioned you on the phone today he warmed right up. He's much more likely to open up to you.'

'What about Amy?'

'She's fine.'

We both look into the back, where Amy is sleeping peacefully in the car seat.

'If she wakes up, I'll come and get you. Here, take these.' She holds out a small notebook and pencil. 'In case he tells you anything new – it's always best to write stuff down. You think you won't forget it, but you'd be surprised.'

I get out of the car and slide the notebook and pencil into the pocket of my jeans. The wooden gate opens soundlessly into an immaculately kept garden and I walk stiffly up the path, conscious of every step, every breath. Barraclough must have been watching from the window, because he opens the door almost before I've rung the bell. I am expecting to feel something when I see him, a deep stirring of suppressed memory, but when a stooped man in his seventies opens the door, there's nothing. He's lost his hair, and no longer has the moustache I saw in the newspaper reports. I would never have recognised him if I'd passed him in the street.

'Mr Barraclough?'

'Cassie,' he says. 'I'm so glad to see you. Come in.'

I follow him through into a silent front room, all muted colours and unsaid words. The sofa is pristine apart from a darkened indent at one end, next to which sits a small pine table with a copy of *The Times* and a half-drunk cup of tea on it.

'Sit down, please. Can I get you a drink?'

'No, thanks.' I extract the notebook and pencil from my pocket and perch on the edge of the armchair. He settles into what is evidently his usual seat opposite. I take a quick look around the room. On the left of the mantelpiece, there's a picture of a slightly younger Barraclough, smartly dressed, with his arm around a kind-faced woman in a mauve trouser suit. To the right, a black and white wedding photo. Barraclough and the woman, younger again, him in a morning suit and her in a white lace dress clutching a bouquet of mismatched flowers, both smiling shyly at the camera.

'So you've been talking to Alison Patchett for her article?' he says.

I pull my focus back to him. 'Yes, a bit. I know a lot of people think we shouldn't stir things up, but . . .'

'A lot of people weren't as affected by that day as you were,' he says. 'You do what you like.'

'Oh. Thanks. I thought you might think we shouldn't go poking around in something that's done.'

'It was a terrible day. The worst of my career. I understand why people want to move on, try to forget it. But for someone like you, who was there, who lost a loved one, it's different. For me too. I'll never forget it.' The words pour from him, and I taste the stillness of the house on my tongue. Barraclough doesn't have anyone to talk to. 'Racing through the town, following the trail of devastation,' he goes on. 'When I saw you outside the house, it should have been an enormous relief, but I didn't know where he was. I ran towards you but all I could think was that I would hear a shot before I reached you, see you crumple to the ground.'

'Alison said the reports were wrong. That I wasn't covered in blood?'

'Not a drop,' he says. 'Your mother had managed to get you out of the house.'

I frown as a flicker of memory washes over me then fades just as quickly. 'What did she say about it, afterwards?'

'She was in shock. She'd seen her husband shot, and a man kill himself, right in front of her. She knew she'd managed to get you out somehow, but she didn't know how. Has she ever said anything to you?'

'No. She never really talked to me about it.' I so wish she had now. I wish I'd tried harder.

He nods sadly. 'People don't. I know why, of course, but it's a pity. Do you think ... you could ask her now?'

He may be older, but his brain hasn't slowed down. Something wasn't right in our house that day, and, like me, he wants to know, to understand.

'She's got early-onset Alzheimer's. She barely knows what day it is.' I'm aware how harsh I sound, but there are times when I can't be bothered with the niceties, with trying to make it sound better than it is. I want to live in the moment, to celebrate who she is now, but it's too hard. All I can see is what I've lost.

'Oh, I'm sorry to hear that.' He does sound sorry, but also disappointed. Mum can't help him with these loose ends he wants to tie up.

'I found something,' I say, wanting to give him an offering in the hope that he'll return the favour. 'In a file of stuff that Mum had kept about the tragedy. There was a photo of her with Elaine Green.'

He looks at me sharply. 'They knew each other?'

'Apparently. She never said, though.'

'She didn't tell us, either. Why would she have held that back?'

'I don't know, but Alison and I think ...'

172

'What?' He leans forward, intense.

'We've been wondering if the shooting was as random as everybody thinks.'

'We investigated that at the time,' he says, drawing back, as if he'd been expecting me to say something else. 'There were no links between any of the victims.'

'We went to see Anne Mooney, Graham Mooney's wife.'

'Ah, how's she doing?' he asks.

I've always known the first responders on that day must have suffered, but I've never seen it as clearly as I do now; the memory of it is still etched on his face.

'She was alright,' I say. 'She let us have a look through his files. I found out that my mum was having driving lessons from him at that time, which she's never told me. And every week there was a woman calling herself Elaine White who had the lesson straight after. Alison and I thought it might have been—'

'Elaine Green.' He looks troubled. 'I did think at the time that something wasn't quite right, that maybe there was more to it than met the eye.'

My pulse throbs in my neck, blood zipping through my veins. Until he spoke I'd been wondering if we were barking up the wrong tree, putting two and two together and coming up with eleven. Eleven victims.

'But the powers that be, they weren't that interested in investigating it further,' he says. 'There was no doubt who had done it, and he was dead. There was talk that he'd had a conspirator, someone who'd helped him plan it, but that was gossip, nothing in it. There was nothing

173

concrete to suggest it was anything other than random. The town was traumatised enough; there was no need to go poking around in fresh wounds.'

'But what made you think there was more to it?' I say.

'It was just a feeling. Nothing more. When I interviewed Elaine Green, I sensed she wasn't telling me the whole truth, but I put it down to what she'd been through. She was a shell. Nothing left. The last time I spoke to her was a few months afterwards, in the hospital. When she got out, she moved house and no one saw her again after that. I believe she moved right away, changed her name. A new life.'

'Didn't she give evidence at the trial?'

'No. She was considered too traumatised and vulnerable. Her evidence was read out in court but she didn't have to appear.'

'There's something else I've heard,' I say cautiously. I don't want to admit that it was Paul I heard it from, not yet. 'Another rumour, I suppose.'

'Yes?' He sits very still.

'The story was that Elaine might have been ... seeing someone else, behind Travis's back.'

'Oh.' He sounds almost disappointed, as if I've given the wrong answer. 'No, I never heard that.'

'But ... there was something, though?'

He looks down at his hands, rubbing one thumb and forefinger together as if trying to get out a stain. I hardly dare to breathe, as if he'll clam up if I so much as shift in my chair.

'I suppose I can tell you,' he says eventually, still staring down. 'She asked me not to tell anyone at the time, and I respected her wishes, but I don't see why it would matter now.'

He pauses again, and again I remain silent, not wanting to give him any reason to change his mind.

'The last time I saw Elaine Green was a few months after the shooting. She was an in-patient in a psychiatric ward. I didn't need to talk to her officially. We'd done all the interviews. I felt ... I don't know, that someone ought to look in on her. She didn't have any friends or family visiting.'

What about Mum? Didn't she go and see Elaine in the hospital? I don't have long to ponder this question, though, because what Barraclough says next blows a hole through everything Alison and I have learned so far.

'The last time I saw her, Elaine was pregnant.'

Chapter 26

15th June 1994 | Suzanne Persimmon

It's unusual for Suzanne to meet a client in a location other than the office, but she has to be flexible. There's no reason why she shouldn't meet her here, on a bench just off the main high street. There can be reasons someone wouldn't want to be seen going into the Citizens Advice Bureau, especially a woman in a certain type of situation. The most dangerous time for a woman experiencing domestic violence can be when she finally makes the decision to leave. That's why Suzanne always advises them to prepare everything in advance, get their passport and any other important documents out of the house. And always, always have someone with them when they tell the abuser they are leaving.

Suzanne doesn't know what's going on with the woman she's waiting for. Her brother is the one who made the appointment – it's too hard for her to make phone calls, apparently, which is a worrying, if common, sign. It's hard to get a sense of someone without the nuance of voice and body language, but she knows that whatever is going on, it's nothing good. It never is, in her line of work. That's why she likes it, though. She used to work in advertising, but it left her with a bad taste in her mouth. Figuring out how to flog stuff to people that they don't need. How to make them want it so badly they'll spend money they can ill afford, get into debt, only for them to realise it hasn't made them happy after all, because nothing can. Nothing you can buy, anyway. She was so thankful, when she fell pregnant, that she had left that corporate world. Not only because the hours and demands would have been incompatible with motherhood, but because she won't be ashamed of her work, when the baby gets older and asks what her job is. 'I help people,' she'll be able to say.

In this job, she makes a positive difference to those who have found themselves, often through no fault of their own, in a hopeless situation. Those who through poverty, bad luck or poor money management have found themselves in insurmountable debt; those in danger of losing their home through no fault of their own; the abused and discriminated against, who don't know where to turn; and of course women who have fallen blindly in love with men who want to control them, or own them, or hurt them. Men who slowly but surely have isolated them from their friends, battered at their self-confidence until they thought no one else would ever want them, and then taken every little hurt, every injustice they have ever suffered, and used it against the women, women who thought they had no one to help them. But they did. They had Suzanne and her colleagues.

The first thing that happens is the screaming. At first, she thinks it's teenage girls mucking about, trying to attract boys.

A mating call. Then a woman runs past on the high street, her bright red hair flying out behind her like a pennant. She's in a business suit and she has kicked off her shoes. She doesn't see Suzanne, sitting on her bench in what is little more than an alleyway off the high street.

Suzanne walks slowly to the top of the alley. First she glances left, in the direction the businesswoman was running. Then she looks right and her heart leaps into her mouth and, terribly, she understands. She ducks back into the passage, pressing herself against the wall, her heart thundering. Surely he'll go past, the man with the gun. But she hears his footsteps now, and they are slowing. Oh, God. Her breath is coming in little ragged puffs. She looks in desperation down the alleyway but it's a dead end, a high locked gate, no way out. Nonetheless she runs towards it, hoping against hope that there's a way through, a way out. She puts her hand on the cold metal grille of the gate. It will not move.

The footsteps are behind her now. She can hear him breathing – a deep, grunting, sweaty sound. She will not look. She closes her eyes, and her heart brims with the unbearable knowledge that her baby won't remember her.

Chapter 27

'Pregnant? Was it ... Travis's?'

'I assume so. There was no suggestion there was anyone else involved.'

'Did she have the baby?' My thoughts whir round and round like a hamster in a wheel.

'I don't know. That was the last time I saw her. She became very distressed while I was with her, and the doctor in charge of her care asked me not to come again.'

'What was she distressed about, that time? The shooting?'

'No.' He looks troubled. 'It was the baby. She didn't want it.'

'Could she not have had a termination?' I force myself to say the word casually, as if it has no special resonance for me. As if I hadn't gone back and forth when I'd first found out I was pregnant, going so far as to book an appointment to discuss termination, only to cancel it again. Twice.

'It was too late by the time she found out. She was just over twenty-four weeks.'

In an attempt to give myself time to think, I flip my notebook open and write: *Elaine was pregnant. 24 weeks when she found out.*

'How could she have got so far through the pregnancy without knowing?' I shake my head in disbelief. You hear these stories of women who didn't know they were pregnant until they went into labour, but I can't see how it could happen. I think of myself at twenty-four weeks pregnant: I felt huge, ankles swollen and riddled with heartburn, Amy rolling and twitching inside me.

'She didn't look pregnant, not really,' he says. 'She was quite large anyway at the time, I think partly because of the medication she was on. Plus the drugs would have stopped her periods. It was one of the staff that suspected, so they tested her. She got very distressed while she was telling me about it. When the doctor took me aside afterwards to suggest I didn't come again, he told me something else too.'

'What?' I sit with my pencil poised, anxious to record every detail.

'When they told Elaine she was pregnant, she withdrew into herself. She was dealing with a lot of trauma, but she'd been doing well, they thought. But the pregnancy sent her spiralling. She was adamant she didn't want the baby, but it was too late for a termination. They had to change her medication, because there was one drug in particular that was unsafe to be taken in pregnancy because it could cause miscarriage. They explained all this to her, and told her what changes they were making to her drug regime, and why. The next morning, they found her passed out in her room. She'd somehow managed to get hold of a supply of this particular drug that was unsafe for the baby, and taken an overdose. She recovered physically, and didn't miscarry, but, when they talked to her about it, it became obvious that she hadn't been trying to kill herself. She'd just been trying to get rid of the baby.'

'Oh, my God. Poor Elaine.'

'Yes.'

In the silence, I write mindlessly in the notebook, as if I might forget this terrible story.

'And you don't know what happened?' I ask. 'Whether she had the baby? If it was OK?'

'No.' He looks ashamed. 'I took the doctor's advice not to visit her again. But . . . it was difficult. Distressing. I . . .' He appears to be steeling himself to reveal an unpleasant truth. 'I was glad of the excuse not to go. I bitterly regret that now.'

'You shouldn't be too hard on yourself. It sounds as if you went above and beyond.'

'It wasn't enough, though, was it? That's the problem with police work. You're constrained, all the time, by budgets and regulations and overwork. You see so many distressing situations, but a lot of the time there's nothing you can do. Or you can't do what you really want to do. You can't save everyone. And on top of all that, you're trying to have a private life.' He stands up and walks to the fireplace, picking up the photo of him with the woman in the mauve trouser suit. 'Peggy used to say I was married to the force. I know she didn't feel I was giving her enough attention. But I never felt I was giving *anything* enough attention. There were so many demands on me, I felt I was failing at everything.'

'That's how I feel,' I say, unable to hold it in. 'I've got a baby, and I'm trying to look after my mum as well, and now there's all this.'

'There are no demands on my time at all now,' he says, replacing the photo on the mantelpiece. 'I sit here and I don't know how to fill the days.'

'I'm sorry,' I say, ill at ease with his loneliness.

'No, it's alright. But let me know if you find anything out, won't you?'

'I will.'

He sees me out, closing the door gently behind me. I walk down the path, clutching my notebook, and he retreats back into the stillness of his house, with only his memories and regrets to keep him company.

Chapter 28

We enter the Farnwood Estate and sweep past the track that leads to the old quarry. Alison slows as the drive becomes bumpier, swerving every now and then to avoid the larger potholes. I fiddle with my phone and look again at the texts Guy sent me last night and this morning. The first one came in at 11.53pm. I know exactly where he was. On the train, heading home to his leafy idyll in Kent. Drunk. But even though I know this, know it deep in my bones, my heart still gave a stupid, treacherous lurch when I saw it. *I miss you.* I had to physically restrain myself from texting straight back: *I miss you too. I wish you could meet our daughter. I love you.* The second one pinged in at 7.05 this morning. He'll have taken his phone into the en-suite as soon as his alarm went off. Bleary-eyed and dry-mouthed, he'll have checked to see what he texted me. Sworn. Rattled off a second text. *Sorry about that. Bit too much to drink. Ignore me.* Not a word about our daughter, about how I am coping alone with the seismic change that has been wreaked upon my life. Yet still I struggle to feel the anger I know is appropriate to the situation. I'm just desperately sad.

'He gets to live here?' I say as we pull up in the gravel drive, goggling at the chocolate-box red-brick lodge with wisteria growing around the door. I don't know how she did it, but Alison has persuaded me to talk to Paul again.

'Yep,' says Alison, switching off the ignition. 'He's head groundskeeper. Comes with the job.'

We would pass the lodge on those primary school trips to Farnwood, but it never occurred to me that somebody actually lived in it.

'Do you think he's still out ... I don't know ... groundskeeping?'

'Nah,' says Alison. 'I know a woman who cleans up at the house. She reckons he's always home by six, and it's ten past. And look, his car's here.' She indicates the beaten-up Land Rover at the side of the house.

'Do you honestly think I should ask him if Elaine had a baby?'

'Yes! Even if he won't tell you, you can see how he reacts.'

'Easy for you to say.' I mentally recoil from the memory of his face contorted with fury.

'Hmm, although ...'

'What?'

'If he says she did, or even if he doesn't, I don't think we should tell anyone else yet. It wouldn't be right to go spreading rumours like that.'

'When did you get so virtuous?'

She shoots me an exasperated look. 'I'm being cautious. Call it journalistic instinct. Now, go on, we haven't got all night.'

Amy has fallen asleep, which gives me a prick of disquiet about the likelihood of her sleeping tonight, but on the other hand means I can easily leave her in the car with Alison. Now it comes to it, though, I'm not sure I can go through with it.

'Maybe you should do it,' I say, eyeing the front door.

'Are you kidding? After what he said to you about journalists? He knows who I am. There are no secrets in a town this size. He'd slam the door in my face before I'd said a word. No, it's got to be you. Go on, before you lose your nerve.'

'I've already lost it,' I say, but under my breath. There's no point arguing with her. With a final glance at Amy – 'She's *fine*,' says Alison, exasperated – I haul myself out of the car and towards the bottle-green front door. The scent of barbecuing meat vies with the wisteria as I knock and wait.

I'm peering through the stained-glass panel on the door when the sound of footsteps from my right makes me jump.

'Can I help you?' Paul is in shorts and a T-shirt, tall and broad-shouldered, his skin heavily tanned. I suppose he mostly works outside. He has a pair of barbecue tongs in one hand and a mildly curious expression, until he clocks who I am. 'What do you want?' His tone isn't entirely unfriendly, but neither is he inviting me in for a beer and a burger.

'I'm sorry to bother you again, but I'm still trying to find out what really happened that day.'

He looks behind me towards the car, where Alison is tapping away on her phone. 'I thought you said you weren't a journalist.'

'I'm not.'

'*She* is. That's Alison Patchett, isn't it?'

She was right about small towns and secrets.

'Yes, but this isn't for the article. It's just for me. She won't put anything in that I'm not happy with. Or that you don't want in it.'

'What's she doing here, then?'

'She's the only person I know with a car,' I say, embarrassed.

The hand holding the tongs drops to his side and he smiles. 'You really are a sad case, aren't you? OK, come round to the garden and we can talk for a bit while my burger's cooking.'

There's a large, square lawn in need of a cut, bordered by overgrown flowerbeds. A small barbecue is balanced on chipped, uneven patio slabs.

'Sorry, it's a bit of a mess,' he says. 'I spend so much energy making sure the gardens up there are immaculate, I can't be bothered when I get home.'

He lifts the burger and inspects the underside, then lays it down again, rejecting it as not charred enough.

'I'm sorry if I was a bit ... aggressive last time I saw

186

you,' he says, still busying himself with the barbecue. 'I'd had a little too much to drink.'

'That's OK.' It's better than OK, in fact. If he feels bad about our last encounter, he'll be on the back foot and more willing to help me.

'What I said about my mother ... forget it. It was the drink talking. When I'm drinking, I can get ... Sometimes I say stupid stuff, make things up ... I get fed up with the rubberneckers, you know. I'm sure you *do* know, given who you are.'

'Yes.'

I don't believe for a second that he was making it up about Elaine's affair. It was too raw to be anything but the truth.

'I had a year's break from it,' he goes on. 'Moved to London. Like you, I think?'

'Yes.'

'Flora always said it would be good for me to get away. I'd always wanted to, but something always stopped me. When I met her, it was the perfect opportunity to begin again. But ... like I said, it all went tits-up, and here I am, back where I started.'

'Yeah, I know the feeling.' I'm back where I started too, although everything is different, including me, and my friends have all gone.

'So what is it you think I can tell you?' he says bullishly, any brief sense of kinship receding. I'm uncomfortably aware of his height, his strength, his proximity. I know he said it was the drink, but what if he loses it, like last time? I'll ease my way in gently, look for an opening.

'You said you haven't seen your mum since around that time?'

'No.'

This isn't going to be easy.

'You were fostered?'

'Yes. And before you ask, it was fine. Val and Ian were perfectly nice.'

'It can't have been the same, though. Not like having your parents around.'

'You do remember who my father was, right? That wasn't exactly a barrel of laughs either. And she was ... I was better off with Val and Ian.'

'I used to fantasise about being fostered by my friend's parents,' I say, a memory striking me unexpectedly. 'I remember being on a long car journey with Mum – one of our caravan holidays, it must have been – we always went away in June, to avoid ... you know. I spent the journey concocting an elaborate fantasy about her crashing the car and me being the only survivor, and my friend Stella's parents offering to have me live with them and change my name to theirs. Stella had three older brothers and they lived in one of those big houses on the Tunston Road. They were always having parties and big family dinners and colourful, fun arguments. I even had the decor for my bedroom picked out. I was a tiny bit disappointed when we arrived unscathed.'

'Right.' He's still not saying much but there's a smile in his voice. The burger sizzles and spits as he flips it.

'So I guess what I'm saying is, I know what it's like to have a … less than ideal background,' I say. 'To have people think they know all about you before you open your mouth. To be famous for something that happened to you, something that wasn't your fault.'

'I know you do.' He pours himself a glass of wine from a bottle balanced on the windowsill behind him.

'The thing is,' I say, deciding I'm going to have to launch in and hope for the best, 'I went to see DI Barraclough.'

Paul looks up sharply. 'Barraclough? He's not still working, surely?'

'No, he's retired. I talked to him about my … concerns, and he … he didn't completely laugh them off. And he mentioned something else, about your mum.'

'What?' The bond I'd thought was tentatively building between us slips away, untethered by my words.

'He said … that the last time he saw her, a couple of months after that day … she was pregnant.'

Paul places his wine glass down deliberately on the windowsill.

'He was mistaken.'

'Are you sure?' I realise how lame the question is as it comes out of my mouth. Am I really asking him if he's sure whether or not he has a brother or sister? But either he's lying, or he really never knew anything about it.

'Perfectly sure,' he says.

'But ... if you haven't seen her yourself, isn't it possible ...?'

'We had supervised visits for the first three years,' he says. 'It's only since I turned sixteen that I've not seen her at all. If that's all, I'd like to eat my dinner in peace now.' He steps towards me, herding me like a sheep around to the front of the house. 'You can tell your mate that,' he says, nodding towards the car.

'OK, thanks,' I say, reluctant to leave. 'Maybe we could ...' But he's gone, disappeared around the side of the house.

I head back to the car and get in. 'Well, that was pointless. He implied he made up the stuff about Elaine having an affair, and said that she definitely wasn't pregnant. He said he would know, because he saw her for the first three years, but he hasn't seen her since he was sixteen.'

I slump into the passenger seat, checking the back where Amy slumbers on peacefully.

'Not quite,' says Alison, flushed with excitement.

'What do you mean?'

'While you were in there, Paul had a visitor.'

'What? Who?'

'A white car pulled into the drive behind me, but as soon as whoever was driving saw my car parked here, they slammed on the brakes and reversed straight back out.'

'Did you see who it was?'

'She was only here for a minute, and I wouldn't swear to it in court, but I'm pretty sure it was Elaine Green.'

Chapter 29

'She was asking so many questions,' Mum says as I put a cup of tea down on the little table beside her chair.

'What? Who was?' I say vaguely, still distracted by the thought of Elaine Green fleeing her son's driveway like a criminal at the sight of an unfamiliar car. Does this mean she didn't move away at all – that she still lives in the area? It certainly indicates that Paul was lying when he said he hadn't seen her since he was sixteen.

'The lady who was here.'

'What lady?'

'The one who was here.'

We could go on like this forever.

'What's this?' I pick up the envelope from the arm of her chair – stiff cream card, my name on the front in elegant, inky-black handwriting.

'I don't know.'

Did whoever came bring it? I slide my thumb under the flap and pull out an invitation, all pink balloons and elephants. Chloe Riordan and Shaun Allbright are delighted to invite me to the christening party for their daughter, Phoebe, this Sunday. That's in four days' time. I'm clearly a last-minute addition to the guest list. I experience a weird stab of guilt about not having Amy christened. It's not the thought of a hell I don't believe in that bothers me, more that it hasn't occurred to me to celebrate her arrival into the world in any way. No silver spoons and special gowns for Amy. No cake with an icing baby on it, no sparkling wine, no enormous teddy bears. No proud daddy joking about how she won't be allowed a boyfriend till she's thirty. She just gets me and only me, day after endless day.

Chloe must have dropped it round while I was out. I turn it over to see a handwritten message. The handwriting is scrappy, barely legible. Someone else must have written the envelope. *Sorry for the short notice! The girls from baby group will be there but do feel free to bring a plus one (as well as Amy!)* it says chirpily. The girls from baby group? She makes it sound as if I'm part of the gang, one of 'the girls'. I was at baby group for about five minutes, and Della and I haven't exactly got off to a flying start. The only one I can imagine being friends with is Karen.

The thought of going makes my body clench, as if my skin is tightening over my bones. I pick up my phone to text Chloe with an excuse, but Mum's hand closes over my arm, her fingers digging in.

'Why was she asking all those questions?'

'She was probably just asking how you are. Being friendly.'

'No, it was . . . other things.'

'Like what?' God, it's hard not to get irritated. Impossible, in fact. Another thing to add to the pile of guilt I'm amassing.

'Oh, I don't know.' Mum's face clouds over as I've seen it do before, her eyes drifting back to the telly, but there's a difference this time. More . . . I would say calculating, but that can't be right, can it? I have the distinct feeling she could tell me if she wanted to, but this time she's choosing not to.

'What did she ask you?' I say again, with the growing sense that I've missed something here, something important. 'When? Was it today?'

She doesn't answer, her hands slack in her lap. She really has gone now, that momentary flash of cognition extinguished. I want to grab her, shake her by the shoulders, shout, bring her back to me. She was here for a second. My mum was here, as she used to be. Not the blank-eyed near-stranger I've become used to, but the woman who encouraged me to live my life, who sent me out into the world with the knowledge that I could do anything, who was there for me no matter what.

There were ways in which I envied Stella and her clan of brothers, her house always filled with chatter and laughter, alive with energy, but there's a unique relationship that exists between a single parent and an only child, however imperfect or fractured. Natalie said something similar in the pub the second time I met her. It was always me and Mum. No one else to bounce off, or argue with, or laugh with. A memory strikes me of a summer day when she came home from work with an enormous watermelon. I'd been home alone, loafing about the house all day, so I must have been into my teenage years. Even though there was no one else to see it, I was unfathomably embarrassed by this huge green fruit, by the thought of her walking home with it in her arms, a spherical, mutant baby. I refused to eat it on these grounds, my mother becoming more and more exasperated as she told me how much it had cost, how difficult to transport home on foot. In the end, she was so overwhelmed by fury at my teenage truculence that she hurled it to the ground with some considerable force, whereupon it split open, spraying the kitchen, and us, with vibrant pink pulp. For a second we stood in silence, Mum as horrified as me at what she had done. Then a smile began to play on her lips, and a snort escaped my nose, and we found ourselves incapacitated by laughter, crouching on the floor, sticky with watermelon juice, black pips in our hair.

A squawk from the hallway drags me into the present. Amy is awake in her car seat, straining at the straps, arms flailing. I get her out and as she pats at my face with both hands, I wonder if we'll have any moments like that watermelon day. With a jolt like a mini electric shock I realise I'm looking forward to it, to my relationship with Amy when she's older. I turn over this new and surprising emotion, examining it from all angles. I won't allow any topic to be off limits, like Mum did with the Hartstead massacre and my dad. I'll be open and honest about everything. What if she asks me about these early days with her, though, about how I felt? How honest can I, or should I, be about that?

I take her upstairs and into our bedroom, laying her down on the bed. Did Mum have a group of mum friends when I was a baby, before Dad died? A gang with whom she shared experiences, swapped horror stories of sleepless nights and explosive nappies? Did I grow up with visitors to the house, women who would put their babies down on the floor to play with me? How did I learn to share, to interact? Who did I play with? I'll never know now.

I pull my phone from my back pocket and tap out a quick text to Chloe, accepting her invitation as if this alone will ward off my demons, protect Amy from social failure. As I put my phone onto my bedside table out of Amy's reach, I frown. The book I've been trying to read for months, which I keep on my bedside table in the hope of one day finishing it, is on the floor. I don't remember knocking it off this morning. *She was asking so many questions.* Has Chloe been in my room? I look around, but it's hard to tell if anything else has been moved.

A question tugs inside me, one I want to, but can't, ignore. I get up, moving Amy into her cot just in case, although she can't yet roll over from back to front. I walk into Mum's room and kneel down on the floor, bending to look under the bed. The purple folder is where I left it when I replaced the photo after showing it to Alison, pushed against the wall. As I pull it out, I notice my hand is trembling. I leaf through the letters and newspaper cuttings until I get to the packet of photos. Slowly, I take them out and look through them. When I get to the end I go through them again, slower this time, rubbing each photo between thumb and forefinger in case two are stuck together, but the outcome each time is the same, and eventually I have to accept it. The photo of Mum and Elaine Green has gone.

Chapter 30

15th June 1994 | Melissa Bradshaw

Melissa is never getting married. She has friends who have been happily wed for years, but they don't work in family law like she does. She doesn't know how anyone could see what she does day in and day out, and still think it was a good idea. Fraser wants to, but what does he know? He manages a jewellery shop, he sees only beginnings – the nervous young men asking for advice, clueless about their girlfriends' ring size; the new fathers, brimming with respect and awe for the wives who have just pushed an actual human being out of their bodies, buying diamond-encrusted eternity rings.

She wouldn't normally see clients out of the office, but the nervous, softly spoken man on the phone insisted on meeting outside the coffee shop on the high street. She supposes he has some reason for not wanting to be seen going into a lawyer's office. She sees a lot of people who are planning to divorce spouses who are unaware of what their partner is planning. Sometimes they are men who want to protect their assets; sometimes women with darker reasons for making their plans so secretly. Melissa is under so much pressure from the partners to bring in new business, she wasn't going to quibble. Plus it's nice to get out of the stuffy heat and stultifying silence of the office.

She's a few minutes early, so she takes a steaming black coffee and a pastry, and sits at an outside table on the pavement, the only customer to do so. She savours this rare moment of guilt-free nothingness, ignoring the mental clamour of work to-do lists and DIY jobs that Fraser needs to do at the weekend, and concentrates on being in this moment. The deliciousness of the scalding coffee on her tongue – asbestos mouth, Fraser calls her – and the way the sweet pastry flakes on her lips. There's a soft drip-drip where the hanging baskets have been watered, the scent of damp earth filtering through the traffic fumes and cooking smells from the café.

Melissa breathes deeply, closing her eyes for a few seconds. The small stresses of her world – tricky clients and unsympathetic bosses, Fraser's growing desire to get engaged, her mum's upcoming hospital appointment – recede, and her shoulders drop for what feels like the first time in months. She doesn't register the popping sound or the distant screams. It's only when there's a louder crack that her eyes snap open, in time to see the shoeless, suited woman racing past, a woman who gasps a single word: 'Run.'

Melissa stands, uncertain, looking down the street. What does she mean? Run where? From what? Then a man emerges from an alleyway she's never noticed before, and she pushes her chair back, jogging the table, spilling her coffee onto the documents she's brought with her. It cascades onto her foot, scalding the bare skin either side of the T-bar on her shoes.

When Fraser comes in to identify her, he will see that foot poking out from beneath the sheet, and for a second – despite the fact she hasn't come home or been in contact – he will experience a wash of relief so great that his knees will give way. Melissa doesn't have a mark like that on her foot: two perfect, scarlet semi-circles dissected by a white line.

For a second, he will believe it's not her.

Chapter 31

The hall is festooned with pink and white bunting. A wall of noise hits us as I push the swing doors open, and Natalie hides a wince. I gave her a million opportunities to back out, but she said she was happy to come – knowing, I think, how anxious I was about it. There are babies wailing, sticky-fingered toddlers charging around high on sugar, and, everywhere, mothers. Mothers who are somehow, amazingly, carrying on adult conversations with other women while simultaneously feeding or burping babies, wiping small faces, blowing noses, kissing imaginary hurts better and answering question after inane question. I can see a couple of men holding babies – there's even one wearing a baby-carrier similar to mine – but mostly they are clustered together clutching bottles of beer, leaving the child-wrangling to their partners. Tom Glover is laughing among them – relaxed, in his natural habitat. A man's man. Ryan hovers at his elbow, sipping self-consciously from a bottle of beer.

Jesus, he's only fourteen. An apprentice, a man's man in training. Give him a few years and he'll have a kid of his own to ignore.

Della is making her way over to us, a glass of wine in one hand and Harry on her hip. He's looking around, his bright blue eyes huge. Karen trails behind with Theo in her arms, holding him in the same position as she was in the church hall, facing out, swinging him up and down. He's crying in a low-level, gripey way that I reckon is one stage before full-on screaming. Her hair needs a wash and she keeps reaching around to pull her top down at the back where it's riding up.

'He's taking it all in, isn't he?' says Natalie to Della, in the manner of one who knows it's the sort of thing one is expected to say about a baby.

'Oh, yes, bless him. You should put Amy facing outwards in that thing.' Amy is slumbering peacefully in the baby-carrier against my chest. 'It's much better for stimulation.'

'Maybe, when she wakes up.'

'Hmm. What is she, twenty weeks?'

'Eighteen and a half.'

'Harry's just over six months now – a Christmas baby like me, poor thing! Only one set of presents and no party!' Her laugh tinkles like broken glass.

'Do you find it good, that carrier?' Karen asks. She's trying to sound casual, but I sense desperation. 'I've got a similar one but he didn't like it. I'm debating whether to give it another go.'

'It's been a lifesaver,' I say. 'Definitely worth trying again.'

'Oh, then I will, thank you.'

As I predicted, Theo ratchets it up a notch, glowing scarlet as he really goes for it. Karen jiggles him ever harder, swaying from foot to foot.

'Careful with him, Karen!' says Della, raising her eyebrows at me. I deliberately ignore her, not wanting to collude in the shaming of Karen, who could so easily be me.

'I think I'll take him outside a minute,' Karen mutters. I go to protest, to tell her no one minds, but she's gone before I have a chance, pushing her way through the swing doors.

'God, she didn't push the doors open with Theo's head, did she?' says Della.

'No, of course not,' I snap. 'I think we'd better go and find Chloe.'

'Wait.' She takes a step closer. 'Cassie, you haven't heard anything from Ryan, have you? He hasn't been ... bothering you?'

'No, I haven't seen him since I was at your house. Why do you ask?'

Natalie shifts uncomfortably beside me. She didn't sign up for an awkward heart-to-heart. I told her we would swoop in, coo over the baby, hoover up a slice of cake and leave after one drink, max.

'He's been very secretive recently. More so than usual, I mean.'

'That's teenage boys for you, isn't it?' I say brightly. I don't want to get into this any more than Natalie does.

'I worry about who he chats to, on these forums. True crimes and all that. I try to keep an eye on what he's doing online but he's got it all locked down, password-protected.'

I sigh. Della seems genuinely worried. 'Will he talk to you about it at all?'

'No, he closes down. I'm of no interest to him, I wasn't even born when the Hartstead shooting happened. He used to ask his dad about it but ... he didn't get any-where, put it that way. Tom doesn't like talking about it. Listen, will you let me know, if he does try and get in touch with you? You read these terrible stories, don't you, about teenagers who do awful things, and it's always the parents who get the blame.'

'What about his mum?' I ask. 'Could you talk to her?'

'You're joking, aren't you? She hardly sees Ryan. He's meant to have this supervised contact with her every week but she always finds some reason to cancel it, and she certainly won't have anything to do with me. It's ridiculous; she was completely off the scene before I met Tom, but she's one of those women. I think she's jealous.' Della smooths her perfectly highlighted hair.

'Who wouldn't be jealous of you? Drinks, ladies?' James from the pub pops up at my elbow proffering a tray of sparkling wine.

'Thanks,' I say. Natalie and I both take one. 'What are you doing here? Are you a friend of Chloe's? Or ...' Chloe's partner's name eludes me.

'I'm the hired help,' he says. 'I know Shaun from the

pub and he asked if I'd give them a hand with the drinks and that. How's my little friend?'

'Er, I'm … alright, I suppose.'

He leans in, eyes dancing. 'I meant Amy, actually.'

'Oh, Cassie,' says Della pityingly, and I attempt a laugh to cover my embarrassment.

'She's OK. Asleep, thank God.'

'Great. I'd better get on with my duties. See you later.' He moves on to the next group.

'God, he's good, isn't he?' Della says, looking after him approvingly.

'What do you mean?' I say.

'Oh, you know, charming the pants off us saggy-tummed mums with bags under our eyes.' Della has nothing under her eyes but immaculately applied highlighter and her stomach is unfeasibly taut in her slim-fitting bright print dress, so I can only assume she is referring to me. 'I bet he's got some young hottie waiting for him at home.'

'How old is he?' says Natalie.

'About my age I think, mid-twenties,' Della says. 'But that means nothing to men, does it? Try internet dating, you'll see what I mean. The men are always looking for a woman five years or more younger than them. Thank God I'm not single, I'd have to shack up with an OAP! Ooh, there's Liz – I'll see you later.'

Natalie and I stare after her, both of us seemingly winded.

'God, she's awful, isn't she?' says Natalie eventually, taking a swig of her wine.

'Well ... it must be hard, having Ryan living with them, and the baby and everything. And Tom doesn't strike me as a barrel of laughs.'

'You really are a nice person, aren't you?' says Natalie, tapping her nails against her glass.

'Not sure about that,' I say, automatically putting a hand on Amy's back. 'You should be inside my head for the day.'

'Lots of women find it hard, these early days with a baby,' she says. 'There's no shame in it. I know my mum did.'

'*They're* not finding it hard, though, are they?' I indicate the room at large. 'They're finding it easy. They love it.'

'You don't know that,' says Natalie. 'You're comparing their outsides to your insides. You look as if you're coping great from the outside. What about that woman with Della earlier? The one with the crying baby.'

'Karen?'

'She's probably looking at you thinking, *Wow, look at her, chatting to her friend, drinking wine, casually carrying her sleeping baby. She's doing fine.* And you are. You're doing brilliantly.'

I look down, trying to stem sudden tears. 'Thanks,' I mutter, unable to say more for fear of bawling my eyes out.

'I mean it,' she insists. 'You're doing it all on your own, and you've got all that stuff with your mum to cope with too. I ... well, I admire you. I just hope you're not taking on too much with this stuff with Alison. You've got so much on your plate. I wish ... '

'What?'

'Nothing.' She shakes her head. 'Come on, let's go and find the girl of the hour, then we can get out of here and go to the pub.'

Chloe is chatting to an elderly couple, him florid and bursting out of a waistcoat, her frail and spindly in a faded linen dress. We wait next to them as they coo over Phoebe, Chloe gamely letting them pinch her cheeks and smother her in kisses, until they finally depart for the food table.

'Hi, thanks so much for coming, Cassie – and ... '

'Natalie. We met briefly in the pub the other day.'

'Oh, yes.' Her eyes slide back to me, barely registering Natalie. I'm used to being the centre of attention, the one everyone is curious about, but I've always thought it's hard for those close to me, destined to be forever the less interesting one. That was one of the things I loved about Guy. He knew about what had happened to me as a child, but it was never the most interesting thing about me.

'Everything looks lovely,' I say. 'Are you having a good day?'

'Yes, amazing,' says Chloe as Phoebe spits her dummy out and lets out a wail. Natalie bends to pick it up and passes it to her. Chloe steals a quick look over to the group of men in the corner before she licks it and sticks it back in.

'Jesus, Chloe.' One of the beer-drinking man's men

pops up beside us, tall and balding, shirt straining over his paunch. He snatches the dummy out of Phoebe's mouth, handing it to Chloe. 'How many times? That floor is disgusting – don't lick it and give it back to her.'

Phoebe's crying starts up again, and Chloe lifts her onto her shoulder.

'Fine, Shaun,' she says, deliberately controlled. 'Could you get me another one from the changing bag, then, please?'

'Get it yourself, I don't know where you've put it,' he says. 'Martin, mate!' He claps a passing pink-shirted man on the back. 'Let's get you a beer.'

As soon as she sees that Shaun is engrossed in conversation at the makeshift bar, she puts the dummy back in and Phoebe settles. 'Luckily Daddy's not there to see how often I do that, is he?' she says to Phoebe with a guilty smile.

'See, I told you,' Natalie says to me.

'What?' Chloe looks from her to me.

'I was just saying to Cassie that everyone finds it tough at times. Having a baby. She's not the only one.'

'Oh, of course it is,' says Chloe, sympathetically. 'I love her to bits,' she goes on, 'but it's so hard. I only got about three hours' sleep last night. I'm bloody knackered.'

It's kind of her, and of Natalie, but I know Chloe doesn't really feel the way I do. Yes, the lack of sleep and time to yourself is hard, everyone knows that, but not everyone resents their baby like I do. Not everyone stares into the darkness as they pace around and around their bedroom in the chill depths of the night, their baby on their shoulder, fantasising about the life they'd be living if she'd never been born.

'Chloe! Where's the cake?' a female voice bawls.

'Oh, God, I'd better go,' says Chloe. 'Thanks so much for coming.'

'Does that mean we can leave?' I say as she bustles off towards the hall's kitchen. 'We've done our bit, shown our faces. No one will remember what time we left, only that we were here.'

'It's up to you,' says Natalie neutrally.

'What? You want to stay?'

'God, no! But you did say you wanted to make more effort, make friends with other mums, get Amy socialising with other babies as she gets older. We haven't been here very long.'

'Sod it, I'll start next week. I'll go to that God-awful baby group, anything, as long as we can go to the pub now.'

'OK, you're the boss. And to be honest this place is giving me a headache.'

We escape into the vestibule and are almost free when a voice calls my name.

'Oh, shit,' I say under my breath.

Ryan lets the doors swing shut behind him, beer still in hand.

'Where are you going?' he says plaintively.

'We're making a move. Amy's getting a little ... ' Amy slumbers peacefully on in the carrier on my chest. Bad choice of excuse.

'I wanted to talk to you a bit more,' he says, his eyes fixed on mine.

'Another time. I really have to go.' My skin prickles. Absurdly, I am something close to afraid of this gangly, spotty youth.

'No, please don't. I only want to talk to you. I know you're trying to find out more about what happened that day. I could help you.'

'I don't think that's such a great idea, Ryan.' I instinctively cradle Amy's sleeping form.

'I could try and talk to my dad again, ask him about my grandad. He might know something.'

'No, it's not a good idea. I don't want to cause any problems in your family.' I grab my jacket from the peg and scoop up the changing bag. 'Let's go,' I say to Natalie. She's looking at Ryan, part horrified, part intrigued. 'Natalie!' I shake her arm.

'Sorry. Yes, right.'

I almost run from the building, aware that Ryan is still standing there staring fixedly after us.

'What was that about?' Natalie says, once we're outside in the car park. 'Who even was that?'

'Ryan – Tom Glover's son. You know, the one I told you about in the pub the other day.'

'Ohhh, him. OK, he is a bit weird.'

'Yeah, just a bit. Always makes me feel as though I need a shower after I've seen him. Shall we go to the pub?'

In the car park, Karen is struggling to strap a still-bawling Theo into his car seat.

'Hang on a sec,' I say to Natalie, and cross over to Karen's car.

'Are you leaving?'

She jumps, cracking her head on the top of the inside of the car.

'Ow, shit!' She puts a hand gingerly to the top of her head. 'Yeah, I just can't cope with any more of this in public.'

'I know how you feel.'

'Do you?' She eyes Amy suspiciously, still peacefully asleep in the carrier.

'Yes. I know I'm making it look easy, but this is a rare good day. Why don't you come to the pub with me and my friend?'

'You're joking, aren't you? With him?'

Theo writhes and strains against the bonds of the car seat, screaming rhythmically.

'Me and Natalie won't mind. Go on.'

'No, I'd better get him home. He might fall asleep if I drive around for a bit. But . . . thanks.'

The screaming is muted as she gets in and closes the door, and fades to nothing as she drives off. I find myself hoping I'll see her again.

At the pub, I feel a small pulse of disappointment that James won't be working there. I give myself a mental shake, mindful of Della's comment about charming the haggard mums. It's drizzling in that peculiarly miserable summer way, so we sit down inside with our drinks, Amy squidged up against my chest.

'That Della's a right charmer, isn't she?' says Natalie.

The knot in my stomach uncurls. 'She is pretty awful.'

'Mind you, with a stepson like that, who can blame her? You should stay away from him.'

'Don't worry, I intend to. Oh, I haven't told you! Alison thinks she saw Elaine Green at Paul's house.'

'Oh! Really? Well, she is his mum, I suppose.'

'Yes, but . . . everyone thought she'd moved away.'

'Perhaps she did. Maybe she was just visiting.'

'But he said he never sees her.'

'He might not be inclined to tell you the whole truth, I suppose.'

'I guess so. Alison thought . . . ' I peter out, unsure what it was that Alison thought.

Natalie fiddles with the stem of her wine glass. 'Don't take this the wrong way, but do you think you should be a bit careful of Alison?'

'What do you mean?'

'I know you've become friendly, and I like her too, but . . . don't forget she's a journalist, that's all.'

'I won't. I do trust her, though, not to put anything in the article about me that I'm not happy with.'

'Yes, I'm sure she wouldn't do that.'

Her emphasis on *that* gives me pause.

'What *do* you think she'd do, then?'

'Oh, Cassie, I don't know what I'm saying, but I get the feeling you need to be a bit cautious. I don't know if it's something she's said, or done, that's subconsciously put me on my guard – maybe it's my imagination. Ignore me. Forget it.'

'OK. But if you do think of anything more ... concrete, will you promise to tell me?'

'Of course. Anyway, back to Della and the Stepford Mums.'

I settle down in guilty anticipation of a minor bitching session, and push Natalie's doubts about Alison far, far to the back of my mind.

Chapter 32

15th June 1994 | Manisha Mehta

Manisha's first emotion on waking is relief. In her dream, she was back at St Margaret's and about to sit an exam she hadn't revised for – hadn't even been to any of the lessons. She lies curled on her side, panic subsiding. School is far behind her. It's been almost a year now since she left. Funnily enough, it's always exams she dreams about, never the bullying; never Hilary Masters and her gang of hangers-on, or what it was like to be the only Asian girl – the only non-white girl, in fact – in the entire school. The questions she could cope with – after all, those girls had never met anyone like her before, and they were curious. She could manage the questions about what she ate, and what she wore at home, or whether her parents were going to make her have an arranged marriage. It was when the whispered insults began that she knew she was in trouble.

At first it was just in the corridors. 'Paki,' Hilary would mutter at first, low enough that no teacher would ever hear. 'Stinking Paki.' After a while, she became more brazen. 'What's that smell?' she would say airily to whichever acolyte she was bestowing her presence on that day. 'Can you smell ... curry?'

Manisha never told the teachers, or her parents. It would only have made things worse. Instead, she waited. And she worked. In the mornings, working meant the hotel. She helped her mum with the breakfasts. If anything, she went to school smelling of bacon fat, not curry. After school, when the hotel was quiet, she'd shut herself in her room and study as if her life depended upon it. Which it kind of did. Last summer, the results were put up on a board in the main hall, and, although she was dying to go in and see how she'd done, she waited outside until she saw Hilary Masters coming down the road and into the school driveway. She followed close behind her, almost too close for comfort, and when they got to the board it was Hilary's results she looked for first. The feeling she got when she saw Hilary's two 'E's and a 'U' was almost sweeter than the one she got a few seconds later at her own three 'A's. She sensed Hilary scanning down the column, Manisha's shameful foreign surname only a few rows below her own, and was certain Hilary flinched when she clocked Manisha's outstanding results.

'Congratulations, Manisha!' Her English teacher, Mrs Corelli, had materialised beside her and squeezed her arm. 'You're going to Cambridge!' She had spoken quietly, so as not to upset any other pupils in the vicinity who hadn't received such happy news, but Hilary was close enough to hear, and Manisha wondered if Mrs Corelli had seen, or suspected, more than she had let on over the years. She felt, not the tumultuous joy she'd anticipated, but a sort of peace that spread within *her, filling her body. She knew, she just knew, that she was going to be OK, that she was going to have the amazing life she'd been dreaming about for years.*

She's spent the past year working in the hotel, saving up for university. Her parents have let her live in the flat at the back, which has its own entrance. When the bell rings, she assumes it's the postman with a parcel that won't fit through the letterbox. She quickly pulls on yesterday's jeans and T-shirt, not wanting the postie to see her in her pyjamas. As she hurries down the stairs, she fantasises about the friends who will come knocking for her at all hours at Cambridge, asking her to go out for a drink or a coffee, or simply wanting her company. All she's thinking about on this June morning as she opens the door is how certain she is that her life, her real life, is about to start in earnest.

When she opens the door, there's no one there. She ventures out and peers round the corner down the passage that leads out to the road and the main entrance of the hotel. She barely has time to register the man in the green shirt, or what he is holding, before her dreams are taken away from her forever.

Chapter 33

Anthea Newland from Oakdene House has been phoning to ask if I want the place for Mum. She's like a used car salesman with her messages containing dire warnings about there only being one place available for someone with her care needs, and how I need to confirm asap if I want it. Mum's been quieter recently, and there's been no repeat of the burning pan incident. Maybe she'll be OK here for a bit longer.

She sleeps later and later these days, and normally I leave her to it, figuring her body probably knows she needs rest, but when it gets to eleven o'clock I strap Amy into the dreaded no-longer-bouncy chair and tiptoe up with a cup of tea, pushing the door open slowly, mindful of the day she lashed out at me.

'Oh, my God.'

I stand frozen in the doorway. Her bed is empty.

'Mum!' I put the tea down on the chest of drawers and run into the bathroom, my bedroom, the spare room, but

I can tell from the chill emptiness in the air that there's no one up here. I stumble down the stairs, shouting for her, but she's nowhere downstairs either. Just Amy, who is getting restless after her regulation seven minutes in the chair. Hoping against hope, I check the garden, but there's nothing.

Swearing, I strap the baby-carrier on. Amy seems to have developed extra arms and legs as I race to stuff her into it. She's wriggling and keeps pulling one of her arms away as I try to fit it through. I can't stem the images of Mum in her nightclothes, or, worse, naked, knocking on doors or wandering into the path of an oncoming car, and with a grunt of frustration I wrench Amy's arm through the strap. She screams, a blood-curdling yell, but I ignore her, grabbing my keys from the side and shoving my feet into a pair of flip-flops. As I run down the street, Amy's wailing falls into a regular pattern, like a siren. I realise that not only does she have a potentially broken arm (good luck explaining that one in A&E) but she's also due for a bottle.

There's no sign of Mum anywhere. There's a young couple, teenagers, waiting at the bus stop. They are kissing, absorbed in one another.

'Excuse me.'

They break apart, the girl embarrassed, the boy facing me with a truculent, challenging expression, as if I'm going to tell him off.

'Have you seen a woman? In her sixties ... behaving strangely ... she might have been in pyjamas? Or dressed, I'm not sure ...'

They stare, expressionless.

'No, sorry,' the girl says. 'We were a bit . . . ' She sniggers and he draws her towards him, pulling her into his side.

'Yeah,' he says, his hand snaking down towards her bum. 'Do you mind?'

I run on, faster now, too worried about Mum to be humiliated. There's an old man coming towards me now, wearing an anorak and a flat cap, carrying a small blue carrier bag containing what looks like a single pint of milk.

'Have you seen a woman . . . ' I gasp.

'In her jimjams?' he says, speaking louder above Amy's screams. 'Yes, I passed her back there on Southall Street.' He motions behind him to the next road on my right. 'I did try to talk to her, find out where she lived and that, but she was a bit . . . wild. I'm sorry.'

'Oh, no need. I know what she's like. Thank you so much,' I call back to him, my feet already moving, heels slamming onto the concrete through the flimsy rubber soles of my flip-flops, one arm clasped around Amy in case I didn't fasten her in properly in my haste. I round the corner into Southall Street, my chest burning at the unaccustomed exercise, and she's there, heading away from me, about twenty metres away in her tartan pyjamas, feet bare, hair matted. Thank God.

'Mum!'

She keeps walking. I hurry to catch up with her, but when I'm almost at her elbow I pause, realising I'm scared of her reaction. Frightened of my own mother.

'Mum,' I say, trying to sound calm and together, despite Amy's continued crying.

This time she stops and looks at me, vacant.

'I want to go home,' she says, like a child who's had enough of a party.

'Yes,' I say, laying my hand on her arm. 'I'm here to take you home.'

I can tell she doesn't recognise me, but she allows me to lead her as we retrace my steps up Southall Street and past the bus stop, now thankfully empty. We get a few funny looks, but the streets are quiet and soon we are through the door and standing together in the hallway. Mum looks at me for a steer as to what to do next. Amy is scarlet and bawling, writhing, her limbs flailing wildly. My instinct says I should take Mum up to bed, tuck her in, smooth her hair, comfort her, and with a surge of pure rage I realise I can't do that, because once again Amy's needs trump everything else. Biting back fury, I turn to her.

'Why don't you go upstairs and lie down? I'll bring you up a cup of tea in a minute.'

She shuffles off obediently. When did she start shuffling? She's sixty-three, for God's sake, not ninety.

I can't take much more of the crying, each scream like a knife slashing into my flesh. I take Amy through to the kitchen. Hands fumbling, I unstrap her and lie her down on the floor – possibly not recommended but it's quicker than putting her anywhere else. She's waving her arms and I quickly check the one I yanked through the carrier. It's OK, thank God. Now able to use my own arms, I rip open a carton of ready-made formula, slop it into a sterilised bottle, pick her up and sit at the table, the empty baby-carrier still hanging from my front. Finally, blissfully, she begins to feed. In the silence, my tears fall, dripping onto Amy's body, spotting her babygro. I rarely allow myself to cry these days. I'm frightened that once I start I won't be able to stop, but I can't hold it in today and soon I'm howling – guttural, wrenching sobs. For Mum – or whoever she is now – in her pyjamas, barefoot and confused on the street. For Amy, innocent and blameless – saddled with me for a mother, no father to speak of, disadvantaged before her life has properly begun. For me.

I'm crying so violently I don't hear the key in the lock, and it's only when she taps nervously on the half-open kitchen door that I realise Chloe is here.

'Oh, God, I didn't hear you.' I try to wipe my wet cheeks and streaming nose on my shoulder, both hands being occupied.

'Sorry. You gave me a key, remember? Are you . . . OK? Here.' She grabs a roll of kitchen towel from the side and pulls off a couple of pieces, holding them out to me.

I gesture helplessly, one hand trapped under Amy and the other holding the bottle.

'Here, let me.' She takes Amy from me in one swift, easy movement, making sure the bottle doesn't come away from her mouth, and sits down opposite me, Amy still sucking away.

'Thanks.' I cover my embarrassment by blowing my nose for longer than is necessary.

'It can be difficult, I know,' says Chloe. 'And I'm sure it's even worse for you. When it gets too much for me, I call my mum and she'll come and take over, take Phoebe out for a bit. But you've got all this with your mum as well. I'm not surprised you're overwhelmed.'

I press my lips together, nails in palms, trying to hold it together. Her unexpected kindness is unravelling me, thread by thread.

'You're doing an amazing job, though. You really are.'

'I'm not.' Fresh tears spring from my eyes. 'I'm doing a bloody awful job.'

'You're not, I promise. Hey, she's still alive, isn't she?'

I smile thinly.

'There you go. That's the main thing at this stage. She's absolutely fine, look at her.' Chloe looks at me thoughtfully. 'It's not good for you, though, to be so worn out. My sister does babysitting, you know. She's a qualified nursery nurse so you wouldn't have any worries about Amy. Do you want me to ask her?'

'I can't afford it.' God, how I would love to hand her over to someone else for the major portion of the day.

'What about your mum? Have you thought any more about residential care?'

'I think I have to. She walked out in her pyjamas and bare feet this morning. I didn't realise straight away, I thought she was still in bed. She was on Southall Street before I caught up with her. That place, though … Oakdene. The thought of her in there …'

'I know it's hard. But if it's going to keep her safe, it's probably for the best.'

I'm silent. I know she's right. I've been avoiding it, thinking I could cope – that I *should* cope, for as long as humanly possible. Having Amy has made me more aware than ever of everything my mother has done for me. Not only did looking after her at home feel like the right thing to do, I wanted to do it, however hard. But this morning has terrified me. I love my mother, even in this unrecognisable state – this morning showed me that. But here, at home, there is only me, and I am not enough. Love is not enough.

'I'll call them later.'

'She's my last client today. Why don't you go out for a few hours, by yourself? I'll stay here and look after her and Amy.'

'Oh, I couldn't, Chloe. It's not fair on you.'

'I'll be fine. My mum's got Phoebe; she won't mind keeping her a bit longer. I want to help.'

I think about having a few hours to myself. I could get the bus into Tunston and browse in the shops, sit and have a coffee, read a magazine. All things I would have taken for granted a few months ago, which are now impossible dreams. They shimmer in front of me like a mirage.

'Are you sure?'

'Absolutely. Now, why don't you give Oakdene a call,

222

go and wash your face and I'll see you back here at ... shall we say three o'clock?'

Twenty minutes later, I'm strolling down the high street, light and untethered. Alone. Before I left, I called Anthea Newland to confirm Mum's place at Oakdene House. The thought of it lurks, threatening to weigh me down, but I force it away. I can worry about that later when I load my responsibilities back on. Right now, it's just me.

At the bus stop, I peruse the timetable. There's a bus to Tunston in fifteen minutes. It'll take another fifteen minutes to get there. Going there and back is going to take a precious hour of my time. And although it's bigger than Hartstead, Tunston's hardly a bustling metropolis. Maybe I'll get a magazine and have lunch in the pub here instead. *Hoping James is going to be there?* taunts a little voice in my head. I push it down. I'm hungry, that's all, and it's the nicest place to eat.

There's no one behind the bar, and I can't ignore the fact that my heart is beating a little faster than normal as I study the menu. I hear footsteps coming up from the cellar and I look up, ready to smile, but it fades on my lips as a woman I've never seen before comes through the door and heads towards me, wiping her hands on her apron. I order a sandwich and take my glass of wine over to a table by the window, opening the trashy magazine I've bought and trying to interest myself in its contents. I used to love these gossipy rags, but I leaf through page after page of this one, not reading any of it.

'Hello there.'

223

My head snaps up, and I can't do anything about the smile that spreads across my face when I see James standing there with a pint of beer.

'Hi! I didn't think you were working.'

'I'm not. This is for me. I've ordered lunch too. Do you mind if I join you, or would you rather be alone with your celebrity gossip?'

'Oh, God, no. I don't know why I bought it; I don't know who any of them are. Sit down.' I shove the magazine into my bag, making more of a performance of it than is strictly necessary.

'Thanks. It's dangerous, living above a pub. I've got to the point where I can't even be bothered to make myself a sandwich; I just come down here and get one. And then it seems rude not to have a pint to go with it.'

'You live above here?'

'Yep, I rent the flat. Makes for an easy commute. Where's Her Royal Highness today?'

'Chloe's taken her for a few hours, to give me a break.'

'Ooh, what are you going to do with your freedom?'

It's an obvious question, an innocent one if I want to take it that way, but I'm pretty sure I'm not imagining the question behind the question, the suggestion in his eyes that don't leave mine. I tell myself he's a flirt, a charmer, that I don't want to embarrass myself, or do something I'll regret. So I'm almost surprised myself to hear the next words that come out of my mouth, after I take a gulp of wine.

'Got any ideas?' I say, looking right back at him.

'Let's have a drink and we'll see if we can think of something, shall we?' He raises his glass and I clink mine against it, our eyes locked.

Over our first drinks, the conversation treads familiar ground. He asks about Amy, and we chat about Alison's article and what she's found out so far. The following two glasses of wine slip down so easily I don't know if it's them or James that is making me giddy. All I do know is that I'm happier than I have been in months. We talk about our lives, our pasts, we tell our stories – the ones you bring out when you're trying to impress someone, or amuse them. He makes me laugh so hard that at one point wine spurts out of my nose. I feel like me again. There's that zing between us, electricity bouncing back and forth, a heat that suffuses my body. I'd almost forgotten this feeling existed, and I certainly didn't think I'd be experiencing it again any time soon. I know it's utter madness but there's nothing else I want to do with the hour and a half I have left before I return to my real life and pile my burdens back on, one by excruciating one. The problem is, it's such a long time since I've been in a situation like this, I can't remember how you get from chatting and flirting to the next stage. I'm pretty sure he's interested, but I get the sense he doesn't want to pressure me, so the move is going to have to come from me.

We're getting towards the bottom of our third drinks, and panic seizes me that he's going to think I'm not interested, and leave.

'So, can I see this famous flat, then?' I blurt it out quickly before I have a chance to change my mind.

'Absolutely.' He looks delighted. 'If you're sure you want to.'

'I want to,' I say, a burst of wine-fuelled daring prompting me to press my foot onto his under the table, making it clear there is no misunderstanding.

We slip through a side door I've never noticed. The burgundy carpet is stained and peppered with cigarette burns, and the off-white textured wallpaper is peeling, but I don't care. As he follows me closely up the narrow staircase, I swear there's an actual, physical heat emanating from him, one that meets a correspondent fire in me. I want him to obliterate everything that is pressing down on me, to make me forget, if only for a little while. There's no need to worry any more about how we will move things to the next stage, because as soon as the door closes behind us he presses me up against it, kissing me, his hands on my neck, in my hair, pulling at my clothes.

We break apart for a second, breathless.

'So, this is the hallway,' he says in the manner of an estate agent, and we collapse in giggles. 'Perhaps madam would like to see the bedroom?'

'Oh, she definitely would,' I say.

He takes my hand and we tumble into his bedroom, falling in a tangle on his unmade bed. I don't know if it's the wine, or his vocal and boundless enthusiasm for my body, but as I gradually shed my clothes I don't give a second's thought to my stretch marks, or the loose skin on my stomach. Even before motherhood ravaged my body, with previous boyfriends – including Guy – I'd felt self-conscious, unable to ever fully relax, as if I were watching from the outside with a critical eye. James either doesn't notice my imperfections or couldn't care less, and for an hour I am completely transported. I'm not observing, or thinking. I am perfectly in the moment. I am not Amy's inadequate mother, or a daughter grieving for a mother who is still alive but no longer really here. I don't have to make any decisions, or consider anybody else's needs – other than James's, and they have merged with my own. I do nothing but feel, and it's glorious.

Afterwards, he falls asleep on his stomach, the duvet over his lower half. I'll have to go soon, but I lie back, spent and loose-limbed, luxuriating in my last minutes of freedom. I suppose I should be feeling guilty or regretful, but I don't, and I doubt I ever will, even if I never see James again.

I can see the top of the tattoo at the base of his spine. Curious, I pull the duvet down to reveal the whole thing. As I thought, it's Roman numerals: XV VI MCMXCIV. I'm pretty sure it's a date, so I idly work it out. XV, that's fifteen. VI, six. The fifteenth of June. Oh, my God. My heartbeat speeds up. I can't work the last bit out; my brain isn't working properly. I slip noiselessly from the bed, retrieving my clothes from various locations around the room, and hurriedly dress before going into the hall to get my bag from where I dropped it an hour ago. I take my phone out, hands shaking, and google 'Roman numeral converter'. I type in 'MCMXCIV' and 'convert', but even before it comes up, I know with a cold certainty what it's going to be. 1994.

Icy fingers trickle down my spine and it strikes me how little I know about James. I don't even know his surname.

I sneak out of his front door and down the stairs. Thank God there's another exit to the street, so I don't have to do a walk of shame through the pub. Combing my hair with my fingers, I hurry down the road, unaccountably eager to hold Amy in my arms. The questions in my head, though, can't be quietened: who is James, and why the hell does he have the date of the Hartstead massacre tattooed on his back?

Chapter 34

gamerboy: did you find anything else out?

katiekat2006: no not yet

gamerboy: ok. Where do you live anyway?

katiekat2006: Hartstead

gamerboy: where tho

katiekat2006: near the high street

gamerboy: you can tell me, I'm not gonna turn up at
your house

gamerboy: its ok jk you don't have to say. Do you live with
your dad as well?

katiekat2006: no just me and mum

gamerboy: do you see your dad?

katiekat2006: no

gamerboy: how come? Wanna meet up and you can tell me?

gamerboy: you still there?

katiekat2006: yes, sorry. Ok

gamerboy: if you dont want to, just say. Doesnt matter to me either way

katiekat2006: no I do want to, its just mum. Will have to think of a way

gamerboy: whatever. Doesnt matter

katiekat2006: Ill sort something for def

gamerboy: cool. xxx

katiekat2006: xxx

Chapter 35

'I've tracked down Manisha Mehta's parents.' Alison bounces along beside me as we head into the park in town. It's not much more than a threadbare triangle of grass with a small, fenced play park in the middle, bounded by a concrete path. Without discussion, we begin a circuit of the path. It's a favourite with dog-walkers, as it's one of the only green spaces within the town itself, although there is plenty of beautiful country-side around here. This was where Maureen Featherstone, Travis Green's penultimate victim, met her end. I try not to think about that now.

I've told Alison that Amy is crankier than usual so I wouldn't have to face James in the pub, although I'm not going to be able to use that forever. I might have to use staying home with Mum as an excuse. Well, it won't be an excuse really. I've increased the carers' hours now, so Chloe comes in the morning and the afternoon until Mum moves into Oakdene, but her meagre savings won't last forever. I can't think about what I'm going to do then, and whether I'll have to sell the house. I want to tell Alison about James's tattoo, but I'm too embarrassed to explain how I got so close to it.

'The girl from the hotel?'

'Yep. They run a small hotel in Foxwell now, more of a B&B really. It's only half an hour's drive from here.'

'You want to go and see them?'

'Yes.' She steps in front of the pram, forcing me to come to a halt. 'Graham Mooney was teaching Elaine Green to drive.'

'We think he *might* have been.'

'Yeah, yeah,' She waves a dismissive hand. 'Your mum was friends with Elaine Green. Secret friends.'

'My mum wasn't killed, though.'

'No, but your dad was. And Elaine was having an affair and pregnant. She's supposed to have moved away and Paul isn't supposed to ever see her, but I saw her driving towards his house the other day. Come on, Cassie. Something was going on. Don't you want to know what it was?'

'Yes. No. I don't know, Alison.'

I think of the anonymous notes, the knife in Amy's pram that I can't be sure was put there by my confused mother.

'Does it matter?' I say, aware how weak this sounds. 'We know Travis Green killed all those people.'

'Does the truth matter?' She strides out again and I take a half-running step to catch up. 'Yes, I think it does.

It matters to the families of the victims. And I think it matters to you, too.'

'OK,' I say, unable to withstand the force of her personality. 'I suppose you want me to come?'

'It would make it easier,' she says.

Of course it would. Cassie Colman, tragic tot. Who could refuse to talk to her?

'Alright. When do you want to go?'

'No time like the present! I've arranged for us to see them this afternoon. Chloe will be coming in for your mum, won't she? Why don't we go and have a coffee in the café now and you can feed Amy, then she'll sleep in the car.'

She's thought of everything, as per usual, and an hour and a half later we're pulling up outside a red-brick fifties house with a crooked sign proclaiming it to be the Willow Tree Hotel. There is no tree in evidence, apart from the poorly drawn representation on the sign itself. Amy is asleep, but Alison wants to come in too, so I heave the car seat out. Amy barely stirs. She was awake for several hours in the night, so she has some catching-up to do. Alright for some. My eyes are hot and sore, and my body aches as if I've run a marathon.

Alison rings the doorbell, and looks down at Amy as we wait.

'God, sometimes I wish Katie was still that small – I know it's hard,' she says, pre-empting my reply, 'but at least you don't have to worry about where she is or what she's doing. Katie's so . . . distant, these days. She's so – I don't know . . . separate from me.'

'That's normal, isn't it, at thirteen?' I think of myself at that age, a whole world in my head, a life my mother knew nothing about.

'Yes, but I think it's more than—'

She's interrupted by the door opening, revealing a tired-looking man in a marginally too small grey suit.

'Mr Mehta?' She holds out her hand to be shaken. 'I'm Alison Patchett. We spoke on the phone.'

'Come in, please.'

He gives her a limp shake and we follow him down the hallway, past a small reception desk and into what looks like the admin office for the hotel. A large woman with a fat black plait of hair rises to greet us.

'Thanks for agreeing to see us,' Alison says, once we're all seated. It's a small room, and they've brought in extra chairs, so the four of us are sitting unnaturally close to each other. I have to keep my legs braced so as not to bump knees with Mr Mehta.

'We don't want that day to be forgotten,' says Mrs Mehta softly. 'We moved because we couldn't face the daily reminders of her, but we don't want others to turn away. People need to remain vigilant, to stop this kind of thing happening again.'

'Do you think the tragedy could have been prevented, then?' says Alison. 'Do you think there were warning signs that Travis Green might do something like this?'

'We don't know,' says Mr Mehta. 'We knew nothing of this man.'

'Manisha had never mentioned him? She didn't know him at all?'

'Well, she knew him, after a fashion.'

Alison's eyes flick to me and back to Mr Mehta. 'She knew him? How?' she asks with deliberate calmness.

'Yes,' he says, as if it should be obvious to us. 'He was the caretaker at her school, St Margaret's, until six months before it happened.'

Of course. I remember it from the newspaper reports at the time.

'But Manisha had never spoken to him as far as we knew,' Mrs Mehta goes on. 'She certainly never mentioned him. In a small town like Hartstead ... some of the victims were bound to be connected to him in some way.'

'Yes, naturally,' Alison says smoothly, but I can hear her mind whirring. 'Was she happy at school?'

Mr Mehta looks at his wife. She is looking down, hands twisting in her lap.

'We think she may have had a little trouble,' he says in a low voice.

'With her academic work?' Alison prompts, knowing this not to be the case. The reports at the time made much of the fact that Manisha had been accepted into Cambridge University.

'No, with ... bullying.'

'She never told us,' Mrs Mehta says, still not looking up. 'I used to ask her about it – I had my suspicions. That Hilary Masters ... I saw her once, in the supermarket, after they left school – not long before she was … She asked me if Manisha was around that day to go out with her. I told her she wouldn't be able to because she was working, that she always worked in the hotel Wednesdays and Fridays because we went to see my mother – she was very unwell by then; it wasn't long before she passed away. But when I told Manisha that her friend Hilary had been asking after her – goodness, Manisha's face … she looked horrified. We made her tell us the truth then. If she had only told us at the time, we would have been in to talk to the head teacher, tried to sort it out, but she had always said everything was alright, and now school was finished, so what could we do?'

'It wasn't your fault,' Alison says. 'I know what teenage girls are like; they don't want to tell you anything.'

'You have a daughter?' Mrs Mehta raises her large, luminous eyes to Alison's.

'Oh … yes …'

'She was much happier when she left school and started working in the hotel,' Mr Mehta says, filling the painful silence that follows. 'She used to say you see all life in a hotel. We had a function room, and we'd be having weddings, christenings, wakes.'

'Did she ever see Travis Green at the hotel?' Alison asks. 'Or his wife, Elaine? Can you think of anything she mentioned that could be relevant?'

'Relevant to what?' Mr Mehta asks. 'I thought you were writing about how the tragedy affected the town.'

'I am,' she says. 'But when you mentioned that Travis

Green had worked at Manisha's school, I wondered if there was a connection, that's all.'

A noise makes me jump, and for a second I can't place it. Then I realise it's coming from Mrs Mehta, stifled sobs escaping her.

'I think you had better go,' says Mr Mehta. 'My wife . . . '

Alison seems about to protest, so I jump in. 'Of course we'll go. We're so sorry if we've brought up unpleasant memories for you.'

'It doesn't matter,' he says, standing and herding us out of the room. 'We live this every day. It is not possible for anyone to make it worse for us.'

As Mr Mehta holds the front door open for us, Alison halts for a second.

'Do you still have the booking records from the hotel in Hartstead?'

'Good heavens, no,' he says. 'We didn't have a computer, it was all written in a book, but we got rid of all that when we moved.'

'OK, thank you.'

As I strap Amy's seat into the car, Alison sighs. 'God, that poor couple.'

'I know.' The Mehtas' naked pain, still so fresh after twenty-five years, has shaken me too. There's something else, though: I'm trying to think where I've heard the name Hilary Masters before.

'Interesting what they said about the things you see in a hotel,' Alison says. 'What did Manisha see? Who did she see?'

'Got it!' I say, closing the back door and throwing myself into the passenger seat.

'Got what? You know what she saw?'

'No, not that. Hilary Masters.'

'Who?'

'The girl Mrs Mehta said might have been bullying Manisha.'

'What about her?' says Alison, mystified.

'I knew I'd heard the name before, and now I've got it. She was quoted in a lot of the newspaper articles at the time. She was laying flowers outside the hotel, and she happened to be there when a journalist was there, so he interviewed her. I'm sure she was referred to as a friend of Manisha's, though.'

'What did she say?' asks Alison.

'Oh, the usual sorts of things, about what a great person she was and what a terrible waste it was. But if she'd been bullying Manisha, what was she doing there? And, now I think about it, why was she asking Mrs Mehta if Manisha was around to go out with her that day in the supermarket?'

'Hmm, good question,' says Alison.

As we drive back to Hartstead, I wind the window down and breathe in the heady summer smell of elderflower. The familiar patchwork fields that line the Tunston Road roll past, taking me further and further away from the Mehtas' quiet and empty hotel, and their quiet and empty life.

Chapter 36

'I've been thinking about things the victims have in common.'

'Hmm?' I'm distracted, looking around for any sign of James. I couldn't think of a reason to give Alison not to go to the pub, and I figured I'd have to face him some time. The problem is, I don't know how I feel. Whenever I think of our afternoon together, I get a prickle of excitement. It's the only time since I moved back to Hartstead that I've felt like *me*, and I crave feeling like that again. But James clearly has a connection to the events of 15th June 1994 – in which case why the hell has he never mentioned it? He knows who I am, and that I'm helping Alison with her article.

'They were all out on the street,' she goes on.

There are footsteps coming up from the cellar and my stomach flutters in anticipation, but then I see a cloud of blonde hair, and my shoulders drop.

'Be with you in a sec.' It's the girl who was working the

other day when James and I were having lunch. I hope she didn't see us slipping upstairs together.

'OK, thanks,' Alison says, and turns back to me impatiently. 'Well?'

'Of course they were out on the street. He was walking through the streets shooting people.'

'Yes, but what were they doing there? Graham was waiting on the street for a client, wasn't he? But that's not usual, is it? Wouldn't a driving instructor normally pick the client up from their house?'

'I don't know. That's hardly—'

'I've been looking through the reports,' she interrupts me. 'They say that David Wilkes the estate agent, Suzanne Persimmon from the Citizens Advice Bureau and the lawyer, Melissa Bradshaw, had all left their offices to meet a client. Isn't that a little weird?'

'Estate agents usually meet their clients outside the property, don't they?'

'OK, but what about the others? Why would a lawyer meet someone outside? Surely they'd come to the office?'

'I suppose so . . .'

'I googled the lawyers that Melissa worked for. It was Franklin & Upshott, on the high street. They're still there. I called them and I struck gold with the receptionist. When I told her I was writing an article for the newspaper, she couldn't get her words out fast enough. She thinks I'm going to make her famous. She said they wouldn't still have the records in terms of Melissa's diary, who she was seeing and all that, but she said she'd try to find out what she could. She called me this morning, and said she'd spoken to one of the older partners who's been there since before the shooting, and guess what?'

'What can I get you?' The blonde woman pops up from the floor behind the bar where she's been unpacking a box of crisps. I try to decipher if she's giving me a knowing look. Has James told her what we did? How well does she know him? Does she know what his connection to the Hartstead shooting is? Luckily Alison orders for both of us, her briskness covering my fluster.

'So what did this partner say?' I ask, when we're ensconced at a corner table.

'He thinks there were some personal effects, her diary and other things, that Melissa had with her, which were returned to the office when the police had finished with them. He said they were probably given to her boyfriend, Fraser McKillick. It's not a common name round here, and I found him easily. He's the manager of Goldsborough Jeweller's in Tunston, so I called him at the shop. We're going to see him this afternoon.'

'What?' I've barely recovered from our trip to the Mehtas' hotel yesterday, still tender from witnessing their ongoing pain.

'Yep. He's still got the bundle of stuff he got from the office, and said we're welcome to look through it.'

'What are you expecting to find?'

'I don't know, Cassie. But there's something not right, don't you think? Can't you feel it?'

As ever, Alison is sweeping me along, an unstoppable force, and for the most part I am with her; I want to know as much as she does. But sometimes I question what lies beneath her naked desire for the truth. Is it simply the journalistic nose for a story? Today though, I push down my questions, and when our drinks arrive, I join her in her endless dissection of the events of 15th June 1994. Several times, I almost spill the beans about James but something stops me.

Later that day, we park in the multi-storey car park in Tunston. Tunston is an unremarkable mid-sized town with a scuffed, down-at-heel shopping arcade. To me, though, and I guess to Alison too, it still retains a sort of glamour, it being the 'big town' to us growing up in Hartstead: the place you went shopping for clothes; the first place you were allowed to go with your friends on the bus. We'd spend all day here, although, looking around now, I can't think what we did once we'd exhausted the excitement of Topshop and River Island. There was a lot of hanging around in the precinct and eyeing up boys we were too shy to speak to. Although it was probably different for her and her friends at Callenden, all pony-trekking and tennis lessons.

Goldsborough Jeweller's is on the ground floor of the arcade, sandwiched between a cheap clothes shop and the key-cutting place. Engagement rings nestle in maroon velvet boxes in the window next to watches that would have paid my rent in London for several months. Inside, an anaemic-looking, mousy girl I would never have pegged as a salesperson scuttles off to get Fraser McKillick for us.

'Ladies!' He comes towards us, hand outstretched. Now this is more like it. It's there in his broad smile, his welcoming tone. Salesmanship oozes from his every pore. Amy kicks her legs in the baby-carrier, and he puts a finger lightly to her cheek. 'Hello there, little one.'

'Alison Patchett.' Alison holds out her hand. 'We spoke on the phone.'

'Ah, yes.' His shoulders drop a little, any hope of commission extinguished. 'Come through.' His hand rests on my lower back for a second as he ushers us behind the sparkling counter displays into a small office. He takes a seat behind the desk and invites us to sit in the two chairs opposite. In front of us sits a transparent plastic wallet containing some papers and a small diary.

'You're writing an article for the *Sunday Times*, you say?' he asks Alison.

'Yes, that's right. It's about how towns move on from tragic events like the Hartstead shooting,' she recites smoothly, and I glance at her.

His fingers are drawn to the plastic folder, passing back and forth over the little popper that holds it closed.

'We're so sorry for your loss,' I say quickly. 'I know it's not the same but I . . . I lost someone too.'

'I know,' he says, smiling at me sadly. 'That's why I agreed to see you.'

I sense Alison mentally patting herself on the back for bringing me into this thing.

'How do you think it has affected you?' Alison asks. 'Do you still get asked about it?'

'Most people don't know I was involved. I wasn't in the papers particularly – not like you were,' he says to me. 'At first it was horrendous. Melissa and I ... we were living together. I was going to ask her to marry me; I hoped we'd have children.'

I look down at his hand, where he is sporting a thick gold wedding band.

'I met Genna a couple of years later.' He twists the ring. 'I've been happy. Lucky. But I suppose it's what the whole thing left me with that's been hardest to cope with, when the initial horror of losing Melissa settled into something more ... manageable.'

'What do you mean?' asks Alison.

'The sense that at any moment something unimaginably awful could happen. Lots of people feel like that, I guess, but when that thing has actually happened to you ...' He slides his eyes towards me. 'It's hard to escape the idea that you're right to feel that way.'

I nod as if I understand, but it's so different for me. I don't have any clear memories of that time. I have a vague memory, aged six or seven perhaps, of asking Mum where my dad was. She told me he had been killed in an accident. I don't know if she actually said car accident, but that was what I got into my head and she certainly never disabused me of the idea. I said it in class once at infant school, in front of everyone. The teacher got a funny look and changed the subject, and afterwards

Amelia Greenhorn, her shiny, conker-brown hair in two high plaits like horns, cornered me in the playground and told me what had really happened. I accused her of lying, but it sounded weak. I could feel the truth in her words deep in my belly. As I had my milk and biscuits at the kitchen table after school, I asked Mum about it and she told me briefly that what Amelia had told me was true. It was a shock, and yet somehow not a shock. She didn't say any more and we carried on as we had been. I don't have the *before* and *after* that Fraser has, the rip in the framework of a perfect world.

'And is this . . . ?' Alison indicates the folder on the desk between us.

'Yes, those are her things. The things she had with her that day.'

'May I?'

Fraser pushes the folder towards Alison. 'Sure.'

She opens the flap and pulls out a few sheets of typed A4 paper stapled together. I lean over. *What You Can Expect If You Choose Franklin & Upshott To Handle Your Divorce*. There's a dark stain across the bottom half of the page.

Alison looks at Fraser, not wanting to ask the question.

'Don't worry, it's coffee,' he says. 'She was at the café on the high street when it happened.'

'Do you know why?' Alison asks casually, as if it's not the reason we are here. 'Would it be usual for her to meet a new client somewhere other than the office?'

'I don't think so, but she didn't talk about her work

much. We had other things going on. Her mother hadn't been well, and we'd bought a house that needed loads doing to it, plus I think she preferred to leave her work at the office.'

'Mm-hm,' says Alison, but I can tell she's not listening. She has opened the diary to June 1994, and is keeping her face determinedly composed. She angles it towards me, and I read the first entry for Wednesday 15th June. *10am*, it says. *The Coffee Station. Nigel Waterford.*

The name rings a bell, but it takes me a few seconds longer than Alison, with her journalist's memory for facts. I get there, though, and when I do, the room tilts around me. Graham Mooney had a ten o'clock appointment on 15th June 1994 with a new client, too. A client named Nigel Waterford.

Chapter 37

As soon as Chloe arrives for the afternoon shift on Monday, I'm out the door. I've been in the house with Mum and Amy all weekend and I'm pretty much ready to explode. I've arranged to meet Natalie at the pub for a drink, but as I walk down the street Amy screams and squirms in the pram. I know she's tired – she had a couple of horrendous nights and barely napped all weekend – but she won't give in to it.

There's a light touch on my arm.

'Sorry to make you jump,' Natalie says, out of breath. 'I've been trying to catch you up. I was calling you, but . . .'

'Oh, hi! Yeah, I didn't hear you over this racket,' I say grimly. Every cry is a scratch on my soul, like nails down a blackboard but a million times worse, with no idea of when it's going to end. 'She's exhausted but she just won't sleep.'

'Shall we walk for a bit?' Natalie says. 'Maybe she'll go off and we can go for our drink in peace then.'

'That would be great,' I say gratefully.

We pass the pub and carry on up the high street towards the park where Maureen Featherstone was killed as she walked her dog. A phrase from the reports I can't keep away from echoes through me: *Maureen Featherstone was taking her dog for its regular morning walk when she was mown down*. I hear Alison's voice in my head, asking questions. Did she take her dog there every morning? Did Travis Green know that?

Over Amy's cries, I tell Natalie parts of what Alison and I have discovered as we make our way round and round the green. As per Alison's instructions, I don't mention Elaine's pregnancy, and I can't bring myself to tell her about James's tattoo, but I explain how we suspect there was more to the shooting than anyone realised at the time.

'Are you going to get the police involved?' Natalie asks into the blissful quiet, Amy having finally dropped off, tear-tracks staining her cheeks.

'I don't think so. We don't have any actual evidence, only theories. I don't think they'll do anything.' They didn't do anything when I found a penknife in my baby's pram, after all.

'And Alison's planning to publish this stuff?'

'I don't know. She keeps saying she's doing this for me, but . . . ' I stop, conscious of being a bit disloyal. Alison has begun to feel like a real friend and I'm close to slagging her off behind her back here.

Natalie doesn't say anything, and I can tell she's letting

me decide if I want to confide in her, not wanting to push me into saying something I'm uncomfortable with.

'I ... feel like she might have more of an agenda than she's saying,' I say eventually. 'It could just be the story, wanting to get a big scoop, but I'm not sure.'

I regret the words almost as soon as they're out of my mouth. I'm not sure what I'm saying.

'I know what you mean,' Natalie says. 'I sometimes get the feeling that ... '

'What?' I stop and look at her, but only for a second because Amy starts to shift. 'Sorry, we need to keep moving.'

As we set off again, a small, tan barrel of a dog comes bounding over and bounces into the wheel of the pram.

'Jasper! Come here!' A woman of about my age comes running over. 'I'm so sorry. Jasper!' She grabs the dog by the collar and clips his lead on. 'He's a nightmare, but he is getting better.'

She moves to pull him away, and then stops. 'It's Cassie, isn't it? Cassie Colman? I'm Janine! Janine Murphy. From St Margaret's?'

'Oh!' I recognise her now. She was a scrawny, gawky thirteen-year-old, but she's grown into her face, all dark eyes and sharp cheekbones. We were inseparable for the first three years of secondary school, until she disappeared off to Callenden. I used to imagine what her new friends were like, all skiing holidays and swimming pools in the garden, as I sat with Chloe in the dinner hall at St Margaret's. 'How are you?'

'I'm good, yeah. Visiting my parents for the weekend. Is she yours?'

'Yes. Amy.'

'Wow. And I thought having a dog was a responsibility! Are you local?'

I tell her I am, and we go back and forth for a bit about our lives, but it doesn't flow. Absurdly, the sense of betrayal I felt when she went off to private school and abandoned me creeps back in. I'm beginning to extricate myself from the conversation when something occurs to me.

'Do you remember a girl called Alison Patchett at Callenden? She would have been two or three years above you.'

Janine frowns. 'It doesn't ring a bell.'

'I suppose you wouldn't have known everyone.' At St Margaret's there were six classes in every year, over a hundred and fifty students. I barely knew everyone in my own year, let alone the others.

'We sort of did, at Callenden. There were only two classes of twenty in each year, and they were very hot on mixing up the years and everyone getting to know everyone else. Community. Alison Patchett, you said?'

'Yes.'

Natalie eyes me curiously. I briefly introduced her at the start of the conversation, but she's not spoken throughout it.

'No, I don't recall anyone of that name. Still, that's not to say she wasn't there. It's been over ten years since I left. I'd better get on, I told my parents I wouldn't be long. It was nice to see you again, Cassie.'

She walks off briskly, keeping Jasper on a tight lead.

'What was all that about?' Natalie asks, as soon as Janine is out of earshot.

'Janine and I were friends up until the third year of senior school. Then she left to go to Callenden. That's where Alison went, supposedly.'

'What do you mean, supposedly?'

'I don't know. She doesn't talk about her past very much, does she?'

'I've never thought about it,' Natalie says. 'What are you saying, that you think she's lying about where she went to school? Why would she do that?'

'Oh, I don't know. I'm probably being paranoid. Ignore me.'

We continue to walk in silence, both absorbed in our own thoughts. Whether Alison went to Callenden or not, the thought that troubles me most is that I asked Janine the question in the first place. It's made me realise that however much I may have felt recently that Alison and I have become friends, I don't quite trust her.

Chapter 38

'I need a drink after all that walking. Shall we?' says Natalie.

I can't think of any reason to give Natalie for not going to the pub without telling her what I did with James, which doesn't feel like an option. As Natalie helps me get the pram through the door, I cast around for James. Oh, God, he's behind the bar.

'I'll grab that corner table,' I say hastily, 'there's room for the pram next to it. Can you get me a Coke?'

I wedge the pram between the table and the wall, and pretend to fuss over Amy to avoid having to look in James's direction. I don't actually touch her; although I'd love an excuse to get out of here, I can't handle any more screaming.

'Hello again.' Paul Green looms over the table, looking taller than usual under the low ceiling. I throw a quick look over to the bar, where Natalie is laughing with James. Paul follows my gaze, then looks back at me with an expression I can't decipher. What does he know about James?

'I'm glad I've seen you,' he says. 'There was something I wanted to say.'

'Do you want to sit down?'

'No, thanks, it'll only take a minute. I can see you're busy.' He looks over to the bar again and my cheeks burn. 'It's about my mother. I know you saw her that day, as you left my house.'

'Oh. Yes, we did. Well, Alison did.'

He looks around and bends in closer. 'I know you probably think I'm angry at my mother after what I said to you in the pub that time. And I guess I am – or I was – I mean, like, my younger self is angry at her. And that can come out when I'm drunk. But I understand now the hell she must have gone through after my father . . . did what he did. I try not to blame her any more for not being able to look after me. I just . . . didn't want to tell you anything about her, and it was simplest to say that I hadn't seen her. It was only partly a lie, anyway. I see very little of her. We've only been talking recently because she's anxious about the twenty-five-year anniversary, and she'd got wind that there was going to be something in the papers.'

'Why are you telling me now?'

'I didn't want you to get the wrong idea, to think I had something to hide. I know what your friend's like, what all journalists are like. She's looking for dirt. I didn't want you to think you'd found any. I don't know what you're trying to achieve, but . . . leave my mother alone, OK?'

'So does she still live around here?' I can't let this opportunity pass, to find out more. But he doesn't reply, simply disappearing out towards the garden without looking back.

'Who was that?' Natalie says, putting my wine down. She looks flushed and distracted, and I worry that James has mentioned our afternoon together. Surely not.

'Paul Green, Travis Green's son.'

'What did he want?' She settles herself into the seat opposite.

'Telling me to keep my nose out, basically. Same old, same old. Alison's right, you know, Natalie. There's more to this thing than meets the eye.'

'And now you think there's more to Alison than meets the eye?'

'I don't know. I think I'm just on edge.'

Natalie runs a finger around the top of her glass. 'She was very keen to befriend you.'

'Oh, charming! It couldn't be that she genuinely wants to be friends with me,' I say, trying to make it sound like a joke, as if it hasn't crossed my mind.

'Oh, I didn't mean it like that, Cassie. Forget I said anything.'

'It's fine,' I say, relenting. 'You're right, in a way. She did approach me because of who I am, in the first place, but I thought we'd become more than that. I thought I could trust her.'

'I'm sure you still can,' says Natalie. 'Are you worried about your friend not remembering her?'

'No, I suppose not. I know Callenden's small, but Alison is a couple of years older than us. Janine could easily have forgotten her.' I know I don't sound convinced.

'I don't know … be careful, won't you? Something feels off, like there's a load of stuff going on here that we don't know about. I don't think it's necessarily to do with Alison, but don't think you have to pursue things just because she wants you to. She needs you – you give her access to people who'd never normally speak to her. But do you need her? You've got a lot of other things going on in your life, what with Amy, and your mum.'

The fact that she cares warms me inside. She changes the subject, and we talk about other things. After an hour or so, I realise I need to get back for Mum. Chloe will have left by now and, although we haven't had a repeat of the fire, or the escape act, I don't like leaving her for too long. Amy will probably wake up soon anyway.

James has been busy at the bar, and I've been studiously avoiding him, but as we leave, Natalie holding the door open for me to push the pram through, there's a tap on my arm. 'Can I have a quick word before you go?'

His tone is deliberately neutral, but I can tell Natalie's interest is piqued. Maybe he did say something to her at the bar. I look down at Amy, willing her to start screaming, but she remains resolutely fast asleep.

'Um, sure. I'll see you later in the week, Natalie?'

She takes the hint and goes, glancing back at us once, quizzically.

'Are you avoiding me or something?'

I think he's aiming for levity, but he misses it by a mile, sounding more like a petulant child. 'No,' I say. 'I've been busy ... Amy, and Mum and—'

'It was my tattoo, wasn't it?'

'What? No. I've been busy, honestly ... '

'I didn't tell you about it because I wanted to get to know you in a normal way, like two regular people. I didn't want it to be this huge thing between us.'

'What do you mean?'

'The date: 15th June 1994. I know who you are, but that's not why I'm interested in you. There's nothing weird going on. I just like you. I'm sorry if it freaked you out. I should have told you before you saw it.'

'It's OK,' I say, trying to keep my voice steady. I can't stop thinking about the way he spoke to Paul Green that time, whispering in his ear. And about other things too – the knife in the pram, the threatening notes. 'I've been thinking I should take a step back from helping Alison with her article. It's probably not appropriate.'

'I don't know; I think it's a good thing to have someone who was actually involved helping her. Might stop it becoming too sensationalist. Look, do you want to meet for a drink one evening? We can talk about it properly. Could you get a babysitter?'

'Not really. It's not fair to ask them to look after Mum too.'

'What about Chloe?' he says.

'I can't ask her. She's already done me a big favour having Amy the other day, when ... um ... and I certainly can't afford to pay her. Let's ... why don't we ... ' I swallow, my mouth dry, suppressing a shiver as I remember how his hand felt as it trailed lightly across the curve of my hip. But getting in any deeper with him would be a huge mistake. I have no idea who he is. 'I don't think we should, you know, see each other again.'

'Oh. I see.' He steps back. 'It is the tattoo, isn't it? I would have told you. As we got to know each other better. But forget it.'

'Is it ... do you ... ?' Suddenly I want to know, curiosity overriding fear.

'Sorry,' he says shortly. 'I like to get to know someone before I share personal stuff with them. I thought that was where this was heading, but I guess I was wrong. I need to get back to work.'

He disappears into the bar, leaving me to open the door and hold it with one hand, while awkwardly shoving the pram through with the other.

Shit. I handled that badly. Why didn't I just wake him up and ask him about the tattoo at the time? I know why, though. I was frightened. I panicked. And I have to face facts. Somebody doesn't want me to find out what really happened on 15th June 1994, and, even if it's not him, James is mixed up in this somehow. It would be madness to get involved with him.

Chapter 39

A car horn toots outside on the street.

'That'll be Alison. I won't be long, Chloe, but if I'm not back by the time you have to leave, don't worry, Mum'll be fine.'

It didn't take Alison long to locate Hilary Masters, and no doubt she's spun her a line as to why we want to come and see her. I kneel to strap Amy into the car seat and pick it up.

'Bye, Mum.'

Chloe follows me out into the hall, fiddling with her necklace. 'Can I have a word?' she says.

'Is it about Oakdene? I've told her millions of times that she's moving there, but she can't retain it – or she doesn't want to.'

'No, it's not about that.' She looks down, her hand stealing to her necklace again.

'You'll have to be quick, Alison's waiting for me.'

'People are starting to talk.' She finally meets my eye.

I put the car seat down, my arm aching already.

'About what?' Has James been shooting his mouth off? Who has he told?

'You and Alison.'

'Oh. What are they saying?'

'Originally, I thought her article was going to be good, about how Hartstead has moved on, the positive stuff about living here. But people are saying you and her are going round stirring up trouble, asking questions.'

'I'm helping her get background information.' It sounds thin, even to me.

'But why, though? Why are you helping her?'

'Why not?' I say, face flaming. I may be questioning Alison's motives myself now, but it doesn't mean I want other people gossiping about her, or me. 'Is there a problem, Chloe?'

'It's alright for you,' she says, speaking rather fast. 'But for some, it might stir up memories, things that could make them ... angry.'

'What are you talking about?'

She picks at her chipped nail polish, and I think of a perfectly varnished set of nails holding a chubby baby hand.

'Is this something to do with Della?'

She looks up. 'I didn't say anything. She didn't ask me to say anything.'

'What do you mean about making someone angry?' I think of Della's unwillingness to meet my eye in the pub that day, Tom Glover slamming out of the house leaving her to pick up the pieces. 'Is it Tom? Does he … he doesn't hurt her, does he?'

'No! Nothing like that. He can be difficult, but he doesn't hit her.'

'I'm sorry,' I say. 'I don't want to make her life hard. But I'm not in charge of Alison. I can't control what she writes.'

'But you're helping her.'

'I'm sorry, but I'm not responsible for Della's husband being *difficult*.'

'It's not easy for her,' Chloe says hotly. 'She's got Ryan to deal with too. She didn't sign up for that. Tom was hardly seeing him when he and Della first got together. They'd never got on very well, but when Social Services said his mum wasn't fit to look after him they had no choice but to take him in. She does her best, but it's not easy when it's not your kid.'

'I'm not saying anything's her fault. But – and sorry if this sounds horrible – those are her problems. They've got nothing to do with me.'

'Jesus.' Chloe looks disgusted for a second, but then Mum calls out and she remembers herself, remembers that she's effectively working for me. 'I'd better go and see to her,' she says and disappears into the front room.

The horn sounds again, and I'm grateful to be able to leave without saying anything more. Outside, I stand confused on the pavement, unable to see Alison's silver Ford Focus.

'Cassie!' Alison's head pokes from the open back

window of a dark green car parked a few spaces down. As I walk nearer, the car seat banging against my leg, I see a taxi firm's logo on the side.

'What's wrong with your car?'

'Get in and I'll tell you on the way,' she says, opening the back door and shifting over to the far side to make room. I take the middle seat and strap the car seat in next to me.

'Tunston now, please,' Alison says to the driver.

'So?' I say as we make our way towards the Tunston Road. Alison and I are uncomfortably close. I can see the dried foundation in the creases around her eyes and a stray chin hair that I long to tweeze. I could've put Amy in the passenger seat, but I felt weird about her being alone in the front with the driver, a large, unkempt man in his sixties.

'OK, two things: firstly – and don't freak out . . .' she says. I keep my expression neutral in an effort to keep any hint of mistrust to myself.

'Someone slashed my tyres.'

'What?'

The driver jumps at the sound of my voice and Amy stirs in the car seat.

'I said don't freak out.'

'What d'you expect? Are you sure? It couldn't have been a flat tyre?'

'What, all four of them?'

'Do you think it's the same person who sent the notes? And put a penknife in Amy's pram?'

'Who else would it be?'

I recoil at her sharpness.

'Sorry,' she says quickly. 'I'm a bit on edge.'

'It's OK. I wonder ...'

'What?'

'It might be nothing, but as I was leaving the house Chloe said something to me. She said people are talking about us – saying we're stirring up trouble, that your article isn't going to be what you said it was.'

'What people?'

'People in general, I think, but also ... you know Tom Glover's wife, Della?'

'Stepmother to the freaky teen, yes.'

'Chloe implied that our ... investigation – it's making Tom angry and he's taking it out on Della.'

'He's hitting her?'

'No, Chloe said not that. But she said he's *difficult*. And that us bringing up all this stuff from the past, and asking questions about Tom's dad, is making it worse. For Della.'

'God, that's awful. Poor Della.' Alison looks uncharacteristically concerned. 'Maybe I should talk to her.'

'What do you mean?'

'Oh ... never mind. Are you thinking she slashed my tyres?'

'I don't know. I can't imagine it.' Della, with her skinny jeans, her immaculate fingernails, sneaking onto Alison's drive under cover of darkness with a sharp knife?

'Or Tom, then?' says Alison.

'That seems more likely, I suppose. But whoever it was, somebody wants us to stop what we're doing.'

'Which is exactly why we shouldn't,' says Alison. 'There's something going on, something we can't see. Don't you want to know what it is?'

'Yes, but . . .'

I can't stop thinking about James's tattoo. He's mixed up in this in some way, but I still can't bear to tell Alison about my abortive non-relationship with him. I shouldn't be ashamed, but I am. It's not so much the sex I'm embarrassed about – it's the intense loneliness, the need-iness that's implied in how easily I was drawn to him.

'You said there were two things?'

'Yes.' She burns with a fierce, intense excitement. 'I've found Elaine Green.'

Chapter 40
15th June 1994 | Maureen Featherstone

Maureen won't be able to keep it from him much longer. Eric isn't the most observant of men, but he can't fail to notice soon. He's due to retire at the end of the year, and then she'll certainly have no hope of hiding it from him. If she's still here by then. He's going to notice sooner than that anyway. The weight that's dropping off her, the exhaustion that shrouds her like a cloak; the lines the pain etches on her face – more each day. If she'd been able to have any treatment, she would have had to tell him. There would have been multiple appointments, visible side effects. But, as it was, they told her they were afraid there was nothing they could do apart from attempt to manage her pain. They were afraid? *she had thought at the time. How did they think she felt?*

Pickles yaps around her feet, sniffing and licking at her ankles. They say dogs can tell, but, if he knows, Pickles doesn't seem too bothered. He just wants a walk. She's already let him out for a pee in their postage-stamp garden, but that's not enough.

Slowly, she laces up her shoes, locates her jacket, keys, Pickles's lead. 'Come on, then. A quick spin around the park,' she warns him, as Pickles leaps and barks in excitement. 'We're not going to the woods today.'

Until recently, they'd had two walks every day. Always around this time she'd take him for a turn around the recreation ground, and later they'd go for a longer walk in the woods on the outskirts of town. She's not been able to manage that recently, though. Pickles has to make do with the rec.

To be honest, anyway, she's been a bit put off the last few times she's been to the woods. She'd taken her usual route which led away from the main path – there was a clearing where Pickles liked her to throw the ball. But there'd been this couple, pressed up against a tree, kissing passionately. So engrossed in each other they didn't notice her. She didn't look too closely but she doesn't think they were young – if it had been teenagers it wouldn't have been so bad, but there was something a bit unsavoury about it. You certainly wouldn't have wanted a child to see it. The last time she went that way, she'd caught a glimpse of them through the trees and turned back before they got to the clearing, Pickles yapping furiously at being done out of his ball-chasing. The trees were dense in that part and it was dark, but she'd thought there was someone else there – heard the crack of twigs underfoot, the rustle of leaves; felt a presence. She'd hoped they would turn back too, or else come upon the couple and have the guts to tell them their behaviour was inappropriate.

Usually Pickles will strain at the lead as they pass the gate to the fenced-off children's play park area. He loves children, although increasingly these days they are frightened of him as he jumps and tries to lick their faces, cowering behind their mothers' legs. It still hurts her to see it, even after all these years, how they cling to their mothers, viewing anyone else with suspicion. It's not the sharp pain it once was, knowing she will never be that special person, the one a child goes to for comfort when all else has deserted them, the one who can make everything alright with her enfolding arms. But it's a pain nonetheless. These days she supposes it would have been IVF, or surrogacy, but in those days, you kept quiet and accepted it. Built another life for yourself. A good life, yes, but one in which she never saw Eric showing a solemn little boy how to hammer in a nail, or swinging a little girl around, pink-cheeked and giggling. Never knew the solitary late-night pleasure of watching a child sleep, breathing in the scent of their warm head, tucking the covers around them a little more tightly.

There's no one in the play park today, and Pickles ignores the gate in favour of sniffing around the base of the scrubby little trees that line the concrete path. One circuit is enough for Maureen, and as they make their way back towards the town, and home, she's already anticipating sinking into her usual chair, the one where she spends more time than she lets on to Eric.

She's the only one of the eleven to know instinctively what's going on as soon as she sees him. The others have looked in blank incomprehension, not understanding until the final seconds, but Maureen is already closer to death than any of the others. She recognises it, although it hasn't come in the form she expected.

She has been consumed with worry for weeks about how to tell Eric, but, as she feels her life ebbing from her, she realises he is going to find out in the worst way possible. There will be a letter from the hospital, and she won't be there to snatch it from the mat and hide it with the others. She imagines his face, already lined with sorrow at the loss of her, uncomprehending at first. Then, slowly, understanding will dawn and he'll put the letter down in horror. Will he feel betrayed that she didn't share it with him, that she has denied him the chance to love her in sickness as he did in health? Or will he understand that she was only trying to save him from pain? That she had taken her vows seriously all those years ago, when she had promised to love and to cherish him. That this was her final act of love.

Chapter 41

'Where is she?' All thoughts of Della and Tom fade away.

'She lives in a village outside Tunston. She's been here all along, can you believe it? I thought we could drop in there now, on our way to see Hilary Masters. Take her by surprise.'

'I don't know, Alison.' The thought of seeing Elaine, meeting her, makes my stomach churn, as if I'm standing on a precipice waiting to step out. 'How did you find her?'

'I've been asking everyone I speak to, either for the article or just anyone I meet in the normal way of things. Yesterday I struck gold. I was dropping some stuff off to a charity shop in Tunston, so I asked the woman working there if she knew of Elaine, like I ask everyone. Turned out she lives on her road! The old dear was lonely and keen to chat, so it was easy to get it out of her.'

'Right.' I shift in my seat and fuss with the straps of Amy's car seat. This is a side of Alison I haven't seen before, and I don't think I like it.

'Elaine's only been living there a couple of years, and I got the impression she's moved around a lot, never getting to know anyone. The woman in the charity shop told me where she lives and everything. Said she keeps herself to herself, doesn't talk to anyone, uses a different name – which explains why I've struggled to find her before. I struck it lucky, because this woman said not many know who she is, but she remembered the case and recognised Elaine from the newspaper photos when she first moved to the village – asked her straight out if it was her. Apparently Elaine begged her not to tell anyone.'

'Maybe we should ... I don't know ... write to her, or try and get her phone number? Rather than showing up and doorstepping her?'

'No, she's more likely to give something away if we surprise her.'

Jesus. 'She's a person, you know, Alison.'

'I know,' she says, injured. 'I'm not totally heart-less. But ... don't you want to see her? Find out what she knows?'

She knows I do, that's the problem.

'I doubt she'll tell us anything.'

'You're probably right. And I'll be sensitive. But let's at least give it a try.'

It's useless to argue, and soon we're pulling up outside a row of tiny, terraced cottages.

'It's the end one,' says Alison.

I peer through the mud-splattered taxi window. The rest of the cottages are all rendered and painted, but the end one is long overdue an upgrade. The paint is flaking, and the dark wood door is scuffed and doesn't fit properly in the doorway. There's one window downstairs, to the left of the door, shrouded in net curtains. Upstairs there are two small, dirty windows, the curtains drawn at both of them. I open the car door, but Alison doesn't move.

'Are you coming, then?'

'I can't, can I? There's no way she'll talk to me.'

'What? Well, what am I going to say to her?'

'Just say you have some questions about that day, questions that need answering for your own peace of mind, that type of thing. See what you can get her to tell you. I'll wait here with Amy.'

'The meter's still running,' warns the taxi driver.

'Yes, I know,' says Alison irritably. 'Be as long as you like,' she says to me. 'Don't worry about the taxi.'

She's right. There's no way Elaine will open up to a journalist. But there is a tiny chance she might talk to me.

I have a choice. Alison can't make me knock on that door. But of course it's not Alison making me. I want to see Elaine; I want to know whatever it is my mother can't, or possibly won't, tell me about what happened that day. I get out of the car without another word, and take the few steps to the front door, which opens right on to the street. I lift my hand and knock. After a minute or so of silence, I knock again, and then hear the sound of slow footsteps.

'Who is it?' The voice is low and uncertain.

'My name's Cassie Colman.'

Elaine says nothing, but I can feel the tension in her silence on the other side of the door, the air shimmering between us with unsaid words.

'Could you open the door, Elaine?'

There's another moment's silence, thick, even with the door between us. A car speeds by, music blaring from the open window.

'Cassie?' The word is unfamiliar on her lips, as if she can't twist her mouth into the right shape to speak it.

I wait again, holding my breath, and then the handle moves, and I want to shout out to her not to, that I'm not alone, that Alison is in the car, but I don't. The door opens a short way, and a face peers out over the security chain – older, of course, lined and pale, hollow-eyed, but unmistakably Elaine Green. It's like a kick to the stomach, to see that she is alive, real.

'Cassie?' she whispers again, staring at me. I think of the picture of her and my mother, the wind in their hair. A lump rises in my throat.

'Hello.' I just about manage to get the word out.

'What do you want?'

'To talk to you.'

'Talk about what?'

'I have some questions about what really happened that day, in Hartstead.'

'No.' It's little more than a whisper.

'Elaine, please. I know you were friends with my mother. I just want to talk. She ... ' I move closer. Elaine shrinks back, pushing the door, the opening now a mere sliver. 'She has dementia. I can't talk to her about anything any more.'

I came here because Alison thought Elaine might have answers about what happened on that June day in 1994. Now I'm here though, all I can think is that she's a link to Mum, to the woman she was before Travis Green changed the course of her life forever. What could Elaine tell me about her?

'Sylvia has dementia?' She lets the door fall open a little, the security chain stretched taut.

'Yes. She can't answer any of my questions.'

'Oh, I *am* sorry to hear that. Very sorry.' She looks distraught.

'I'm sorry to come here and ambush you like this. It ... it wasn't my idea.'

In the taxi, Alison fusses over Amy in the car seat, head down. 'Who's that?' Elaine says.

'A friend who's come with me. And my baby.'

'I can't help you. Please, go away.' She sounds constrained, as if she has something in her throat. 'Leave me alone.'

I know what Alison would say. She'd want me to throw the things we know in Elaine's face, ask her about the affair, the pregnancy, the rumours of an accomplice. See how she reacts, if she gives anything away. But I can't do it to her, to this faded, broken, bird-like woman.

'I think ... that you loved my mum, that you and she were close. Is there any message you'd like me to take to her?'

She shakes her head wordlessly, shrinking further away.

'OK, I'll go. But ... can I give you my phone number, or my address? In case you do ever want to talk? Or ... to come and see my mother?'

She doesn't reply, but she doesn't close the door either, so I scramble in my bag for a scrap of paper and a pen, scribble down my address and mobile number and pass it through the gap. She takes it without reading it, crumpling it in her hand. I go to say something else, unsure as I open my mouth what it's going to be, but before either of us find out, she has closed the door. My shoulders sag and I head back towards the car. Before I get in, I take a final look at the house and something flashes in my peripheral vision. I suppose there was time for Elaine to get up the stairs and into the front bedroom, but she would have had to have moved pretty fast. She must have done, though, because what other explanation could there be for the movement that catches my eye at the upstairs window, that of a curtain dropping back into place?

Chapter 42

We stand on the pavement outside Hilary Masters's house. Alison peppered me with questions about Elaine the minute I got into the car, but once she realised I had learned nothing we sank into an unusually uncomfortable silence – possibly an angry one on her part, although she didn't make it explicit. I wait for her to ring the doorbell. She straightens her skirt and re-tucks her shirt.

'She does know we're coming, doesn't she?' I say, suspicious.

'Yes, yes. Is Amy still asleep?'

'You can see she is, Alison. She's right here. What's going on?'

She wrinkles her nose. 'I may not have told her exactly *why* we were coming.'

'Alison! Why not?'

'I had the feeling she wouldn't see us if I told her what it was really about. If Mrs Mehta is right, and she was bullying Manisha, she won't want that brought up, will she?'

'What did you say, then? How did you find her?'

'On Facebook. I told her I was researching an article for the local paper about the centenary of St Margaret's.'

'Oh, for God's sake.' My churning resentment about her having forced me to confront Elaine alone bubbles up.

'I know. Sorry. But we're here now.'

I look up and down the road. We drove through a warren of lookalike streets to get here, lined with identikit bungalows and semis. I can't carry Amy very far in the car seat, she's too heavy, and I haven't brought the pram or the sling.

'Fine,' I say, defeated. 'But you can do the talking.'

Alison straightens her skirt once more before ringing the bell.

I know Hilary must be mid-forties, but she looks younger, apart from the telltale smoker's lines around her mouth. She's smartly dressed in tailored trousers and a fine-knit V-neck jumper, giving a professional impression spoiled only by faded pink, fluffy mule slippers.

'Hi, I'm Alison. We spoke on Messenger.'

'Yes, hi. Ooh, hello!' she coos at Amy, who is still fast asleep. 'Come in.'

We follow her down the cream-carpeted hall, a hint of stale cigarette smoke lingering in the air. There are two large framed photos on the wall, each of a blonde young woman in a mortar board, a proud, strained smile on her face.

'Your daughters?' Alison asks as we pass.

'Yes.' Hilary stops for a minute and regards them fondly.

'Both went to uni, they did. Not like their mother. I didn't do too well at school. I was surprised you got in touch with me, to be honest.'

She's not surprised, though, not really. I can tell. She still has a touch of the queen bee about her. She thinks someone has asked around, looking for the stand-out popular students of her year.

'So, was there anything specific you wanted to ask about?' she says, once we're seated in her small, painfully neat lounge. There are no books in here, or ornaments other than picture frames with more photos of her beloved daughters on the dust-free MDF shelves. No magazines, abandoned cardigans or shoes, half-drunk cups of coffee or even a stray TV remote to be seen. It looks like a house no one lives in.

'Well, yes,' says Alison.

I pretend to fuss over Amy, tucking her blanket in more securely, almost hoping that she'll wake up, so I can occupy myself with soothing her. There's a loose piece of fluff on the carpet near the car seat that has escaped Hilary's eagle eyes.

'I am writing an article,' Alison goes on. 'It's actually for the *Sunday Times*.'

'Oh?' Hilary sits up a little straighter, far from displeased. Does she honestly think a national newspaper is going to run an article on the centenary of a tiny provincial town's school, heavily featuring a middle-aged nobody who failed her exams there twenty-five years ago?

'Yes, but I'm afraid it's not about the centenary. In fact, it's not about St Margaret's at all.'

276

Hilary tilts her head, confused but still smiling.

'The article is about how towns move on from tragedy . . . like in Hartstead.'

Hilary's mouth is still stretched into the facsimile of a smile but she's clearly in a huge panic.

'What's that got to do with me?' Her eyes stray to the mantelpiece, her hand reaching to her trouser pocket. Cigarettes, that's what she's looking for.

'We saw your name in the reports at the time,' Alison says smoothly. 'You were a friend of one of the victims, I believe? Manisha Mehta?'

She's keeping what Mrs Mehta said up her sleeve, then.

'Yes. Yes, that's right.' She looks from Alison to me, and back again. 'Though we weren't that close.' She can't tell which way the wind is blowing. What's interesting is that she hasn't reacted with the anger you might expect, given that Alison's admitted we've lied to her and gained access to her home under false pretences. She's obviously got something else on her mind.

'Cassie here was . . . involved in the events of that day,' Alison continues.

'Cassie? Not little Cassie Colman?'

'Yes,' I say. She softens and I take my chance. 'Hilary, there's some evidence to suggest that the shootings may not have been as random as they appeared. We think Travis Green may have deliberately targeted his victims. As a . . . friend of Manisha's, we thought you might be able to shed some light.'

'No!' She springs up and crosses the room to pull out a

pack of Marlboro Lights, a lighter and an ashtray from a concealed drawer in a side table. 'Do you mind if I . . . ?'

'I'd rather . . . ' I gesture towards Amy.

'It's my house, isn't it?' she snaps. 'I'll open the window if you're that bothered.'

'OK,' I say weakly.

She perches on the windowsill, lighting up and sucking down a lungful of smoke, which she ostentatiously blows out of the open window.

'I don't know what makes you think I can help,' she says.

'There are certain things we've found out,' says Alison. 'It seems there was more going on than met the eye.'

'It was nothing to do with what happened that day.' There's something of the cornered animal about Hilary. 'Manisha was in the wrong place at the wrong time, that's all.'

There's a subtle change in the atmosphere, and it takes me a few seconds to realise it's caused by Alison. Her antennae have pricked up. Hilary thinks we know something about her.

'Are you sure about that?' says Alison.

'Yes! OK, the reports at the time were wrong, Manisha and I didn't get on at school, but I'm not a racist. Just because she was Indian, it doesn't mean that was why I didn't like her.'

'No, of course not,' says Alison soothingly. Has she ever worked for a tabloid? She'd be very good at it. 'Hilary, nobody's accusing you of racism. And we're certainly not saying that anything's your fault. We're just trying to get a fuller picture of what happened that day. I'm sure what you did had nothing to do with it.'

She's chancing her arm here, betting that Hilary's hiding something. I think back to the Willow Tree Hotel; Mrs Mehta bumping into Hilary in the supermarket. Why had Hilary been asking about meeting up with Manisha? She always worked Wednesday and Friday, Mrs Mehta had told Hilary.

'I mean,' Hilary goes on, mistakenly sensing an ally, 'everyone's so quick to cry racism nowadays. But it's not racist to think that people should fit in to the country they're living in, is it? These Muslim women with their faces covered, you can't see what they're thinking. It's not right. If they want to live in our country, they should abide by our customs. If I went to live in their country I'd have to obey their rules, wouldn't I, or I'd get stoned to death?'

Hilary takes another drag. This time she doesn't bother with the window, instead blowing a defiant stream of smoke into the room. I fight the urge to shield Amy with her blanket.

'Why did you ask Mrs Mehta about Manisha's work days?' I blurt out, unable to think of a more subtle way of phrasing the question.

'I don't know what you're talking about. I've no idea what happened. I didn't know Travis Green.'

There's a silence. 'That's ... not what Cassie asked you,' Alison says slowly. We exchange a glance.

'Did Travis Green ask you to find out what days Manisha worked at the hotel?' I say, the words forming

279

before I've had a chance to think through the implications of what I'm asking.

'That was nothing to do with the shooting.' She looks from me to Alison, and back again. Unthinkingly, she lifts the cigarette to her lips and takes another drag, ash falling unheeded onto her lap. 'It was going to be a ... prank. I don't know, really, what it was; he just asked me to find out what days she worked. That was all.'

'When was this? When he still worked at the school?' says Alison, deliberately casual.

'No, it was ages after that. I saw him in town. He must have remembered me; he came over. I suppose I was flattered. He wasn't bad-looking, even though he was old, to me. You know what girls are like.' She attempts a giggle: a silly girl who didn't know what she was doing. She doesn't fool me. She might not have known what he was really up to, but, whatever it was she thought Travis was planning, she must have known it wouldn't be anything good. He must have had the measure of her, had seen how she'd treated Manisha at school and realised she could help him. The question is, why did he target Manisha?

'Why did you go and lay flowers outside the hotel?' I ask, although I know the answer. I don't believe she'd had any idea what he was planning, but she'd realised afterwards that she'd helped him, however unwittingly. Hilary Masters had had a guilty conscience.

'Everyone was doing it,' she snaps, stubbing out her cigarette and standing up. 'The town was in shock. I was the same as everybody else. I think you'd better go now.

And don't you dare quote me in your article. In fact, if you so much as hint at my name, I'll get lawyers on to you.'

She doesn't speak again, even to say goodbye, and Alison, Amy and I are soon out on the pavement. I move the car seat out of the sun, into the shade of the front wall of Hilary's neighbour's house, while Alison calls a cab to take us home.

Thankfully, our second cabbie of the day isn't inclined to talk. Alison tries to engage me in speculation about what we've discovered, but I shut her down, telling her I had a bad night and want to try and catch a twenty-minute nap while Amy's still thankfully asleep.

I close my eyes and rest my head against the window, but I'm wide awake. On one level, I'm trying to process what we've learned from Hilary, but uppermost in my mind is her blatant racism, which has left a bitter taste in my mouth. More than that, though, it's Alison's collusion in it that's bothering me – and, tacitly, my own. Shouldn't we have challenged Hilary's views? Isn't it our duty to call out comments like these wherever we come across them? OK, we wouldn't have got what we wanted from her if we'd confronted her, but has that become more important than anything else?

I've been struggling with my identity from the day I became a mother, but since getting involved with Alison it's been getting ever more muddied. Who the hell am I?

Chapter 43

I stand outside, trying unsuccessfully to unclench my jaw. It's a perfectly innocuous-looking building, modern red-brick with gabled windows, surrounded by neatly tended flowerbeds. It looks nice. Institutional, but nice. I've been inside it before, so why are my feet rooted to the spot, my legs like jelly? Several (mostly middle-aged) people have passed me on their way in or out for the fifteen minutes I've been standing here. Some have been visibly upset, others matter-of-fact, smiling at Amy asleep on my chest.

'Are you OK?' says a familiar voice behind me, and I jump.

'Karen! Um, yeah, I'm fine. Just trying to … work myself up to going in, I guess.'

'I know how you feel. It never gets any easier.'

'Who are you … ?'

'My dad. He's been here a year. You?'

'My mum moved in yesterday. Does your dad have dementia?'

'Yes.'

'How have you found Oakdene?'

'It's good. To be honest – and I feel bad admitting this – it was a burden lifted when he came to live here. To know that someone else was looking out for him apart from me. And my useless brother, I suppose, not that he ever did anything much.'

I've often wished I had a brother or sister to share the responsibility, the guilt, the grief, but I guess it doesn't always work out that way.

'I'd better get back in,' she says. 'I only came out for a quick breath of air; it's so hot in there. I'll leave you to it.'

A few minutes later, I sign in and make my way towards Mum's room. The smell of whatever they had for lunch pervades the hallway and I feel an unfair lurch of nausea. It's not an unpleasant smell – if I smelled it in a friend's kitchen I'd probably ask eagerly what was cooking – but in combination with the hushed corridors and quasi-medical atmosphere it turns my stomach. Leaving Mum here for the first time yesterday is an experience I never wish to repeat. She'd been having a bad day anyway, lost in the fog – although perhaps that made it easier, not harder. It might have been even worse if she'd been fully aware of what was happening.

Her door is ajar and I peer through. She's sitting upright in the armchair, staring, mouth agape, at the TV. I knock softly and go in.

'Hi, Mum.'

She looks at me and her expression clears. 'Cassie! Can we go now?'

She sounds so like her old self that it's all I can do not to help her pack and bustle her into a taxi. I try to focus on how I felt chasing after her in the street, her pyjamas an incongruous bright spot on that grey street, that grey morning.

'They say you've got to stay here for a bit,' I sit down next to her on the bed.

'What? No, I want to go home!'

'I know, it's just for a bit longer.' I have no idea how to explain it to her, whether I'm doing the right thing by colluding in her delusion that her stay here is temporary. The problem is, I don't know what else to say.

'Have you had lunch?' I ask pointlessly. Of course she's had lunch. Lunch happens at the same time every day here, whether you want it or not. She doesn't reply, so I try again. 'How are you feeling?'

Is this how it's going to be from now on? Me asking her a series of questions, her giving one-word answers like a surly teenager, barely giving me enough time to think of my next one. Will we ever have a real conversation again? There are so many things I want to ask her, but I can't pretend it's only the dementia that's stopping me. There's always been a wall up around the subject of my father and the Hartstead tragedy.

'I'm absolutely fine, I told you.' Her attention drifts back towards the TV.

'Have you met any of the other . . . people staying here?'

'What people?'

I look around the room, searching for conversational inspiration. The photo albums Anthea suggested I bring to ease the transition are on the bedside table. I think of the photograph of Mum and Elaine, and wonder where it is now. The thought follows that although I showed her the photo, asked her if she knew who it was, I never actually said Elaine's name. I try to imagine saying the words out loud, but the thought of it makes me shaky. It was never said between us, that I mustn't bring up the past, or ask about my father, but I got the message from her own silence. But the gap between us grows wider every day. Soon there will be no chance of bridging it. We'll stand either side of this raging river that is going to carry her away, our voices lost in the roar of the water.

I square my shoulders. 'Mum?'

She continues watching the TV as if she hasn't heard me. 'Mum!'

She looks at me vaguely.

'Did you ... did you ever know a woman called Elaine Green?'

'No,' she says automatically, but I can tell it's her default answer, the one she gives because she has no idea what I'm talking about, or whether or not she ever knew an Elaine Green.

'In the old days,' I persist. 'Before ... when I was little.'

'Elaine Green ... oh!' A pop of recognition.

'You do remember her?' I lean towards her, our knees almost touching.

'No, I don't think so. No, never heard of her.' The cloud has descended again. At least I think it has, unless ... No. Surely I can't think she's exaggerating her lack of recall because she doesn't want to talk about it. At the very least, she would have heard of Elaine because of all the publicity at the time.

'Are you sure? She was about your age. She was married ... with a child.'

'No. No, she didn't.'

'What? She didn't what?'

'Nothing. I don't know.' She turns back to the TV.

'A child, you mean? She didn't have a child?' I had meant Paul, but is Mum talking about the other baby, the one Elaine was pregnant with at the time of the shooting? Did she know about that?

She remains silent, as if she hasn't heard me. I can't tell if she's in a world of her own, unreachable, or if she has deliberately removed herself to avoid my questions. Thinking again of the missing photo, I try a different tack.

'I see you've got the photo albums out. Have you been looking at them?'

'Them?' She dismisses them with a wave of her hand. 'Oh, they wanted to look through them with me.'

'Who? One of the staff?' The words come out quicker than I meant them to.

'Yes,' she says, in the voice she uses when she doesn't

know the answer, but is afraid to admit it.

'Are you sure?' I say, although I know badgering her will make it harder to determine the truth, not easier.

'Yes!'

'A man or a woman?'

'Oh, for God's sake, I don't know. Now be quiet, I'm watching this.'

We sit in silence for a while, but I can't settle. I need to know who's been looking through the albums with her. I tell her I'm going to the toilet, and retrace my steps towards the lobby.

'Cassie!'

I look behind me to see a familiar face peering out of one of the rooms.

'Hi, Karen. How's your dad?'

'Not great, to be honest.'

There's a pause in which it seems neither of us have anything to say, and I wonder if she's regretting calling out to me. I notice that her top's on inside out, but don't say anything.

'I'll let you get back to him.'

'OK.' She makes to turn into the room, but then seems to change her mind. 'Can we stay out here for a minute more?' she says, and I realise she's on the verge of tears. 'Only ... I can't have the same conversation again. I've been here two hours and he keeps asking me the same questions over and over. I love him, although we've always had a tricky relationship to be honest, but it's so hard and horrible to see him like this, and Theo barely slept last night and I'm so unbelievably tired. But the thing is ...' She puts her hands to her eyes momentarily, drawing a shaky breath. 'When I get home, I won't be able to sit down and rest or decompress from all this, because Theo will need me. I already know he's crying because I've had six bloody texts from my husband asking when I'm coming back. Theo won't take a bottle, you see. Oh, God sorry, I don't know why I'm telling you this.' She sags against the wall.

'It's OK, there's no need to apologise.' I rub her arm, unsure if she's a hugging sort of person. Unsure if I am any more. 'I understand, kind of. Every situation's different, but I know what it's like to be the one that everyone relies on. The one who has to be OK, all the time. The one who can't take a break because otherwise everything will fall apart.'

'Yes. That's it. Thank you.' Her voice cracks. 'That's exactly it.'

'I need to go and talk to the receptionist now, but ... do you want to have coffee some time? You could come to mine if that's easier?'

'I'd love to. Yes, thank you.'

We swap phone numbers, and I make my way towards reception. At the end of the corridor, I look back. Karen is leaning against the wall outside her father's room, frowning at her phone, wiping away tears with the back of her hand.

The receptionist is engrossed in her computer, her face a perfect mask of foundation, painted nails tapping urgently at the keyboard.

'Excuse me, I wanted to speak to someone about my mother's care.'

'Is there a problem?' She drags her eyes from the screen and observes me disapprovingly, giving the impression that if there is indeed a problem, it will be mine rather than hers.

'No, nothing like that. Someone's been looking through my mum's photo albums with her, and I wanted to know who it was.'

'It'll be one of the care assistants. It's one of the first things they do with a new resident. Helps us to get to know them, talk to them about their lives and families.'

'OK, great.' She's talking to me as though I'm a total imbecile but I'm too relieved to care. I was being paranoid. 'Does she have a particular assistant who looks after her that I could speak to?'

'I'll have a look who's on today, wait a moment please.' As she taps at the computer, I look over the visitors' signing-in book on the desk in front of me. There's my signature from earlier, the last one in the book, along with the time I arrived and the name of the resident I'm visiting. At first my eyes keep moving automatically up the page, but then they stop and slowly skim back down. There it is, a few entries up from mine, dated this morning at ten-fifteen. My mother's name: Sylvia Colman. I look across to the visitor name and signature columns, but they are both filled in with an illegible scrawl.

'Excuse me.' My throat feels thick, stuck together.

'Hmm?' she says without looking at me. 'Oh, here we are, it's Gabriela Pawlowski. She's been on all week, so it would have been her.'

'OK, thanks.' It barely registers. 'It says here someone visited Mum earlier today – look.'

She leans over the book. 'Yes, that's right.'

'Do you … do you know who it was?'

'Sorry, no. We get lots of visitors, I couldn't possibly remember them all,' she says shirtily, as if my mild enquiry had been a damning criticism.

'Would this Gabriela know?

'It's possible.'

'Can you call her? Get her to come and see me?' The words tumble out like water.

'She's very busy, you might have to wait.' Her fingers fly over the keyboard again, the subtext being *I'm very busy too, please stop bothering me.*

'That's alright, I'll be in Mum's room.'

'Oh, you're in luck, this is her now.' She sounds almost disappointed. 'Gabriela!'

A pretty young woman with mousy hair pulled into a neat French plait comes over to the desk.

'This lady wants to talk to you.' With that, she returns her full attention to the computer, duty discharged.

'Can I help you?' The young woman's voice is softly accented.

'Yes, I believe you've been looking after my mother, Sylvia Colman? She's only been here since yesterday.'

'Oh, yes, Sylvia.'

'Can I ask, have you looked through her private things with her, photo albums and so on?'

Gabriela looks worried. 'Oh, not yet. That is part of my job and I know it is very important to get to know the residents, and I am going to do it very soon. I have been so busy today—'

'It's alright, don't worry. I just ... wondered.' So it wasn't Gabriela who looked through the albums with her. 'I see from the visitors' book that she had another visitor this morning.' I point to the scrawl in the book.

'Oh, yes.'

'Did you happen to see who it was?'

'No, I am so sorry. I was busy with another resident at that time. She had had an ... accident and it took me a little time to clean her. But your mother did tell me when I took her in to lunch that she had had a visitor.'

'Did she say who it was?'

'Yes.' She looks pleased to be able to give me some of the information I want. 'It was your sister.'

'What?' This throws me completely. I've got so tangled up in the lies of the past that for a second I think perhaps I do indeed have a sister I don't know about. 'I don't have a sister.'

'Oh ... perhaps I misunderstood ...' Gabriela looks frightened, as if I'm going to march off to Anthea Newland and demand she be fired. 'My English is not so good.' Her English is perfect. 'I ... I thought it must be your sister because I am sure Sylvia said that she had had a visit from her daughter.'

Chapter 44

My head aches and my limbs are like lead, but I can't sleep. Who the hell has been visiting my mother? If it were just something she'd said herself, I could rationalise it – she's confused; at her last appointment the doctor said her memory impairment is very severe now. But somebody signed in to the home. And that somebody sat with my mother, and looked through her photo albums, and presumably told her she was her daughter.

I think of Alison, of her hunger when she talks about the article. Is her writing career on the rocks? Does she need this story to be a huge success? Or is it something else, something more than journalistic instinct? Is she on a personal quest of her own? She's the only one I can think of who would have an interest in looking through my mother's things. But, if she'd wanted to, she could have just asked me. It's not as if I've said no to any of her other requests.

I turn the pillow over again, bashing it into shape.

It's an old one, worn thin and lumpy with overuse. Tomorrow, I'll go and get myself a new one. I skate over how I'm going to afford it now the house may have to be sold to pay for Mum's care, and indeed where and how I'm going to live. I've struggled to sleep these past few nights, unused to being the only adult in the house.

I'm just drifting off when my eyes ping open. Something has woken me, but I don't know what. It's not fully dark in here, indistinct shapes – the chest of drawers, piles of abandoned clothes, an open pack of nappies – looming out of the half-light thrown by Amy's nightlight.

I stand in the middle of the room, uncertain, silvery knives and slashed tyres flashing through my brain. For once, Amy is slumbering peacefully in her cot next to me, all long lashes and plump cheeks, her musical mobile dangling above her in silence. I think I hear a faint sound from downstairs, like someone moving around. Is my mind playing tricks on me? I'm almost tempted to get back into bed and pull the duvet over my head, but then a deep-buried, tiger-mother instinct to protect Amy kicks in, a flame of anger igniting inside me. If there is someone down there, how dare they break in, trying to scare me or whatever it is they're doing? I steal out of the room, leaving the door wide open so as to be sure to hear Amy if she cries, and creep down the stairs. The streetlight illuminates the hallway through the frosted glass panels in the door. Nothing is out of place. I go into the living room first, adrenaline surging through me. Nothing appears out of place, but ridiculously I fling the curtains back, as if someone could be crouching behind them. I peer out of the window into the street, but everything is still and quiet apart from an urban fox sauntering down the middle of the road as though he owns it. I step silently down the hall and into the kitchen, hyper-aware of the blood rushing round my body at twice its normal speed. It feels several degrees cooler in here, and when I flick the light on I immediately know why: one of the glass panels in the back door is missing, only jagged, splintered edges to show where it once was. Oh God. Nausea rises but I shove it down. This is no time for histrionics. I need to call the police. They can't brush this aside. Then I hear something from upstairs. It takes me a few seconds to identify it but when I do my blood runs cold. A light, tinkling chime. Twinkle twinkle, little star. It's the music from Amy's cot mobile. A mobile that only plays the music if it's turned on from a switch on the thing itself, high above the cot. A switch way, way out of Amy's accidental reach.

Suddenly I'm running, all thought of treading quietly forgotten, taking the stairs two at a time, a roaring in my head. On the landing, I stop, hand clapped over my mouth, blood frozen in my veins. I left our bedroom door wide open, but now it's barely ajar, the glow from Amy's nightlight a thin sliver of soft orange. I am drenched in sweat, my pyjama top sticking unpleasantly to me. I force my leaden legs along the landing, and push open the door. My eyes are drawn first to the cot, and thank

God, thank God, Amy is there. The relief is so great that my knees buckle and I almost fall. The mobile turns, taunting me with its tune. Twinkle twinkle, little star. The blue light from it dapples across the rise and fall of her tiny chest in its stripy sleepsuit. Her light, regular breathing speaks to me: I'm OK, I'm OK. I look fearfully around the room, but everything else is as I left it. Heart thumping, I drop to my knees and peer under the bed, but it's as it always is, nothing more than Mum's ancient suitcase and a thick layer of dust. There is no one here. As I climb back to my feet, I hear the click of the front door. I dash out of our room and into Mum's, at the front of the house. I press my nose to the window, looking first one way and then the other. I just catch a glimpse of a figure dressed in black, running, but there's no time, and not enough light, to register anything more before the figure turns down a side street and disappears.

Back in our room, I pick Amy up and hold her against my shoulder. She murmurs, but settles almost instantly, her face in the crook of my neck, hot breath against my skin. I take a lungful of her warm, baby smell. I never got that thing about sniffing babies before I had her. On the odd occasion I'd held one, I'd always thought they smelled a bit gross, like dandruff and sweat and blood. But lately, I can't get enough of the sweet, baby-shampoo, washing-powder, fluffy-haired scent of her. The house is silent, and I know that the intruder has gone. Nevertheless, I hold my baby closer than ever as I dial 999.

Chapter 45

'Jesus, Cassie. You must have been petrified. What did the police say?'

Alison takes a sip of her tea. She's sitting in Mum's chair, which feels weird but I didn't want to say anything. She'd suggested meeting in the pub, but I'd said I couldn't go out until the door had been fixed. This was partly true, although I'm also avoiding James. I'd called Natalie as soon as the police left – she's got a work deadline, but she'd stayed on the phone with me, talking calmly and reassuringly, for over an hour, until Alison got here.

'Not a great deal. They had a good look around, but said they couldn't find any fingerprints. They're going to check the local CCTV, not that there is any on this street, helpfully.' It was a different officer from the one I saw when I found the penknife, but this one was equally uninterested, particularly given nothing had been stolen. I told her about the cot mobile, but she tried to imply that I must have been mistaken, or the mobile faulty.

Alison looks down at her tea. 'Cassie, would you ... do you think we should leave it? I mean, I know you want the truth, and obviously I want the story, but it's not worth anyone getting hurt over. If something happened to Amy, or you, I'd never forgive myself.'

I am touched, and I realise that despite my recent doubts, Alison and I have genuinely become friends. I am so used to thinking of myself as alone and essentially friendless, I haven't noticed that I'm falteringly putting down roots in Hartstead: Alison; Natalie; Karen, who I've invited to come over for coffee next week. I shut down any thoughts of James.

'No,' I say. 'Whoever's doing all this, I don't think they're going to hurt me. I ... this sounds weird but I don't think they want to. If it was anything more than empty threats, they would've done something by now.'

It doesn't feel real here in the lounge, sunlight filtering through the window, Amy at my feet practising her new-found sitting-up skills and playing with the mini rolling pin that's still her favourite. The thrill of fear that ran through me in the night feels like something born out of my fevered imagination, like a nightmare.

'Why don't you come and stay with us for a while?' Alison says. She senses my hesitation. 'Please, Cassie. I don't want to go into it, but I've had experiences that are not a million miles from this. I'd feel so much better if you'd come to us.'

'Amy wakes in the night a bit.' A lot. 'I don't want to disturb you and Katie.'

'You won't. Katie's a teenager, a full marching band in her room wouldn't wake her, and I sleep so badly it won't make any difference.'

How extraordinary, how terribly wonderful it would be, even temporarily, to wake in the morning in a house that contained someone who didn't depend on me for everything, didn't look to me to provide their every waking and sleeping need. Someone who would make me a cup of tea, ask me how I slept.

I need to do something first, though, to banish the last of my doubts, before I find myself living with her.

'Alison, there's something I need to ask you.'

'Yikes, sounds serious,' she says, smiling down at Amy, who has bopped her on the leg with her rolling pin.

'Yeah, it kind of is. The other day . . . I bumped into a girl I used to know from school. She went to Callenden when we were in Year 9.'

'Oh. I see.' She strokes Amy's soft hair, smile fading.

'She . . . she didn't remember you. I know you would have been a couple of years above her . . . wouldn't you?'

She closes her eyes briefly. 'I should have told you before.'

She's going to wear out that patch of Amy's hair at this rate. 'Told me what?'

'I *was* at Callenden. But I went by a different surname then.'

'Oh.' It's a more prosaic explanation than I was expecting.

'Patchett was my grandmother's maiden name. I

298

wanted to choose something that had meaning, but it had to be a name he wouldn't recognise.'

'Who?' It comes out quieter than I intended, almost a whisper.

'Katie's dad,' she says, as if it should have been obvious.

'Oh. What . . . ?'

'I'd just left school. That summer after A-levels felt as if it would go on forever. I got a job in a pub in Tunston. That was where I met him. He was older than me. Quite a bit older. I was flattered, I suppose. He was so sophisticated compared to the boys I knew. He came in all the time. I thought it was to see me. It was only much later I realised that no one spends that much time in pubs except alcoholics.'

I think of Paul. Alison had said Katie's father had been friends with him. If this was what they'd had in common, no wonder she hadn't wanted to dwell on it. Amy starts to grizzle, and Alison lifts her onto her lap and bounces her gently. I stay quiet, allowing her to tell me in her own time. I get the sense that these are unfamiliar words for her, ones she rarely allows herself to speak aloud.

'When I got pregnant, he asked me to move in with him. My parents were horrified, wanted me to get rid of the baby, but I thought I was in love. I thought it was this romantic, *Romeo and Juliet*-style love story. By the time I realised what he was really like, it was too late. I'd fallen out with my parents, and couldn't admit that they'd been right about him all along.'

'Was he . . . violent?'

'Yes,' she says into Amy's head. 'I know what you're thinking. Why didn't I walk out? Well, it's not that easy.'

'I know. I wasn't thinking that.'

'Most people do.'

'Not me,' I say firmly.

'In the end it was Katie that saved me,' she says. 'I couldn't do it for me, but the day he threatened to hurt her I just walked out of there with her in my arms. I didn't even take a bag.'

'That was brave.' I reach out and touch her arm. It's not enough, but I want her to know I'm hearing her.

'I was lucky. I knew my parents wouldn't turn me away, once I'd left him. A lot of women aren't so fortunate.'

'Did he try and come after you?'

'Yes. It was horrendous. I had to move away from my parents in the end, because he kept showing up there. That was when I started using Patchett as my surname.'

'Was that what you thought about the note, before you saw mine – that it was from him?'

'Yes. He hasn't bothered us for years, but when I saw that, my first thought was that he was back. I was kind of pleased to find out you'd had one too. I'm always petrified he's going to try and secretly get in touch with Katie.'

'Why didn't you tell me about him before?'

'It's a big thing to tell, I suppose. Not the sort of thing you tell someone when you've only just met them, and, once I did know you better, I didn't know how to bring it up. Also, it's become a way of life for me, to keep silent about it. It's always felt safer. I'm sorry. Are you upset?'

'No. Of course not.' I'm relieved, if anything, callous as that sounds. I realise I've always had the sense that Alison was keeping something back, and I suppose I was scared it was something to do with me. I feel the last of my doubts about her drain away.

'Come and stay, then. Please.'

'OK,' I say, digging the nail of my fourth finger into my palm to stem the grateful tears I am close to, the ones that will expose my loneliness. 'Just for a bit. Thank you.'

'Oh, you'll be doing me a favour,' she says breezily, pretending not to notice. 'Katie's always an angel when there's another adult around. If it's only me, she's utterly vile. Now, I've been thinking, we should—'

She's interrupted by the doorbell.

'Sorry,' I say. 'Can you keep an eye on Amy?'

'Sure.' Alison puts Amy down on the floor and sits cross-legged next to her as I leave the room.

Two anxious faces greet me when I open the door. Chloe is standing slightly behind Della, carrying a cardboard box.

'Can we come in?' Della asks.

I stand aside to allow them in. They pass me and head for the front room.

'Oh!' Della stops short at the sight of Alison.

'Hi,' Alison says. 'Do you want me to leave you in peace?' The question is ostensibly directed at Della and Chloe, but really she's asking me, and I feel a rush of gratitude.

'No, please stay,' I say. Something about Della and Chloe's demeanour suggests I may need a friend.

'Yes, do stay,' Della says, with none of the antagonism towards Alison I expected.

Alison sits back on her chair, lifting Amy on to her lap, and looks at Della expectantly.

'Sit down.' I wave the two of them towards the sofa, and take the only other seat, a hard chair near the window. They lock eyes as if seeking permission from each other, and gingerly lower themselves on to the sofa as if it might explode. Chloe places the box on the floor beside her.

'So, what's all this about?' Alison takes charge, as I had secretly been hoping she would. 'Because if it's about not writing the article—'

'It's not,' says Chloe quickly. 'Della?'

Della is the least composed I've ever seen her. I'm thinking how tired and unwell she looks when I realise it's because she isn't wearing any make-up.

'I didn't know what to do, who to talk to. I was ... I *am* ... scared.'

'Della,' Alison says tentatively, 'is this something to do with your husband? Cassie told me he gets upset about the rumours that his dad was Travis Green's collaborator. Are you ... are you frightened of him?'

'No! He can be tricky, but Tom wouldn't hurt me.'

'It's not always about physical hurt, though, Della,' Alison says. 'I know he's got a temper. Do you ever feel you're walking on eggshells, regulating what you say or do to make sure he doesn't get angry?'

'Oh, for God's sake, this is nothing to do with Tom!' Chloe says. 'It's not Tom she's frightened of.'

Silence rings in the air for a few seconds, heavy with the implication of what Chloe has said. It's Alison who breaks it.

'Who is it, then?'

Chloe's hand creeps into Della's and gives it a squeeze before she speaks.

'Ryan,' she says, the word echoing around the room, into every crevice. 'She's afraid of Ryan.'

Chapter 46

'What do you mean, you're afraid of Ryan?' Alison says, looking from Della to Chloe and back again.

'He's always been a bit ... strange,' Della says. She's usually so bright and glossy – brittle, but never subdued like this. 'I knew he was ... interested in the Hartstead shooting, and he likes these true crime programmes and books and things.'

I look again at the cardboard box. Of course. It's the one I saw in Ryan's room.

'I rarely go into his room. It's such a pit,' Della goes on. 'Every now and then I make him tidy up a bit so I can run the hoover round, but that's about it. But, this morning, Ryan was out and my friend has taken Harry for me, so I decided to blitz the whole house. It was a good opportunity to properly clean his room for once. I was getting everything out from under the bed so I could hoover, and I found this.' She points at the box.

'I saw that in his room. That time I came to your

house.' He must have hidden it under his bed after my visit.

'I probably shouldn't have opened it. I'm not sure what I was expecting to find.'

'What's in it?' Alison cuts to the chase.

Della looks at Chloe, who opens the box. The square of green material is on the top. Unease trickles through me. Chloe passes the cloth square gingerly to Della, who lays it on the sofa next to her, then takes out a bundle of old newspapers.

'So there were these,' Della says. 'They're newspaper reports from the days after the shooting.'

I recognise them from my own long-ago research. 'Where did he get them?'

'I don't know. I haven't said anything to him yet. Online, I guess. I know he's been visiting these weird forums and sites where people discuss famous shootings and mass murders, because . . .' She picks up the green material between her thumb and forefinger.

'What *is* that?' Alison looks in fascination.

Della and Chloe exchange another look.

'I didn't know, but when I looked through the box I found the paperwork that came with it. Ryan ordered it online from one of these horrible sites that deal in serial killer merchandise. It came with a "certificate of authenticity", although I don't suppose that means anything; in fact I'm sure it's probably not real.'

'What do you mean, not real?' Alison looks as if she's holding herself back from reaching out for it.

'Supposedly, it's a piece of the shirt Travis was wearing the day of the shooting.'

'Jesus!' Alison recoils as if from a physical attack, and a pulse of revulsion throbs through me. 'What the hell?'

'These sites are so horrible,' Chloe says. 'Della called me when she realised what she'd found, and we looked at the site Ryan got this from. It's sick, really sick.'

'I saw it in his room.' I find my voice. 'I don't know how, but I knew there was something not right about it. It's real. I know it sounds mad, but I can feel it.'

'Oh, come on, Cassie,' says Alison. 'There's no way you can know that. You're just spooked.'

'Maybe,' I say, but I know better.

'That's not the only thing,' Della says nervously, putting the cloth back on the sofa.

She reaches into the box again and pulls out a folded piece of paper. She unfolds it, and slowly holds it up so both Alison and I can see it. It's the size of a large poster, and for a minute my brain struggles to catch up with what I'm seeing.

In the centre of the paper is my face, twenty-five years younger, a blown-up version of the photo that was used in all the reports at the time. My hair is pulled into two small golden bunches, and I'm squinting against the photographer's lights. Immediately above this is a smaller picture of my dad, again a familiar photo not only from the newspaper archives but from the meagre selection of photos my mother has from my childhood and before. I used to pore over this photo in the album, trying to see a resemblance to me, or divine a clue as to what my father was like, in the absence of any information from Mum. Spread around my picture, like the numbers on a clock face, are photos of all the other victims, in the order in which they were killed, my dad in pride of place at twelve o'clock.

'Jesus,' Alison says again. 'Do you know why he's so obsessed with the shooting?'

'No. Tom never talked about him much before we had to take him in a year ago. He used to go and take him out every now and then, but he never came to stay with us. I'd only met him a few times. I made an effort when he moved in, I really did. But he just stayed in his room. When I got pregnant with Harry a few months after he arrived, I guess that sort of took over. It was easier to leave him to his own devices, which was what he seemed to want anyway. I knew he spent a lot of time online, but I didn't know what he was doing.'

'You said you're frightened of him – what do you mean by that? Do you think he might try to hurt you?' Alison says.

'Not just me,' she says. 'I also found this.'

She pulls out another piece of paper and unfolds it to A3 size. Silently she holds it out to me. I cross the room and take it from her.

'Let me see,' says Alison.

I lower myself onto the arm of her chair. Amy reaches out and grasps the edge of the paper, crumpling it in her fist. Alison puts her down on the floor, handing her a rattle. I stare at the paper blankly.

'Oh, my God,' she says.

It's a hand-drawn map of Hartstead. Well, part of Hartstead. Ryan has included only the streets where Travis wreaked his havoc, along with arrows showing the direction he took. At the scene of each shooting he's drawn a circle, coloured heavily in red.

'The thing is,' Della says, 'it's not Hartstead in 1994.'

'What do you mean?' Alison tears herself away from the map.

'Look.' Della points to the site of the red circles. 'This is where Melissa Bradshaw was killed, outside the old café. But that's not there any more. It's Costa now. And Ryan's labelled it Costa. And here, he's marked Tesco's on the high street, but that wasn't there then. I don't think this is a replica of Travis Green's route. I think it's a plan.'

My head swims, and I grip the back of Alison's chair to stop myself losing my balance.

'Some sort of copycat thing, you mean?' Alison says.

'I don't know. It might be a silly teenage … joke,' Della says. 'But what if it's not? Think of all those school shootings where it's kids that do it.'

'Why did you bring it to me?' I ask. I wish I'd never seen any of it. That piece of cloth, this ugly map. I want her and Chloe to take it away. 'You should take this to the police.'

Della shrugs helplessly and looks at Chloe.

'Della didn't know what to do,' Chloe says. 'If we go to the police, she'll have to tell Tom first, and she was worried about that.' She looks back at Della.

'Sometimes he ... flies off the handle at Ryan, loses his rag. It makes everything quite difficult. I know I've got to tell him, but I suppose I wanted to see what you thought first. You understand about that day.'

'If you think there's the slightest chance Ryan's going to do something ... criminal, you have to tell the police,' says Alison. 'But talk to Ryan first. Confront him with all this, see what he says.'

'But Tom ... he's going to go crazy ... Oh, God, what's the time?'

Alison checks her phone. 'Quarter to twelve.'

'We need to go. Tom's going to be home soon. He's only working a half day. Come on, Chloe.'

'But what are you going to do?' Alison asks.

'I don't know. I shouldn't have told anyone.'

'No, it's good that you did. You did the right thing. Talk to Tom, and then Ryan. See what he says. And if you want to ask my advice, or Cassie's, let us know. OK?'

'OK. Thanks.'

They pack up Ryan's little collection and go, leaving Alison and me alone again, with only Amy's babbling breaking the silence.

'You don't think he ... '

'Ryan? I don't know, Alison. I know he's a bit of an odd one, but he's just a kid. Isn't he?'

'I guess. But, like she said, look at all those school shootings. And who's he talking to online? There are all sorts of weirdos out there. I've written pieces about them.

He could have someone whispering in his ear, encouraging him. *Grooming* him.'

I think of the christening, when Ryan sought me out. 'I know what she means, a bit. I've felt frightened of him too. At Phoebe's christening, when he was asking me about helping with the article. It's hard to put your finger on it, but I felt very uneasy.'

'Let's see what he says when Della talks to him. *If* she talks to him.'

'You think she won't?'

'She can deny it till she's blue in the face, but that woman is frightened of her husband. He may not be hitting her, but that's the not the only way to abuse someone.'

'God, poor Della.'

'Indeed. Right, do you want to start packing up some things for you and Amy?'

'OK. Before I do, though . . . '

I need to tell Alison about James's tattoo. If I trust her enough to stay with her, I should be able to trust her with this too. I pick Amy up and fuss over her needlessly, trying to think of a way of introducing the subject.

'Cassie?' Alison isn't fooled by this uncharacteristic display of fond mothering. 'Are you OK?'

'There's something I haven't told you,' I say into Amy's head. 'Haven't told anyone, in fact.'

'Yes?' She's deliberately neutral, but clearly intrigued.

'It's about James.'

'James?' She can't place him.

'From the pub.'

'Oh. OK. What about him?'

'He has a tattoo on his back. It's a date, in Roman numerals.' Maybe she'll be so interested she'll forget to ask me how I know this.

'Not ... ?'

'Yes. 15th June 1994.'

'Oh, my God! Did you ask him why? When did you even see it?'

I don't say anything, but my glowing face does the talking for me.

'Oh.' Alison fails to suppress a smile. 'Blimey, Cassie. He's gorgeous.'

I have a brief flashback of James's lips on my skin, and my stomach flips. Heat stains my cheeks further.

'Cassie! My God, what did he do to you?'

I snort with unexpected laughter, and in an instant I'm twenty-three again, sitting up in bed, Aisha cross-legged on the other end with a cup of tea, dissecting the night before, or what we could remember of it. It was so much fun living with her, and I wish briefly that I hadn't allowed Guy to encourage me to get a place of my own, so he could come and go more discreetly. Which, if I'm brutally honest with myself, is basically what our relationship consisted of. Him coming, and then going.

'It was only one time,' I say to Alison.

'When?'

'A week and a half ago.'

'Why didn't you tell me?'

'I don't know. I was embarrassed.'

'Embarrassed that you slept with the hot barman? I'd be shouting it from the rooftops!'

'I don't know, Alison – it's not the kind of thing a proper mother would do.'

'Happy mummy, happy baby!' She smirks.

'Well . . . he is pretty hot.' We both laugh. 'But it ended a bit weirdly,' I go on.

'Because of the tattoo?'

'Yes. He fell asleep, and that's when I noticed it. When I worked out what the date was, I freaked out and left. The next time I saw him, he tried to talk to me and I brushed him off. I was scared, I suppose, of what it meant – the tattoo. We had a sort of row, and I haven't spoken to him since.'

'So you don't know why he has it?'

'No. He wouldn't say.'

She looks thoughtful, and then her face lights up. 'He could be Elaine's child, Cassie! He must be about the right age. Which would make Paul his half-brother. That would explain that time you saw them having that argument, or whatever it was.'

'It's possible, I guess. But there must be loads of people in this town who have cause to commemorate that date. There were eleven victims for a start, so there's their families and friends. Plus lots of others were affected – people who witnessed stuff.'

'We should ask him.'

'He was pretty pissed off with me last time I saw him. He won't tell me anything. Plus, if he is Elaine's child . . .'

'What?'

'He could be the one who's been trying to stop us finding out what happened – the notes, your tyres. The penknife in Amy's pram. It was after that day in the pub when we saw Della, and she tried to apologise to me about Tom and Ryan. James was there that day too.'

'If James is the one who did all those things, all the more reason to ask him.'

'But he could be dangerous. Also, like I said, he's not going to tell me anything now.'

'He might tell *me*, though,' she says. 'Maybe it's not some big secret. If he didn't want anyone to know he had any connection to the shooting, surely he wouldn't have had the date tattooed on his backside.'

'Back,' I correct her.

'I know.' She grins. 'I just like thinking about his backside. The point is, he may be happy to talk to me for the article. We won't know until we try.'

'Until *you* try, you mean. He won't talk to you if I'm there.'

'We don't know that! Have you apologised for running away?'

'No, not as such.'

'Let's go, then!'

'Now? I can't – the back door . . .'

'OK, what time's the glazier coming? You said he said he'd be here before twelve, right? It's nearly that now, and it won't take him more than half an hour to fix one pane of glass. We'll go straight after.'

Chapter 47

An hour and a half later we're standing in the sunshine outside the pub.

'I don't know about this, Alison.'

'God, you really don't like confrontation, do you?'

'Does anyone?' I'm rattled, pissed off with her for her cod psychology. And its accuracy.

'I don't mind it. It's always better to get things out in the open. That's one of the things I've found so hard with Katie getting older. We always used to talk about everything, but now she barely speaks to me unless she wants money.'

'I think Amy's going to wake up.' I peer into the pram.

'Cassie, she's absolutely fasto. You're being ridiculous. What have you got to lose?'

'Fine. Open the gate for me, then.'

Once we're settled at a table in the garden, Alison offers to go and get the drinks. 'I'll get him to come out here and we can talk to him together,' she says.

'Fine,' I say again, having seemingly reverted to being a sullen teen.

It's quiet in the garden. There's the occasional passing car, the murmured conversation of the couple on a nearby table, birdsong. I inhale the still, warm air and have a bit of a word with myself. Objectively, James hasn't done anything wrong. I'm the one who ran out after we slept together and refused to see him again. If I paint him as the baddie and go in on the defensive, he won't want to tell us anything, and rightly so.

'Fucking calm down!'

Paul Green stumbles out of the pub, a half-empty pint of beer in one hand, his phone in the other, pressed to his ear. He staggers over the step down to the garden. He probably thinks he's whispering, but we can hear every word. 'Please, don't do anything stupid. You're overreacting. It's not the end of the world if people know the truth, is it?'

Alison pushes the door open with her hip, a glass of wine in either hand. Paul's standing too close and it almost hits him.

'Jesus Christ!'

'Sorry, I didn't see you there.'

He mutters briefly into his phone and shoves it into his back pocket, glowering darkly at Alison.

She hurries over to me and puts the drinks down. 'James isn't here, but the girl behind the bar says he's due in any minute. What was all that about?'

'Can't you leave it alone?' Paul looms up behind her, making her jump. 'You're a vulture.'

Alison goes to speak, but he cuts in.

'Don't give me that crap about writing about how towns recover from tragedies.' He's slurring his words, speaking much more loudly than is necessary. I think of the connection I felt with him the day I went to his house – his dry humour, his likeability. He's a different man when he's been drinking. There are spittle flecks at the corners of his mouth. 'You want to stir things up, things that should be left in the past.'

He takes a gulp of his beer, slopping it into his mouth, his chin wet.

'Things about you?' Alison asks in a measured tone that belies her excitement at this opportunity to get up close and personal with Paul Green.

'Me? There's nothing to know about me.' He downs the remainder of his pint and slams the glass on the table.

'Who, then? Elaine? Was your father violent towards her?'

Alison's going for it, perhaps reasoning that he won't remember this conversation tomorrow.

'Is that the angle you're pushing? *Poor Elaine, victim of domestic violence*?' He steps backwards and almost trips, then leans forward, both hands on the table. 'I knew things about her. I saw what she was doing. I can … you've got to understand who he was, why he felt like he … needed to get rid of them all.'

'Everything alright?'

James appears as if from nowhere. Despite the drama of the situation, my stomach gives a little leap. It's partly the thought of the confrontation with him to come, but also a little bit his forearms and the way his jeans sit just below his waist. I tighten my grip on the bench either side of my legs.

'Fine,' Alison says tersely, terrified James will frighten Paul off when he was on the verge of spilling the goods.

'Oh, yeah, fine. Great.' Alison's fears are realised as Paul slouches off, fumbling with the gate and disappearing off up the road.

'Shit,' she says under her breath.

'What? Was he threatening you?'

'For God's sake, no!'

James raises his eyebrows.

'Sorry,' she says. 'It's ... I thought he was going to tell us something. It doesn't matter.' She smiles at him, mindful that she wants something from him too. 'I'm glad you're here, actually.'

'Oh, yes?'

'Yes. Cassie wants to apologise.'

'Can she not speak for herself?' It's pointed, but there's a hint of a smile beneath the sarcasm.

'Yes. Yes, of course.' I interlock my fingers and squeeze hard under the table. 'I'm so sorry about ... well, all of it.'

He looks at me gravely for a couple of seconds, then shrugs and sits down. Alison does the same.

'It's OK. I probably overreacted a bit. It's a difficult thing for me to talk about.'

'Oh?' Alison breaks in, *faux* casually. 'What is it exactly that's so difficult?'

He laughs. 'You certainly are a journalist, aren't you? Look, I don't mind talking to you about it, there's no big secret or anything, but I need to see anything you write about me before you send it to your editor, or whatever. OK?'

'OK.' Alison settles herself more comfortably on the bench. 'So?'

'I do have a connection to the shooting. My mother was one of the victims.'

My heart races. Is he Elaine's son? While she wasn't killed in the tragedy, she was certainly a victim of it.

'Who was your mother?' Alison asks.

'Suzanne Persimmon,' he says.

My heart slows a fraction as I sort through my mental file on the tragedy. Got it: the woman who worked for the Citizens Advice Bureau.

'She had a baby?' Alison says. 'That wasn't mentioned in the press, was it?'

'I was only a few months old. My dad didn't want loads of speculation around me, growing up, so he asked the police to help him keep it out of the papers. For the most part they did, although there are a few mentions of me if you know where to look.'

'I'm so sorry,' I say, instinctively reaching out to touch his hand. His fingers curl in on themselves, and I draw mine back as if burned. 'Sorry.'

'No, it's fine, I didn't mean to—' He shoots a look at Alison and collects himself. 'I don't deserve sympathy. I mean, I never knew my mum. You must remember your dad more.'

'Not really; I was only four. Bits and pieces. Him swinging me round. There was this pink plastic tea set, the teapot particularly. I asked Mum about it once and she said he used to play with me with it. What I felt was more ... an absence, I suppose. A missing piece. You must have felt that too?'

'Yeah. Dad ... did his best, but ... I don't think fatherhood came very naturally to him. I didn't want for anything growing up – not material things, anyway. But he never talked about her. Never showed me any photos, or letters she'd written, or told me anything about how she was with me.'

'Did you never ask?' It's Alison who asks this question, of course, not me, because I know he didn't, and I understand why. When something is never mentioned, you accept tacitly that it is not to be talked about.

'No. But when I was about fourteen, fifteen, I started trying to find out more about what happened that day.'

God, he and I have more in common than I thought.

'It was then that I first heard the rumour about there being an accomplice.' He looks embarrassed. 'I got kind of obsessed, I suppose.'

'With finding out if it was true?'

'Yeah. And who it was.'

Alison leans forward. 'Did you ever find out anything?'

'No. I spent years trying to find out where Elaine Green was. I thought if there was an accomplice she might have known who it was. And then, when I turned eighteen, I got the tattoo. It was kind of a ... mission

319

statement, I suppose. It probably sounds crazy, but I was going through a lot at the time. I think because I never knew my mum, and Dad never talked about her, I hadn't had the chance to grieve for her. The tattoo was part of that. But, not long after that, I realised I needed to let it go. It sounds ridiculous, but I'd let it take over my life. So I made a conscious effort to stop thinking about it, get on with my own life. Until ...'

He picks at a piece of wood that's splintering from the table.

'What?' says Alison.

'I overheard you and Cassie talking in the pub one day. You told her there was another rumour, that the accomplice might be one of the victims. I'd never heard that before. It sort of ... brought it all back up. I found myself searching online again for information about the shooting, pumping Paul for details when I thought he was drunk enough to let something slip about where Elaine is.'

So that was what he was doing that day.

'And did he tell you anything?' Alison had to ask, even though of course she and I know where Elaine is – much good that it's done us.

'No, nothing. And I'm not going to ask again. I have to let it go, properly this time.' He looks awkwardly at me. 'I'm sorry I didn't tell you before, Cassie.'

'It's OK,' I say, and it is. He doesn't owe me anything. We hardly know each other, after all.

'So ... we're cool, yeah? You don't have to keep away from the pub?'

'We're cool,' I say. 'Thank you.'

'Are you guys going to the memorial service tomorrow evening?'

'I think so,' I say. 'I'm going to have to bring Amy, though, so I'm not sure how long she'll last.'

'She'll be fine,' Alison says, exasperated. 'We'll be there.'

'Great. Right, I'd better get to work.' He stands up and makes his way inside. I look after him.

'It is a pretty nice view,' Alison says slyly.

'I was looking at the . . . . Oh, OK, I was looking at him,' I say, laughing foolishly.

'Well, never mind that. What about what Paul said? I'm sorry, but he can't claim it was the drink talking again; that's twice he's said that Elaine wasn't innocent in all this. Who on earth was she having the affair with?'

I don't want to think about it. That photo, Mum and Elaine, young and windswept. Friends. Did Elaine betray my mum in the worst way possible?

'Paul said Travis *felt like he needed to get rid of them all*,' Alison goes on. 'That's got to be the connection. Travis was getting rid of everyone who knew about the affair. I mean, he was a nutcase, wasn't he? He sounds like the sort of man who wouldn't have been able to stand being humiliated like that, as he would have seen it.'

'Maybe . . . '

'That's got to be it.' Her excitement is palpable, like a dog that's caught the scent of the fox. 'Peter and Jane lived next door, so they might have seen this other man coming and going when Travis was out.'

'Mmm.'

'And Graham Mooney – people talk when they're driving, don't they? It's a good way to get someone to open up to you: make them drive you somewhere. Something about not having to look at the other person as you're talking.'

Like a priest. Or a barman.

'We should talk to the relatives again. Ask different questions this time. I'm going to phone Sharmaine first.'

'Who?

'My editor.'

She pulls out her phone and dials. *Voicemail*, she mouths at me.

'Hi, Sharmaine, it's Alison Patchett. About the Travis Green story – you know my theory that it wasn't a random shooting? Looks like I was right. He'd found out his wife was having an affair, and was taking out everyone who knew. And she was pregnant, by the lover, and tried to get rid of it. Call me as soon as you get this.'

'We don't know all that for sure,' I say feebly, as she rings off.

'No, I know, but I want to get her excited about it. Right, so one of the victims must have been Elaine's lover.'

'I suppose so.' I look down, tracing the grain of wood on the table.

'What's the matter, Cassie? Are you . . . oh.'

'Yeah.' I force the words out, my throat closing around

them. 'If my mum and Elaine were such good friends, you'd expect it to have been her Travis killed, wouldn't you? It would have been Mum who knew, not my dad?'

'Oh.'

'Yes. What if the man Elaine Green was having an affair with was my dad?'

Chapter 48

katiekat2006: I found something

gamerboy: what?

katiekat2006: a notebook. On mums desk. Not seen it before.
Its not mums writing but I know its about the
shooting cos the heading is Barraclough. Isnt
that the policeman?

gamerboy: yeh, what does it say

katiekat2006: It says, Elaine was pregnant. 24 weeks when
found out. And then on the line underneath,
Didn't want the baby. Deliberately overdosed on
a drug that causes miscarriage

katiekat2006: are you there?

katiekat2006: hey, are you OK?

gamerboy: sorry, my mum came in. Is there anything else?

katiekat2006: no, that's all that's in the notebook

katiekat2006: are you still there?

katiekat2006: ???

katiekat2006: ???

gamerboy: sorry mum again

gamerboy: so do you want to meet?

katiekat2006: what, like IRL?

gamerboy: yeh

katiekat2006: for real?

gamerboy: yeh

gamerboy: or don't you want to?

katiekat2006: sure, if you do. Where?

gamerboy: do you know the quarry on the Farnwood estate?

katiekat2006: yeh. But I can't get up there. Too far

gamerboy: then r you going to the church service tonight?
               For the shooting?

katiekat2006: yeh, with mum though

gamerboy: cant you sneak away from her? There'll be
               loads there

katiekat2006: maybe

gamerboy: towards the end of it sneak away. Theres a lane between the church and the hall. Ill be there. You know it?

katiekat2006: yeh I know where you mean. I'll try

gamerboy: don't let me down k

katiekat2006: yeh k

gamerboy: see you then

katiekat2006: k see you then

gamerboy: k

gamerboy: can't wait to see you

gamerboy: xxx

Chapter 49

Candles dot the churchyard, little glimmering beacons in the twilight. I heard the woman behind me whisper to her friend that they had toyed with the idea of real ones but thought they'd keep blowing out, so instead we've each been given a small white plastic one to hold aloft at the given signal. I shift my weight from foot to foot. Everything aches. Amy's getting so heavy. I don't know how much longer my body will take carrying her around like this.

We are clustered loosely around the graves of those of the eleven who are buried here, waiting for the vicar to kick things off. Travis's grave is conspicuous by its absence, although there will be many present who are thinking of him with a hard stone of hatred lodged in their hearts. And my father's is missing too, his ashes scattered to the winds as per his wishes. Was that the real reason? Or was it that my mother couldn't forgive him for having an affair with her friend? Manisha, too, was cremated, and I wonder now how the rest of them could have been happy for their loved ones to be interred so close together, their proximity a permanent memorial to the worst thing that ever happened to them.

'So, how's the article going?' James says. 'Ready to drag us all through the muck?'

Alison laughs uncomfortably, and Natalie looks at her quizzically.

'Yes, right,' says Alison. 'I don't think my candle's working.' She fiddles with the switch, moving it back and forth to no effect.

'Well—' I begin. We'd agreed that we'd tell people before she sent the copy to her editor, the people that matter at any rate. But Alison interrupts me.

'Oh, it's working now!' she says brightly. 'I haven't written it yet,' she says to James. 'But it's possible that it's going to be a bit more … personal than I anticipated.'

'What a surprise,' he says.

'As I said, you can see it before it goes to press, and if there's anything you're unhappy with I'll take it out. I don't want to say too much yet.'

'It's only Natalie and James,' I say.

'Charming!' he says, but there's laughter in his voice.

'You know what I mean,' I say, suddenly finding my candle very interesting.

'So, when you say personal …' Natalie begins.

'It's not about you guys,' Alison says. 'But I need to be a bit careful.' She looks around. Chloe and her partner Shaun, and Della and Tom, are a few feet in front of us.

Neither of us have heard from Della since we saw her yesterday. A minute ago the two women were chatting animatedly, but they've fallen into silence. I think at first that they've been sensible and left Ryan at home, but then I see him loitering at the edge of the churchyard, in the shadow of a giant yew. I should have known he wouldn't miss an opportunity to revel in the events of 15th June 1994. This is one for the scrapbook for him. I nudge Alison.

'Look.'

'Shit. Do you think Della's spoken to him, or told Tom?'

'I don't know. If she doesn't, do you think we should?'

'Somebody's going to have to,' she says. 'Maybe she's waiting for tonight to be over.'

I can understand that. It feels as though the town has been holding its breath, waiting for this vigil.

Ryan has his back to us now. There's another boy there, tall and broad, but Ryan's addressing himself to someone else, someone hidden from my view by his body. When he moves to the left, I'm horrified to see that it's Katie. I'd thought when Alison and Katie arrived that she was a touch inappropriately dressed for the occasion in a crop top, denim shorts and four-inch wedge-heeled sandals, and I hope to God now that it's not for Ryan's benefit. *Don't say anything*, Alison had mouthed to me wearily as I'd looked askance at the way Katie's bum was hanging out the bottom of her shorts.

Katie's laughing, her usually surly features transformed. Her vivid red hair is pulled up tightly in a perfectly spherical bun. A strand has come free and she's twisting it around and around her finger as she talks, with mesmeric effect on Ryan and the other boy. I nudge Alison again, wanting to alert her to this horrifying spectacle, but she takes it the wrong way.

'Alright,' she says to Natalie. 'I'll tell you properly later, but Paul Green filled us in on a few things yesterday. Things that weren't as they seemed. People who weren't as they seemed. Like Elaine, Travis's wife. Put it this way: I would definitely no longer describe the Hartstead shooting as random.'

It's probably my imagination, but, as her words ring out, I feel a shift in the atmosphere, a little charge that runs around the churchyard.

'I haven't been able to speak to my editor yet,' she continues, 'but I'm pretty sure she'll want to run it as soon as possible, once she knows the truth.'

'The truth?' Natalie says. 'That sounds very dramatic.'

Alison smiles smugly, enjoying the intrigue. 'There's some more personal stuff that we found out about Elaine as well, that I think my editor will be interested in.'

'What happened to your *sensitive* article about towns that have lived through traumatic events?' None of us had noticed Tom edging nearer, but now he is facing us, tense and frowning. Della hangs back anxiously, a couple of paces behind.

'Things took a different turn,' says Alison. 'It's still going to be sensitively written. It's nothing for you to worry about.'

'Sensitive? Yeah, right. I can't believe you've got the front to show up here tonight. Do you have no respect?'

'Yes, I do. I'm from round here too.'

'Whatever.' He takes a step closer. 'What's this secret you're going to reveal? What do you think you've found out?'

Alison flings a panicked look at me.

'Hey, calm down.' James inserts himself into the space between them.

'Who the hell are you?' says Tom.

'I'm ... no one. I just think this isn't the time or the place. You talked about respect. Don't do this here.'

'I'll do whatever the fuck I want.'

'If you want to talk about being sensitive, you might want to look a bit closer to home,' Alison says.

Della flinches. She obviously hasn't told him.

'Not now.' I lay a restraining hand on Alison's arm.

I can sense those nearest to us nudging each other and reaching for their phones to video us for the news later, but then there's movement at the church doors, and the vicar emerges, followed by the members of the church choir. They're carrying real candles, tall ones in wooden holders, and the crowd falls silent as the strains of 'Abide With Me' surge through the warm evening air. I look over towards the yew tree. Katie, Ryan and the tall boy are watching the procession. I decide against telling Alison. There's nothing she can do about it now. I'll make sure she knows as soon as the service is over.

I didn't realise until now that the vicar is the same

331

one as in my childhood. I recognise him, despite the grey hair and careworn face. I'm transported back to the school hall, me cross-legged on the dusty floor, the smell of school dinners lingering in the air.

'Welcome, friends.' His voice is lower than I remember, a little weaker. 'Thank you for joining us tonight, as we honour the victims of the terrible events of 15th June 1994. I'd like to begin with a moment of silent prayer.'

Most people bow their heads, many with their eyes closed. I take the opportunity to look around. They're all here – the bereaved, the descendants of the victims and the merely curious. I can see Mrs Mooney, her glasses glinting in the fake candlelight. Mr and Mrs Mehta are here too, huddled together, holding hands. I spy Fraser McKillick looming at the back of the crowd, an attractive olive-skinned woman at his side. Katie, Ryan and his friend are still under the yew tree, Katie looking at her phone.

Beside me, I sense Alison stiffening.

'Shit!' she whispers. She's spotted them. She beckons Katie furiously, but, instead of joining us, she and the two boys slip into the crowd further towards the front, and we lose sight of them.

'What's she doing with him?' Alison hisses at me.

'I don't know.'

Heads swivel in our direction, many of them shooting disapproving glares.

'Nothing's going to happen here,' I whisper. 'You can go and grab her at the end.'

The service continues, with more prayers, an address

from the vicar, hymns from the choir and ones we have to join in with, half-remembered phrases and tunes from childhood. Throughout, Alison stands on her tiptoes, craning her head one way and then the other, trying to see through the crowd to wherever Katie is. At the end, we are invited to hold our candles aloft as the vicar reads the names of the victims into the silent evening air:

'Peter Frogmore.

'Jane Frogmore.

'Richard Delaney.

'Sheila Delaney.

'Graham Mooney.

'David Wilkes.

'Manisha Mehta.

'Suzanne Persimmon.

'Melissa Bradshaw.

'Maureen Featherstone.

'Gary Colman.'

He pauses at the end of the list and my throat tightens as for a second I think the vicar is, in spectacularly misjudged fashion, about to say Travis Green's name, but he doesn't. As my father's name fades into the twilight, a solitary choirboy's voice, pure and true, sings 'Amazing Grace'. The choir hold their candles high again and slowly make their way back towards the church. It feels as though the entire congregation is holding its breath.

'Can you see Katie?'

I scan the churchyard. 'No.'

'Oh, God.' The crowd mills around, some looking at the

headstones of the victims, others picking their way through the graves to greet friends. 'Where are Natalie and James?'

'I'm not sure. We said we'd go to the pub after; maybe they've gone over there already. Let's wait till it's emptied out a bit here and we'll be able to see Katie.'

We sit at the edge of the churchyard, near the lychgate. Alison is poised on the very edge of the bench, her body taut. The crowd thins until it's only us and Della and Tom, but there's still no sign of Katie or Ryan. After the unpleasantness earlier, none of us is inclined to speak to the others, but eventually I approach them.

'Have you seen Katie and Ryan?'

'No.' Della looks worried, Tom merely impatient.

'Fucking idiot,' he says. I recoil, and he has the grace to look embarrassed. 'Not you,' he says gruffly. 'My stupid bloody son.'

There are footsteps, and two figures emerge from behind the church. Alison stands up, relief etched on her features. It's short-lived though, as she realises that although one of the figures is Ryan, the other isn't Katie, it's the tall boy.

'Where the hell have you been?' says Tom. He leans in towards Ryan and sniffs. 'Is that ... have you been smoking *weed*? In a fucking churchyard?'

'Where's Katie?' Alison doesn't care what they've been smoking.

'Dunno,' says Ryan. His companion sniggers.

'She was with you, last time I saw her.' Alison's words cut harshly through the evening air. 'During the service.'

'She went off somewhere.'

Ryan's friend giggles again.

'Where? What do you mean?'

'She said she had to meet someone.'

'What? Who?'

'Dunno.' He finally clocks Alison's worried air, the sense of urgency. 'Sorry.'

'How do you know her, anyway?' Alison says fiercely. 'You don't go to Callenden, surely?'

'No, he doesn't go to that bloody snobby school,' says Tom.

'Instagram,' says Ryan, as if it should be the most obvious thing in the world.

'Katie's not even on Instagram!'

'Yes, she is. I don't think she wanted you to know, so you couldn't follow her on there.' Ryan looks slightly shamefaced.

'She's probably gone to the pub,' Della says. 'Why don't you go down there and see?'

'She's only thirteen! What have you done to her?' She advances on Ryan, who takes a step back.

'Nothing,' he mutters.

'Why the hell would my son have done anything to her?' says Tom, squaring up to her again.

'I don't know, why don't you ask your wife?' Alison spits.

'What the fuck is going on?' Tom hisses at Della.

'I'm scared,' Alison says to me. 'What if it's Katie's dad? What if he's found us?'

A car horn sounds and we all turn. Natalie is at the

wheel of a small maroon car. The window rolls down. 'Are you looking for Katie?'

'Yes!' Alison says. 'Have you seen her?'

'About five minutes ago.'

'Oh, thank God. Where?'

'She was walking with James towards the pub.'

'With James? She barely knows him.' All thoughts of Ryan or Katie's father are forgotten.

'It did seem a bit odd, and I hadn't seen you guys any-where, so I thought I'd drive back round and see if you were still here. Do you want a lift down there?'

'What about Amy?'

'I've got a car seat here.' She jerks a thumb at the pas-senger seat next to her. 'A friend of mine was chucking it so I said I'd have it – thought it'd come in handy if you wanted me to look after Amy again.'

'We could walk . . .' I don't know if I can be bothered to get Amy out of the carrier and into the car seat.

'Oh, no, come on, Cassie.' Alison pulls at the skin on her neck. 'I'm worried about Katie.'

'OK.'

I manage to settle Amy in the car seat without waking her, and Alison and I pile into the back. Natalie drives towards the pub, Alison staring anxiously out of the window in silence. As we get near the pub, there are groups of churchgoers all heading towards it. Natalie slows down to let a couple cross the road.

'There's a space there,' Alison says, pointing. 'It's free at this time of the night all along here.'

'I'd rather not park on the main road,' Natalie says, speeding up.

There's a thudding noise from somewhere behind us.

'What was that? Did you hit something?' I say, looking through the rear window.

'I don't think so,' Natalie says.

'Why didn't you park down there?' Alison says, indicating the side road we've just sped past. Natalie doesn't reply. 'Natalie?'

There's another thump from the back. Alison and I turn to each other, incomprehension transmuting to horror.

'Natalie!' I lean forward and grab her shoulder. She shakes me off and puts her foot down, skidding round a mini roundabout. 'Natalie, where's Katie? You said you saw her with James.'

'I'm sorry.' She's panicky, on the verge of tears.

'It's OK,' I say, trying to stay calm. 'Let's go back to the pub and find Katie, OK?'

'I know where she is,' Natalie says despairingly, keeping her eyes firmly ahead, tearing across a crossroads without looking left or right. 'She's in the boot of the car.'

Chapter 50

15th June 1994 | Travis Green

Not long now until all eleven are wiped out and there'll be no one left in the world who knows that his slut of a wife has betrayed him. No one to look at her belly as it swells with Richard Delaney's seed. No nosy neighbours peering over the garden wall, remarking to each other right out in the open, in their garden, about the fancy man who visited her next door when they thought Travis couldn't hear them.

He has annihilated the man himself – done what he wished he could have done that day he followed Elaine and saw them together in the woods, saw Elaine writhing and panting in a way she'd never done with him. She'd never said no to Travis, but it always felt like she was waiting for it to be over; as if it was a chore to be got out of the way, like cleaning the toilet or putting out the bins. Richard's wife had to go too, because he couldn't be sure she didn't know.

No more secret driving lessons where she could pour her heart out without having to make eye contact. Travis heard him once, the instructor, when he was dropping Elaine off in

338

town. Travis was meant to be at work but he hadn't gone in (it wasn't long before they fired him, in fact – for unreliability, not anything else, despite the rumours). He knew Elaine was up to something, and he needed to find out what. He'd tried to get it out of her the night before but she wouldn't tell him, despite him being very ... persuasive. 'Take care,' the grey-haired man had said through the window. 'You've only got one life – you need to make sure you live it.' And then he'd seen Elaine embrace a woman he'd never seen before, a woman he now knows to be Sylvia Colman. A woman he is on his way to kill. She had raised a gentle finger to the purple and yellow bruise that bloomed around Elaine's eye, and they'd exchanged a few words and another hug before Sylvia got into the instructor's car and drove slowly away. Elaine used to ask Travis if she could learn to drive when they were first married, and he'd laugh and say he'd take her anywhere she wanted to go. The problem was she couldn't take the hint, and she'd asked one too many times. He'd snapped, he admits it now. He probably overreacted, went a bit over the top. She never asked again though.

He's been getting rid of them all, working his way through the chain. The greasy estate agent who showed Elaine and her lover a poky little flat above a shop in Tunston as Travis watched, unseen, from the café across the road. That busybody do-gooder from the Citizens Advice Bureau and the harpy from the solicitors. Women who listened to the lies his wife told about him, women who were helping his wife to leave him, instead of staying at home where they belonged. The little darkie from the hotel where his whore of a wife had gone with *that man every other Wednesday when they thought he'd be in Tunston all afternoon, signing on. He'd known something good would come out of that job at the school, even if they had asked him to leave in the end. It had been worth it to get the information from that other girl. They'd said he 'wasn't performing satisfactorily' when they terminated his contract, but Travis had seen their faces, seen them squirming. He knew they were uncomfortable with how he looked at the girls. What did they expect, though, with their knee socks and their skirts so short you could almost see their arses? They're all the same in the end, women. Even Elaine, who he'd thought was so different. The old biddy who'd seen her with Richard in the woods the same day as Travis had been almost as disgusted as Travis himself. At least she can't tell anyone now.*

So now there's just Sylvia Colman to go. He knew he'd been right to discourage Elaine from having friends, friends who would pour poison in her ear, turn her against Travis. He is in no doubt that Elaine has confided in Sylvia. She probably knows more than anyone about Elaine's plans to leave Travis, set up home with that piece of shit and have his baby. The gossips of Hartstead would have had a field day. Everyone would know he couldn't keep his wife under control. He can't allow that to happen. He's got rid of everyone else who knows, and now Sylvia Colman has to go.

Chapter 51

'What the hell?' Alison lunges forward, grabbing at Natalie. 'Stop the car!'

We swerve to the left, bumping up onto the pavement and down again. The car seat shakes from side to side. I was so anxious about not waking Amy, I didn't check to see if it was strapped in properly. Natalie takes no notice, accelerating harder. I put my hand on Alison's arm and shake my head at her, trying to signal the need to remain calm. Whatever's going on here, shouting and panicking is going to make it worse. She gets the message and sits back, rigid with tension. I let go of her arm and lean forward, swallowing down my own fear.

'Natalie, I don't know what's going on here, but could you slow down a bit, please? You're going to crash.' *My baby*, I want to say, panic swelling in my throat. *My baby is in the car.*

She ignores me. We're approaching the traffic lights on Stevens Road as they change from green to amber to red.

There's a car twenty metres in front of us and it stops at the lights. Natalie slams her hand on the horn again and again. But she is forced to slow, and, without thinking about whether this is the right thing to do, I reach for the door handle and pull.

Locked. She must have put the child locks on. Natalie pulls out around the car in front and speeds past it, despite the still-red light, and I'm thrown sideways.

'Please, Natalie. What's going on?' I need to try and engage her. She looked close to tears a moment ago; I can't believe she wants to be doing this. She takes no notice, screeching around a corner and onto a back road which leads to the Farnwood Estate. Is she taking us to Paul?

Again it's as if I haven't spoken. She drives faster and faster. The road is barely wide enough for two cars to pass at certain points, and I keep my eyes on Amy, praying to a previously unacknowledged deity to keep her safe, forcing myself to breathe slowly. Alison's hand creeps into mine.

After a few minutes, we swing into the Farnwood Estate. I'm expecting Natalie to keep going up the drive towards Paul's lodge, but instead she swings a right onto a bumpy track that winds uphill.

I'm hit by a memory I didn't know I had. Walking up this track in the dark with only a tiny, fading torch to show the way, with Stella and Bec. We were staying over at Bec's house, and she'd arranged to sneak out of her house at midnight to meet her boyfriend and his friends, a pair of small, mousy boys she was hoping we'd get off with. Bec's house wasn't far from here, and we'd met them at the end of her road and walked here together, swigging from a bottle of whisky the boys had brought. I'd only taken tiny sips, barely able to swallow the disgusting amber liquid; the boys were taking great gulps, laughing at us for being scared of what could emerge from the blackness of the woods on either side. With a lurch of my stomach, I remember what lies at the top of this track: the quarry. Every dire warning from my mother and my friends' parents rings through my head. *Remember what happened to Adam Groundswell.*

After what feels like an eternity but is in reality only a few minutes, the track levels out and Natalie brings the car to a halt, keeping the engine running. There's nothing but inky blackness out of the side windows. In front, the headlights illuminate a large neon-yellow sign with a triangle containing an exclamation mark and the words DANGER: KEEP OUT – DEEP QUARRY. Another memory: the three boys, emboldened by whisky, daring each other to go ever closer to the edge; the girls and I, more sober, pleading with them to stop.

'Natalie, what's going on? Please, can we get Katie out of the boot?' I try my best to keep my voice level, but it's impossible. My mind veers wildly through various scenarios. If only I knew what she was planning to do. Should I try to climb into the front and get Amy out and run? What about Katie? What kind of physical state is she in? Between us, in theory, surely Alison and I could overpower Natalie, but not if one of us is potentially carrying or supporting Katie, and the other holding Amy. I'm paralysed by fear and indecision.

Natalie rests her head on the steering wheel, breathing fast. There's more thumping from the boot. A whimper comes from the baby seat. Oh God, Amy's waking up.

'Please,' Alison sobs. 'I don't know what's going on but it's got nothing to do with Katie. Please let her go.'

'None of this would be happening if you'd left it alone.' It's the first time she's spoken since she told us Katie was in the boot. She sounds unlike herself – desperate, despairing.

'We will. I will.' The words trip over Alison's tongue in their eagerness to get out. 'I won't publish the article. Is that what this is about?'

'She didn't want me,' Natalie says in a small voice. 'Cassie wrote it in a notebook.' Amy's whimper turns into a wail and she raises her voice. 'I spent my whole life protecting her secret, and she didn't even want me.'

I throw a desperate glance at Amy, who is properly crying now. I must try to focus on Natalie though. 'So Elaine . . . ' I almost don't need to ask. It's clear now that Natalie is the last piece of the puzzle. But I do anyway. 'She's your mother?'

'Yes. I'm sorry I didn't tell you. I wanted to. I wish I could have. I wanted . . . don't think I didn't want to be friends with you. I really liked you; it wasn't all pretending. I'd never had friends before, not properly. At school, I could never invite classmates home because Mum wouldn't see anyone. That first day in the pub, I didn't even know it was you at first. And then when you told me your name . . . it was like fate. I was . . . curious, I suppose. You and me, we both grew up under the same shadow. I wanted to see you, to know you. That was all it was at first. I didn't tell you who I was because I didn't want to freak you out. But when you got involved with *her* . . . '

Alison stiffens beside me and I lay a warning hand on her arm. I know Natalie. She isn't a monster. She's my friend. Perhaps my half-sister. She's lonely and damaged, more than I could have imagined, but I cannot believe she would hurt anyone. I don't think she wants to, not deep down.

'I was trying to protect my mother.' A suppressed sob breaks free. 'Every day when I was growing up, she drilled it into me. *Don't trust anyone. Never let anyone in. Don't let the truth out.* I'm just doing what she told me. My entire life has been about making sure nobody finds out why that . . . animal did what he did. That it was her fault.'

'But it wasn't her fault.' My God, poor Elaine. All these years she's been blaming herself? What was it like in their house, when Natalie was growing up? What did Elaine say to her daughter, day after day, that led her here? 'Travis Green killed those people. It doesn't matter why he thought he was doing it. It was nobody's fault, or doing, but his own. No one would ever think otherwise.'

'They would. It *was* her fault. If she hadn't been having an affair, none of this would have happened. She always said no one must ever find out. I was her helper. I always knew I wasn't Travis's child. She wanted me to know that I didn't come from him. She said . . . she said she wanted me, that she loved me because I was part of my dad. I've spent so long protecting her secret, like she said I had to. But now I know the truth. She didn't want me. She tried so hard to get rid of me.'

'Natalie,' I say urgently, leaning forward, my eyes fixed on my screaming daughter in the car seat next to her, every fibre of my being yearning to reach out and pick her up. 'I felt the same. About Amy. I was going to have an abortion. Her father wanted me to, and I thought there was no way I was ready for a baby, especially on my own. I made the appointment and cancelled it twice. I could easily have gone through with it. But it doesn't mean I love Amy any less. I love her more.'

My heart is pouring out of my mouth and I feel the truth of what I'm saying. I love her more. More than I ever thought possible. More than I would have if we lived in a traditional family set-up, with a doting dad on the scene. She is mine, and I am hers. Her screams are like knives in my heart.

'It's not the same,' Natalie says dully. 'I spent my life protecting her. The shooting wouldn't have happened if Mother hadn't had an affair, hadn't been planning to leave Travis. You know, I know you do. He only killed the people who knew about the affair. He was wiping out every trace of it.'

'Yes, I know that. But Natalie, that doesn't make it Elaine's fault. Or my dad's.'

'Your dad? Why would it have been his fault?' Natalie's eyes lose their glaze momentarily.

'Was he not ... is he not ...?'

'My father? No! Richard Delaney was my father. That's why Travis killed him and his wife. What made you think it was your father?'

'I ... don't know.'

Why did Travis kill him, then? How could my father have known about Elaine's affair and not my mother?

'It *was* Mother's fault,' she continues. 'She told me. You can't have understood it properly. Peter and Jane, the neighbours, they were so nosy, they must have seen him coming and going when Travis wasn't there. He couldn't have been sure about Graham, but he'd found out Mother had been secretly having driving lessons, so he must have thought she'd told him what she was planning. Manisha was always on the hotel desk on a Wednesday afternoon. Mother and my dad went there when Travis was in Tunston signing on.' Natalie sounds like a member of the clergy, reciting a familiar liturgy. This is her Lord's Prayer, learned at her mother's knee. I go to say something, but she carries on, ignoring me and showing no sign that she's registered Amy's ongoing distress.

'David Wilkes showed Mother and my dad a flat in Tunston. They couldn't have stayed in Hartstead. She'd been in to see Suzanne Persimmon for advice about the financial side of leaving Travis, and Melissa Bradshaw about the legalities, how she could get a divorce. And Maureen Featherstone ... she must have seen them

347

together, been in the wrong place at the wrong time. He'd been following Mother, you see. He must have been, to have known about everyone who knew.'

What about my dad? The question nags at me like toothache, but I can't be distracted by that now.

'But that still doesn't make it your mum's fault.' Surely, if I can make her see this, she'll stop this thing. 'Plenty of women have affairs, leave their partners. But their partners don't go on a killing spree. That's on Travis, not Elaine.'

Her shoulders sag a little and the urgency goes out of her. 'But Mother always said ... she always said I had to ... no one must know ...'

'No one *will* know, Natalie. Alison and I are the only ones who know, and now we know how important it is to you, we'll keep it to ourselves. You should have told me at the beginning. Why didn't you?'

'I wanted to,' she says, her voice breaking. 'I'm so sorry about the note, and the penknife, and the tyres. I was just trying to scare you, to get you to leave it alone. I only came to your house the first time to speak to your mum, to make sure she couldn't tell anyone, and to get rid of that photo. She knew the truth, Cassie. I was so scared she'd let it slip to you or Alison. I went to see her again in the care home – I had to make sure she didn't have any other photos. She thought ... she thought I was her daughter, so I played along. I wouldn't have hurt her. The second time at your house, when I put the cot mobile on ... I needed you to stop. I was only trying to frighten you enough to stop you. I'm sorry, Cassie. My whole life, Mother always said people can't be trusted. I wanted to trust you, but I couldn't. And now it seems I couldn't trust her either. She tried to *murder* me. She didn't make an appointment at a clinic and cancel it, like you. She took an overdose of a drug that she thought would kill me.'

'She wasn't in her right mind, though!' I say urgently. 'Think of what she'd been through. She was probably suffering from PTSD.'

'I don't care!' she wails. 'I spent so much time and energy making sure nobody would find out what really happened. I've been messaging Katie to find out what you knew.'

'Katie?' says Alison sharply. 'What do you mean?'

'I've been messaging her on Instagram, pretending to be a boy, ever since I first heard you were planning to write an article. I guess you don't know everything about her after all. That was how I knew what you'd found out. But it was only today that she found the notebook and told me about . . . what my mother did to me. And now you're going to put that in your article, and everyone will know.'

'I won't, I promise I won't.'

'You said it in the churchyard. There's some more personal stuff about Elaine, you said. I was trying to stop you publishing the stuff about my mother anyway, like I know she would want me to. But this . . . you can't publish this. Then everyone will know I wasn't wanted.'

'I swear to God I haven't spoken to my editor yet,' says Alison. 'I can make it go away.'

'You two know, though. You know what she did.' Her hollow despair sends a chill down my spine. 'How can I trust you?'

'I'm your friend, Natalie.' I lean forward again, trying not to look at Amy's twisted, scarlet tear-stained face this time because I won't be able to hold it together if I do. 'You've become really important to me since I moved back to Hartstead. I would never do anything to hurt you.'

'Nor would I,' Alison chimes in.

'Ha. Not even for a story?' says Natalie bitterly.

'No! Please, let Katie go.'

'If you go ahead and write about me and my mother, don't think Katie will ever be safe,' Natalie says, uncertainly, as if she can hardly believe what she's saying. 'I'll find a way to get to her, like I did before. It was so easy, getting her to believe I was a boy on Instagram.'

'I won't, I swear,' Alison says. 'Nobody else knows, it's only me and Cassie.'

Natalie's shoulders slump, and she slowly lowers her hands, which have been gripping the steering wheel.

'Can I please take Amy?' I say, unable to bear it any longer.

Natalie undoes the straps with shaking hands, lifts her out and passes her to me. I take her in my arms, and her screams subside instantly, her body relaxing. The taut string within me is released as for the first time ever I know she recognises me. I'm not just any pair of arms; it's specifically me that is comforting her.

350

No one else would do. How could I ever have thought of being without her?

'Can you let Katie out now, please?' I say, trying to keep my voice even.

'OK.'

Natalie opens the car door, and walks slowly round to the boot. Through the back windscreen, the rear lights giving out an unearthly red glow, we see her haul Katie out of the boot.

'Oh, God,' Alison whimpers. A thick strip of black gaffer tape covers Katie's mouth, above which her terrified eyes flicker towards us. Her wrists are also taped tightly behind her back, but her legs are free. Alison presses the button to open the car window and reaches out to Katie. 'Natalie, open the door, please.'

Natalie's hand is on the handle when Alison's phone begins to ring.

'Who's that?' snaps Natalie, snatching her arm away.

'I don't know. It doesn't matter. I'll leave it,' Alison says.

'Give me your phone.' The softness of a moment ago has disappeared and the cold, hard Natalie I don't recognise is back.

Alison looks briefly at me, signalling panic.

'Give me the phone,' Natalie says with grim determination.

Alison digs into her pocket and passes the phone through the window. I try to look at the screen but I can't see who it is. Alison can, though, and in the semi-darkness I see the colour leaching from her face.

'Sharmaine.' Natalie grips Katie's arm like a vice as the phone continues to ring. 'Who's Sharmaine?'

'My ... my editor,' stammers Alison. 'Leave it, please.'

Natalie swipes the screen and holds the phone out in front of her.

'Hello?' she says casually.

'Hi, Alison, how are you?'

Natalie has put the phone on speaker, and Sharmaine's voice echoes out into the night.

'I'm good, thanks!' Natalie says, her voice imitating Alison's upbeat inflections.

'OK. So ... ' Sharmaine sounds excited. Alison looks as if she's been told she's swallowed poison. 'When are you going to get this Travis Green story to me? I've told Christopher all about it, and he's super-keen to get it in asap. If what you've told me is true about his wife's affair, and him killing all those people deliberately, this is huge. We're holding a double-page spread for it at the weekend.'

'Great!' says Natalie, injecting a cold note of enthusiasm. 'What about the baby stuff?'

'About the wife trying to get rid of the baby? Yeah, adds a great human angle, we'll definitely use that.'

Natalie flings the phone at Alison, and screams one word. 'Liar!' She takes a few steps backwards, towards the edge of the quarry, dragging Katie with her. 'I knew I couldn't trust you. How dare you lie to me?'

'No!' The word comes from deep inside Alison, a primal place I recognise. She reaches through the open window, opens the car door and half falls out. I clamber after her, gripping Amy to me.

'Stay back!' Natalie is right on the edge now, squinting in the glare from the car headlights. Katie's ankle buckles in her ridiculous high wedge sandals, and she would have fallen if Natalie wasn't gripping her arm, her fingers pressed hard into the flesh. She stumbles again and a stone is dislodged, tumbling to the bottom of the pit. Her breath is coming in short, sobbing gasps through the tape across her mouth.

'What do you want?' Alison pleads, her eyes never leaving her daughter.

'I need you to see how important this is. I've been trying to stop you, but nothing *works*.' She yanks on Katie's arm and Katie takes a step to steady herself, dislodging more stones. Alison gives a strangled yelp of fear.

'We won't write the story,' I say, realising Alison can't speak. 'I mean, Alison won't write it. Will you?'

'No,' she croaks. 'I swear to God, I won't write it. I'll tell my editor I got it wrong. Nobody else knows what we've found out.'

'I don't believe you.'

She wants to trust us, I can feel it, but it's an unfamiliar sensation. She's not used to having faith in anyone.

'Come away from the edge, Natalie. You're scaring me.' I take a slow step towards her.

'Stay back!' she says again, panicked.

Katie's ankle gives way once more, sending further debris crashing to the bottom of the quarry. She grasps at Natalie to try and steady herself, and now they are spiralling, teetering on the edge. In a heartbeat Alison launches herself towards them, and before I've registered what's happening she has pulled Katie from Natalie's grasp, fear and motherhood giving her superhuman strength. I remain rooted to the spot, cradling Amy in my arms, unable to do anything but hold her and protect her. Katie's legs give way beneath her and Alison lifts her in her arms and staggers away from the drop. As she does so, Natalie loses her footing and slips, landing hard on her knees on a large stone right on the quarry's edge. She reaches out in front of her, towards me, but there's nothing there to hold on to. My stomach is in my mouth. I take one useless step towards her, but there's nothing I can do. A heartrending scream echoes into the darkness as she plunges to the bottom. Then the screaming stops, and there is nothing but silence.

Chapter 52

Paul looks large and out of place in Elaine's small, dishevelled kitchen. One of the cupboard doors is hanging by one hinge, the worktops are stained, and used dishes are heaped in the sink. Elaine wipes crumbs and dust from the table with a dirty dishcloth.

'Sit down, Elaine,' says Paul. I try not to betray any surprise that he doesn't call her Mum, or Mother.

She puts the cloth down next to the sink, and sits beside him. Her hands, dry as paper, twist around and around as if winding an imaginary skein of wool.

I look down and draw a long breath, trying not to make it sound like a sigh. I've refused the offer of tea or coffee. I don't think Elaine wants me here any longer than necessary. Not that it *is* entirely necessary. I didn't tell Alison I was coming, because I want the truth from Elaine. Not about Natalie – about Mum. About me.

'She was a dear little girl.' I look up to find her eyes

on me. Brown with flecks of green. Just like Natalie's. 'I know you'll find that hard to believe.'

'Actually, no, I don't. She was my friend.' It sounds ridiculous, given what I know now about how she lied to me, and frightened me, and put my daughter in danger, but I can't help missing her. I believe she was telling the truth when she said she cared about me, that she never wanted to hurt me. I wish so much I could tell her that – that I understand. If I'd tried harder that night at the quarry, maybe I could have saved her.

'I didn't think they'd let me keep her after ... what I did ... and what with Paul being ... away from me,' Elaine says.

I shoot a quick look at Paul. He remains impassive, his gaze fixed on a spot on the wall about a foot to my left.

'They kept a close eye. Very close. Especially at first. But once they could see I could cope ... she was such a good baby, such a good girl ... ' She pulls a crumpled tissue from her sleeve and wipes her nose. 'It's all my fault.'

'No.' He still won't look at her. 'It was Dad's fault, not yours.' His voice is clipped, and I can't help but think of the drunken outbursts where he hinted at blaming Elaine for Travis's behaviour. Is that a truer representation of his feelings about what happened that day? I can understand how he would have felt that as a teenager who idolised his father and felt abandoned by his mother, but surely he can see now that it was in no way Elaine's fault.

'No. It was too much to put on her. I never should have told her the truth. Look where it led her. I should have known better. I was supposed to be the adult. She changed. When she was a teenager. So secretive.'

'All teenagers are secretive. You weren't to know what was going on in her head. No parent does.'

'You weren't there, Paul. She was eighteen when you came back into our lives, and by then the damage was done. I made her world so small. It was me and her.' She's shredding the tissue now, little flakes scattered across the kitchen table like dandruff. 'I didn't want her to have friends; I didn't want her to fit in. We moved house every couple of years, never got to know our neighbours. I just wanted her home with me. And for nobody to ever know it was my fault that those eleven people died – and don't say it. Don't say it was his fault, because I know it was mine.'

She'll never change her view on that. She has made guilt her life's work. And Natalie's. I feel a twinge of anger towards Elaine. Even with the life she'd had, Natalie was able to be funny and caring and a good friend. Yes, she lied to me, but I refuse to believe she was pretending all the time. Imagine what she could have been like if Elaine hadn't cloistered her away, filling her mind with poison.

I drag myself back to the present. I need answers from Elaine, and this may be my only chance.

'That rumour, that Travis had an accomplice … was there any truth in that?' I ask.

'Oh, no, none at all,' she says. 'I think Dennis Glover encouraged it, though; it kept trespassers away from the farm.'

So Tom was right. His dad had nothing to do with it.

And Della is simply a wife who's scared of her husband. And her stepson. I called her a few days ago. She said she told Tom everything when they got home from the memorial, and that they confronted Ryan together. She said Tom hadn't got angry and had actually been very supportive. She also said Ryan understood what he had done was wrong, and that he'd promised to stop his obsession with the shooting and all things true crime. I wasn't sure I believed a word of it, but I also no longer think Ryan poses any real danger to anyone.

'What about the other rumour? That one of the victims was his accomplice?' I ask.

Elaine stares out of the window, miles away.

'There was no accomplice,' Paul says. 'There were tons of rumours flying about after it happened, almost none of them true.'

How much time and energy had James wasted on that particular wild-goose chase?

'I should have known something like this would happen. I should have tried to stop her,' says Paul. 'I'd been worried about her for a while. I'd seen how close she was getting to you and Alison, and she wouldn't let me tell you who she was. I had a feeling I needed to keep an eye on her, but I had no idea she would do something like that. I was more worried she'd try and hurt herself.'

Elaine stifles a sob at this.

'I'd spoken to her the day before, on the phone, when I … saw you at the pub.' He looks uncomfortable. 'I'm sorry about that.'

'It's OK.'

'It's not really, but ... thanks.' This is the 'real' him, I catch myself thinking, not the slurring, stumbling mess that I've seen in the pub. But how many partners and friends of alcoholics have fallen down that hole?

'I knew she was getting desperate. I'd told her she should come clean with you, trust you, but she ... she found it difficult to trust people. I should have known ...'

'It's my fault.' Elaine doesn't look up. 'I did that to her. My little girl.' The words spew from her.

'I didn't mean that,' he says mechanically. 'I meant I should have known she'd go to the quarry. It always held a kind of fascination for her. And the way she sounded when I spoke to her the day before ... she wasn't rational.'

'What do you mean about the quarry?' I ask.

'There was this time ...' He looks over at Elaine, who nods briefly. 'Not long after I got back in touch with my mother; I guess Natalie must have been nineteen, twenty ...'

'Nineteen. She was nineteen.' Her pain is sharp, like a knife.

'She'd always had a bit of a thing about it. I don't know if it was because she knew Travis used to go there, or whether it was because of the boy who died there – you wouldn't know, it happened when I was a kid.'

'Adam Groundswell, yes. I don't remember it, but my mum used to tell me about what happened to him to warn me about not going up there.'

'Yeah. It happened before Natalie was born, but she

was fascinated by it. She was always troubled, but things had been worse than usual, and then this one day she went up to the quarry and took a load of pills. I don't know if she really meant to kill herself or not, but she called Elaine and told her what she'd done, and we were able to get to her in time.'

There's a small silence, and I can feel us all thinking how nobody was able to get to her in time, this time. The air takes on the quality of an ending. Soon one of us will say *Right*, and stand up, and this conversation will be over and I'll never have another chance to ask the question I need to ask. I steel myself.

'There is one more thing, Elaine. It's about my dad. Why did Travis kill him? You and my mum were friends, weren't you? Did she not know about the affair with Richard? Did my dad know?'

Her fingers stop tearing the tissue, but she won't look at me.

'Elaine?'

'I swore I'd never tell anyone.' She abandons the remains of the tissue and picks at a small scab on her wrist.

'Please, Elaine.' I can't bear to have gone through all this for nothing. Also, there's a memory that's been scratching away at me ever since I saw the picture of Mum and Elaine, and it's suddenly become clearer now. I was outside the house. But I think I looked through the window. I think I saw my mum bending down over Travis Green on the floor. I think I saw her doing something inexplicable.

360

But I can't trust my memory, it's too fragile.

'Don't you think I deserve the truth?'

'I . . . I suppose you do,' she says heavily.

There's a silence that lengthens. I hardly dare to breathe.

'Your mother and I *were* friends. Good friends. We first met in between our driving lessons. We'd just smile at first, never spoke. But one day she had a black eye. I didn't say anything to her, but I asked Graham Mooney during my lesson if he knew how she came to have such a bruise, and he said it was the same way I came to have mine.'

What? This can't be right. I've seen the letters from my dad to my mum. He loved her.

'Graham Mooney knew what Travis was like, because I'd told him once when he noticed me wincing as I got into the car. Travis had hit me across the back the night before. I never normally told anyone; if they asked I'd usually come up with some story. But there was something very kind, very sympathetic about Graham, and that day I'd had enough, burst into tears, told him everything about what Travis was like, about Richard too. That poor, poor man. If only I'd kept my mouth shut.'

'So did you speak to my mum, then? The next time you saw her?'

Perhaps the next part of this story is where Elaine found out that my mum got her black eye from someone else. Please let it be that.

'Yes, I asked her if she had time for a coffee after the lesson. I don't think she wanted to, but I put her on the spot and she couldn't think of an excuse quick enough. So we went to the coffee shop on the high street. I asked her about the black eye, and she made an excuse at first, but I wouldn't let her get away with that. I told her what Travis was like, and it came pouring out of her. She was taking driving lessons in secret, like I was. Your father . . . '

She looks at me closely.

'Is this . . . did you know this already about your father? I'm not telling you something you didn't know, am I?'

'I . . . had some idea,' I manage to choke out the lie. I don't want her to clam up and stop telling this story. As little as I want to hear it, I know I need to.

'When I said I never saw her after the shooting, that wasn't entirely true.' Her voice is stronger now. 'I saw her once. She came to see me and she told me what really happened. I think she needed to let it out, and she knew she could trust me. But if I tell you, you might wish I hadn't. There are some things it's better not to know.'

'I've spent my life not properly knowing things. Mum never talked about the shooting; she never talked about my dad, or what happened to her or me that day. I've had enough. I want to know the truth. I want to face it, whatever it is.'

'Alright,' she says, as the scab she's been worrying at finally comes away, a thin ribbon of blood seeping out from the sore beneath. 'I'll tell you.'

Chapter 53

15th June 1994 | Sylvia Colman

Sylvia's heart sinks as she hears Gary moving around upstairs. After he called in sick to work, he'd gone back to sleep and she had been hoping he'd stay in bed a bit longer. She scurries round the kitchen, wiping up stray crumbs and hurriedly sweeping the floor. She scours the room for anything that might upset him. The stairs creak and she dashes to the kettle, pouring away the old water and filling it fresh before she sets it to boil. For a second she thinks she hears him whistling and her shoulders drop a fraction – maybe it's one of his good days – but then she realises it's a bird in the garden, the cheerful sound leaking in through the partially open window. She panics, unable to recall whether he likes the window open or closed at this time of day.

'Morning!' she trills as he enters the room. She hates this nervy, falsely cheerful version of herself, but she can't work out who else to be. Gary throws himself down at the table.

'God, I slept terribly,' he says. 'I feel like absolute crap.'

'Oh, dear. The kettle's nearly boiled.'

'Oh, great. That makes everything better if the fucking kettle's nearly boiled.'

'Yes, sorry, of course.'

'Mama, mama!' Cassie barrels into the room, holding a pink plastic teapot aloft.

'What's she doing here? I thought she was meant to be at nursery.'

'She's running a bit of a temperature, I thought it was better to keep her at home. We'll go out in a bit, give you some peace.'

'She looks alright to me.'

'Cuppa tea!' Cassie says, holding the teapot up to Sylvia.

Sylvia kneels and pretends to take a swig from the spout.

'Mmm, delicious. Why don't you go and lay out the teacups and plates in your bedroom, and I'll come up in a minute and we'll have a tea party.'

'I want to have a tea party here. Inna kitchen!'

'No, not in here, sweetheart. Daddy's having his cuppa tea in here.'

'I sit with Daddy.' She plonks the teapot down on the table and pulls out a chair, the legs scraping loudly against the kitchen floor. Sylvia's stomach tightens as she sees Gary wince at the sound. Cassie sits on the chair, but now she's too far from the table. 'Push me in!' she orders Sylvia.

Sylvia tries to lift the chair with Cassie on it so it doesn't make the sound again, but Cassie's so heavy and her arm still hurts from where Gary twisted it behind her back last night and there's that screeching noise again and she holds her breath but it's too late, he's snapped and the teapot goes flying across the room.

'That fucking noise!'

'My teapot!' Cassie lets out a wail, and Sylvia reaches down to lift her up, ready to slip from the room with her, already thinking of the fastest way to placate her, to silence her, but she's too late and Gary gets there first, his meaty hand closing around Cassie's delicate wrist. 'Ow!' Her screams get louder, and Sylvia, attuned to her beloved child's every sound, recognises real distress and pain.

She's been feeling this coming for a while. Until now, he's never actually touched Cassie in anger. He's got pissed off with her, sure, but Sylvia has always been able to head him off at the pass, to whisk Cassie out of harm's way. She is a world expert on Gary's moods, and so far she has been able to anticipate them in time to get Cassie away before he boils over. Cassie has never seen him hurt Sylvia, either. Sylvia has shielded her from that, as she has from so much of the day-to-day reality of their lives. She loves Cassie fiercely, painfully, and cannot bear for her innocence to be shattered. Cassie is too young to learn that the world is a cruel, frightening place where even those who are supposed to protect you will hurt you. Sylvia knows, has known for a while now, that it won't be long before she can't stand between Gary and Cassie any more. Before he aims his vitriolic, uncontrollable rage at their sweet daughter.

She swallows down a terrifying urge to rip Gary's arm from its socket, and instead lays a timid hand on his.

'Let me take her upstairs,' she says. 'Please.' She struggles to keep in the sob that is forming in the back of her throat, knowing how important it is to maintain a level tone to avoid accusations of hysteria.

Gary hesitates for a second, and grunts as he pulls roughly away from Cassie's wrist, giving it a final squeeze for good measure. Sylvia scoops Cassie up and holds her close. Cassie buries her wet face in Sylvia's neck as she heads for the door that leads to the stairs.

All three of them jump as the kitchen door, the one that leads to the passage at the side of the house, is smashed open. Cassie stares, not understanding what she is seeing. Gary leaps up, his chair skittering across the floor, and a scream sticks in Sylvia's throat. Travis Green stands framed in the doorway, sweat pouring from him, rifle in hand. The four of them stand there, frozen in this strange tableau.

Travis looks in confusion from Gary to Sylvia, a trembling Cassie in her arms.

'What are they doing here?' he says. 'She should be at nursery.' He looks at Gary. 'You should be at work.'

'They're ... they're not very well,' Sylvia manages.

She's never spoken to Travis before, but she knows who he is, what he's capable of. Her friend Elaine didn't have to tell her. Sylvia had seen the bruises appearing with depressing regularity over the months they'd been friends, and was only too aware what they meant. They matched her own.

'They weren't meant to be here.' Travis's voice rises in panic, and then the phone rings. They all stand there listening to it until it rings out. There's a few seconds of silence, and then it starts to ring again. A police siren wails in the distance, getting louder. Cassie's arms tighten around Sylvia's neck, and Sylvia holds her closer, feeling Cassie's heart beating like a bird's, fluttery and fast.

'Put her down,' he says to Sylvia. 'Get her out of here.'

Cassie has Sylvia in a vice-like grip, arms and legs wound around her like a baby monkey. Sylvia kneels and unpeels her with some difficulty.

'Go next door, to Mrs Flitwick,' she says. 'Do you understand me? Go. I will be there in a minute.'

Cassie whimpers, her eyes fixed on Sylvia, and for a moment Sylvia thinks she's not going to go, but Travis steps aside and Cassie scurries past him into the side passage and away. The sirens wail again, closer still, and Travis waves his rifle wildly in Sylvia's direction, panic flooding his features. He goes to squeeze the trigger and, as he does, Sylvia drops to the floor. Gunfire explodes, plates shatter, and Sylvia lies still. Travis swings the rifle round and sticks the barrel in his mouth, pointing up towards his brain. His finger moves on the trigger for the last time, and there's an earth-shattering bang, and he slumps to the floor, his head a surprisingly dark red, oozing mess.

'Jesus, fuck,' Gary breathes, slumped against the dresser. 'Sylv?' His voice is a child's, asking for its mother.

Sylvia sits up slowly, among the wreckage.

'Oh, my God, Sylvia, are you OK? Aren't you hurt?'

'I fell before he pulled the trigger,' she says in amazement. She gets to her feet and crosses to the bloodied mess that was once Travis Green.

'What are you doing, Sylv? Don't touch him.'

She doesn't look at Gary. The sirens are getting louder and she has no time to waste. Her thoughts are only of Cassie – Cassie with a hairy, meaty hand gripping her slender arm;

Cassie cowering in a corner, afraid; Cassie growing up walk-ing on eggshells around Gary, learning to make herself small, like Sylvia has done.

Without realising what she is thinking, what her uncon-scious brain is planning, Sylvia takes a mental picture of where the gun is in relation to Travis's body and the sodden mess that was once his head. She bends down and takes it from him. There's blood on the handle and her hands slip a little, but if Gary had ever bothered to ask her about her childhood he would have known that she used to go out shooting rabbits with her father when she was a girl. Handling a gun holds no fear for her.

'What are you ...?' Gary is confused, but not scared. Sylvia has made herself so small over the years, it doesn't occur to him to be frightened of her.

'No time to explain,' Sylvia says. 'The police will be here in a minute.'

She raises the rifle, aims it squarely at Gary's chest and pulls the trigger. As police cars gather around the house, she carefully positions the gun back in Travis's lifeless hands.

Chapter 54

'Awww, Theo looks so cute today!' coos Chloe, looking down into Karen's buggy.

'It's a good job he is cute, otherwise I would've thrown him out of the window last night,' says Karen, croaky with exhaustion. She's pale, and her hair is scraped into a greasy, tangled ponytail. 'He barely slept.'

Theo, of course, is peacefully snoozing in the buggy, not a care in the world. It was Karen who persuaded me to come back to the baby group, after I finally made a date with her for the coffee we'd mentioned at the care home that day. Coffee at mine grew into walks in the park and on to evenings over a glass of wine, and Karen, like Alison, is beginning to feel like a real friend.

'You don't want to let him sleep too long today,' warns Della. 'He won't sleep again tonight and you'll get yourself into a vicious ...' She trails off under the weight of Karen's frosty glare.

'Are you serious? You want me to wake him up and . . . *deal* with him? After the night I've had?'

'Sorry.' Della flushes. 'I didn't mean . . .'

'Let's go and get a coffee,' I say, squeezing Karen's arm.

'If you can call it that,' she says darkly. As we walk away, she turns back. 'Sorry, Della. Just tired.'

'Oh, God, don't worry. We've all been there.'

As Pat attempts to dissolve bargain-basement coffee granules in not-quite-boiling water, Karen glumly observes Della, her blonde hair immaculately streaked, face subtly but expertly made up.

'I know for a fact Harry doesn't sleep that well, so how the hell does she look like that?'

Pat passes us two small polystyrene cups containing what I can only assume is muddy water. 'You shouldn't set too much store by appearances,' she says reprovingly. 'Sometimes that's the only thing a person can control, while below the surface everything's in turmoil.'

'Yes, you're right,' says Karen, chastened. 'Thanks, Pat.'

We move towards the others.

'Sod that,' says Karen, under her breath. 'I want to look like a sex goddess mummy, I don't care about the inner turmoil. Bring it on.'

We're still giggling when we reach Della and Chloe, who look at us enquiringly.

'What's so funny?' Chloe asks.

'Oh, nothing, just Pat,' I say. 'I can't stay long today, I'm going to see Mum.'

'Aw, how's she doing in the care home? I miss my little visits!'

'She's doing OK.' How can I put into words 'how she is'? I don't have the words, or rather I have too many – words that the casual enquirer doesn't want to hear. So I tell them what they do want to hear. She's *doing as well as can be expected*, she's *settling in nicely*.

'And what about your dad, Karen?' Chloe says.

'Same as ever,' Karen says shortly. I give her hand a quick squeeze. She won't want to talk about it with Chloe and Della, but I know that the last time she visited, her dad didn't know who she was at all, and got extremely distressed. She's dreading her next visit.

I lose the thread of the conversation after this as Della explains at length the convoluted plot of a TV series she's watching. I sense Karen watching me, and, when I make my excuses and leave, she catches up with me in the foyer of the church hall.

'Are you OK? You were a bit quiet in there.'

'I'm fine.'

Again I'm answering as expected, but it cuts no ice with Karen, who raises a stern eyebrow. 'Is it Natalie? It's OK to grieve for her, Cassie. You and she were close.'

'Partly,' I say, and it's true. Natalie's absence is a nagging pain, always there in the background, sometimes close to overwhelming me. 'But also . . . it's Mum. Finding out what she did.' I told Karen the whole story over a bottle of wine one night last week. I hadn't planned to say anything, but I found it spilling out of me as the pinot

371

grigio flowed in. 'It's hard enough seeing her as she is now, but not being able to ask her about it, to tell her . . . that I understand, I guess. For her to have carried that all those years must have been an awful burden. I wish I could tell her I know, that it's OK, that I understand she was trying to protect me. I wish I could say thank you.'

'It's so hard.' Karen pulls me into her arms for a massive hug. It's one of the things I like about her, that she never tries to put a gloss on things. If they're crap, she acknowledges that, instead of trying to make me count my blessings. 'Want to pop round for a cuppa after you've seen her? My house is a shithole but I have chocolate Hobnobs.'

'I'd love to.'

I try to pretend otherwise but my heart beats a little faster as I approach the pub. I very nearly pass it without incident, but, as I compose my features into a deliberately not-disappointed expression, the door opens and out he comes into the garden with a tray. A customer calls him over and I think he hasn't seen me, but he looks up and shrugs apologetically, making a little phone shape with his hand. I fail to stop a foolish grin from spreading, and wave. Nothing more has happened between us, but there's definitely a spark there, and, for now, the little bit of warmth it gives off is enough.

That's two good things, I think to myself, as I make my way up the path and into Oakdene House. Talking to James later, and Hobnobs at Karen's. Simple pleasures, but these are the things that make up a life.

And there's a third good thing: Alison has asked if I'd officially like to become her lodger. She'd been thinking of getting one anyway, but had been worried about the impact on Katie. However, Katie has surprised her by not only warming to me, but being a natural with Amy, happy to sit on the floor playing with her for hours. She hasn't been out since the night at the quarry. She blames herself for being so gullible as to let Natalie's messages on Instagram fool her into feeding her information. She hasn't been able to tell us much about the confrontation between her and Natalie when Natalie first seized her and bundled her into the boot of the car. She keeps apologising over and over, saying it's all her fault. Alison says we need to give her time, that she'll be OK.

I've put Mum's house on the market, and started looking for a job locally. I can almost believe that things will be alright.

I think, as I sign the visitors' book, about my dad's love letters. I re-read them yesterday with new eyes, and can't believe I ever thought them romantic. His insistence that Mum didn't need anyone but him should have been a massive red flag, but they didn't have the term 'coercive control' back then. He was subtle, too; he never openly slagged off her friends, but there were little digs, suggestions that they weren't good enough for her, that she didn't need them now she had him. Slowly but surely, he was ensuring she had no one else to turn to, was reliant on him for everything. Was that the reason she chose to stay single afterwards – because she understood that being alone is better than being with the wrong person? I know for sure now that that's what she would tell me if she could. She would want me to value myself enough to believe that I deserve more than the poor version of a relationship that Guy offered me; more than gratefully eating the crumbs that fell from the table of his life. I hope for Amy's sake that he can be a father to her one day, and I'll never prevent that from happening, but I will never again think so little of myself that I accept second-best.

It's the rude receptionist today, but, instead of letting her upset me, I think about telling Alison later how she managed to communicate with me without either a single word, or any eye contact whatsoever. 'Thanks so much!' I gush insincerely, and she pulls the book towards her chest like a shield. I've got Amy facing outwards in the carrier and she's burbling and waving her arms, but the receptionist doesn't so much as crack a smile.

'Well, she was friendly, wasn't she?' I say into the top of Amy's head as we walk down the corridor. I stand outside Mum's door for a second, screwing up my courage. God, I hate that it takes courage to see my own mother. 'Here we go.'

'A-ba,' Amy says thoughtfully.

'Huh. Thanks for your contribution.'

Mum is sitting in her chair, her hair freshly washed and shiny. 'Hello!' she says, delighted. I feel my body soften. Looks as though it's a good day.

I sit down on the bed. 'Hi, Mum.'

Her smile falters a little. She may be in a good mood, but she doesn't know I'm her daughter. 'And who's this?' She reaches out and strokes Amy's cheek; Amy bats her hand with a pudgy fist.

'This is your ...' I don't want to distress her. 'This is Amy.'

'Hello, Amy.'

'A-ba,' Amy says again. Sparkling conversationalist, my daughter.

'I had a little girl once,' Mum says casually.

'Oh?' My heart speeds up a little and I grab Amy's little hands to stop mine from trembling. 'What was her name?' I don't know why, but I want to hear her say it.

'Cassie,' she says, as if I should have known. 'My little Cassie.'

I press my lips together, blinking back tears. 'What was she like?'

'She was a lovely little thing, like this one. So lovely. I would have done anything for her.'

'Would you?' My tears are flowing freely now, but she doesn't seem to have noticed.

'Oh, yes. Oh, yes. Anything. Can I hold her?'

I unstrap Amy from the carrier and pass her over onto Mum's lap. She lifts her, bringing Amy's face up close to her own. 'Hello, my little darling. You're so beautiful. Yes, you are.'

She tucks Amy into her lap with the practised ease of an experienced mother. A lump forms in my throat as I realise it's the same way I tuck Amy into me. Have I made it? I may never be a Chloe, happy to dedicate all my time and effort to my child in perpetuity, obsessed with every detail of behaviour and development. I'm still me, with all my flaws, my imperfections; but I'm someone else too, and I'm finally at peace with that. I'm a mother. I've been trying so hard to be a good one that I missed something vital. I thought I couldn't mother her effectively as I am. I thought I needed to mould myself into a different shape, a different kind of mother. But I was wrong. Yes, I'll make mistakes and mess things up, but I am the mother she needs, just as I am.

I am enough.

Acknowledgements

As always, huge thanks to my superstar agent Felicity Blunt, and to my editors Lucy Malagoni and Rosanna Forte and the whole team at Sphere. Thank you for believing in me and my work.

In the course of my research, I read several books that were very helpful. *Somebody I Used To Know* by Wendy Mitchell is an incredible, brave, moving memoir written by someone living with dementia. I'd also like to thank the book's co-writer (and novelist in her own right) Anna Wharton, who kindly read the parts of my novel relating to dementia and offered advice. Other books I found useful include *Still Alice* by Lisa Genova, *Where Memories Go: Why dementia changes everything* by Sally Magnusson and *My Mad Dad: The Diary of an Unravelling Mind* by Robyn Hollingworth. I also learned a lot from the notes my brilliant copy editor Linda McQueen gave me, informed by her own experience of caring for a loved one with dementia. I hope that Sylvia's story in the book is a sensitive and realistic portrayal of what it's like to care for someone with dementia. Any inaccuracies are mine and mine alone.

Thank you to my brilliantly supportive family and friends. Part of this book was written in the lockdown of 2020, so I'd especially like to thank everyone that kept me going through that strange time, including my girls Hattie, Jane, Naomi & Rachel, all my writing pals especially the Ladykillers (ladies, I'd be lost without you), Bill, my dear friends Catherine, Claire and Natasha, and Chris K, for all the unsolicited advice and making me laugh a lot. Extra special thanks to Jon for the cocktails and the crisps, and everything else.

Global pandemic aside, this book has been a long time coming. When I started writing it, my husband was alive. I continued to write it through his illness, and in the aftermath of his death. He was my biggest supporter, and I so wish he could have got to read it. The biggest thank you is due to my sons Charlie & Arthur, who make everything better. We spent a lot more time at home together than any of us were expecting while I was working on this book, and it's a credit to both of them that it was actually pretty fun. They make me laugh every day, they bring me up when I'm down, and their maturity and resilience never fail to make me proud. Like everything else I do, now and forever, this book is for them.